From the Depths of Vispa

The Goats in Space Saga

From the Depths of Vispa
Across the Sands of Aurinko
Into the Forest of Strom
Beyond the Ice of Fyel

From the Depths of Vispa

(Book One of the Goats in Space Saga)

E. E. Oakey

Gallant Gillhew Publishing
Copyright © Text E E Oakey 2019
Copyright © Cover illustration Emma Oakey 2019
Copyright © Chapter illustrations Emma Oakey, Tristan Oakey and James Oakey 2019
The moral right of the author has been asserted

ISBN 978 0 9876441 0 7

Cover design by Ruth Weinekoetter

To my parents for their encouragement.

To Stuart for his support. x

To my boys for their inspiration.

How do you say that?

Seyfert = **Zay**-furt

Tycho = **Tie**-ko

Walf = ½ Wolf + ½ Ralph

Suza = **Soo**-za

Addie = Addie!

Nineveh = **Nin**-uh-vuh

Hawtrey = Hor-tree

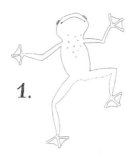

1.

Sublime Nothingness
(Spinning in Space)

Zafe stopped fiddling with the plug and floated over to the window.

Delicate, far-flung stars pricked a dense blanket of inky darkness, but it wasn't always this calm. Colliding galaxies, rogue planets, incoming terrapods; any number of things might be happening outside, but today there was nothing. No events, no anomalies, no arrivals and no departures. No change.

He traced the reflection of his smile in the dark glass.

BEEP. BEEP. BEEP.

The boy's serenity evaporated as the travel agent's face flickered back: black and white on the tiny screen. Her voice emerged amid crackles of disruption.

'— — sooo super to see you. It looks like the frequency has stabilised, but I don't know how long our line will last. So, as I was saying, Zafe sweetheart, you ought -' BLIP.

'Sorry, I didn't catch that.'

Her lips were moving, but there was no sound.

Another BLIP and her voice erupted from the little screen once more. 'And Zafe sweetheart, I've spoken with the doctor and she says that before you set off she'll prescribe you a course of grit tablets and you *must* go to sickbay for your dirt injections.'

'Injections of dirt?'

'Things aren't quite as clean on the worlds as they are on the space station, so it's best to take precautions. Oh, and it's important that you watch your —' She'd fizzled away into grey again.

'WHAT? WHAT DO I HAVE TO … watch?' He was shouting at a blank screen.

Zafe waved his limbs about until he'd drifted over to a kink in the wire, straightened it, unplugged the screen and plugged it back in again. A skewed, wibbling image of the agent reappeared. She was still chatting, completely unaware that for the last minute she'd been conducting their conversation solo.

'— — make your parents so proud, embarking on this adventure and making friends, of course.'

'Friends?'

'I'm sure I didn't get to roam around the Quadmos when I was your age, and get to know some —'

'Yes, um, I wanted to talk to you about that. Actually, I'm not sure ab-' BLIP.

Gone. Her face had disappeared again.

Zafe frantically rekinked the wire and tinkered with the plug, he shook the screen and wrestled with the controls, but the line was dead. Dead as a Dromban sand frog.

It looked like he was on his way.

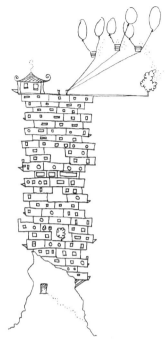

2. Istanglia
(On the Planet of Vispa)

Five hundred years is a long time to wait for a raspberry.

The fruit had been flown to the watery planet of Vispa by spacepod, and Amburg Tower had offered to host the grand event.

An excited crowd of tower-dwellers were listening to a speech by the mayor, Mrs Drinkwater, in which she congratulated the space station botanists, the spacepod engineers — and their parents and grandparents.

By the time she'd thanked the cow-crabs for their dung (delivered to the lab by rocket), the dung collectors and the soil sifters, they were beginning to fear the speech would never end, but she brought it to a successful conclusion by suggesting that if the hard work continued it might be a nectarine next year.

Finally! After an afternoon's queuing the students of
Hundredwater School were permitted to peer and sniff at the
strange, bubbly-pink fruit they'd come to see. But, more
importantly, they were also allowed to add their names to the
Raspberry Raffle.

Although Tycho Gillhew (Year Seven) had never seen a
raspberry before he could tell this one was well past its best. He
also knew that it would still be a lot more appealing than
whatever he'd be having for dinner when he got home. Tycho
crossed his fingers as Mayor Drinkwater delved into the pot of
tickets, unfolded the strip of jellypaper and made the
announcement: Jadri was the winner of the raspberry dinner.

The mayor made her way through the crowd over to the lucky
winner, holding the old-world fruit aloft on a small saucer. And
after yet another speech, Mrs Drinkwater retreated and the rest
of the class gathered round to view the precious bounty up
close. Too close.

Amid a mob of fruit-admiring onlookers, Tycho felt a pang
of disappointment — and a sharp dig in the ribs. There was a
sound of breaking china, a yelp and he was whipped round by
Jadri who looked weirdly angry for someone who'd just won
the only raspberry on the entire planet.

The raffle-winner grabbed his top and kicked his shins while
Tycho pinched, wailed and did everything he could to escape.
His best friend Walf waded in to help but only managed to
elbow Tycho in the face, which seemed to make Jadri even
wilder (Why? It was Tycho who would have the black eye!)
The scuffle stoppe abruptly when they heard the roar of Mr
Antibus, the headmaster.

When class was dismissed two minutes later, just Tycho,
Walf and Jadri remained. The three of them returned to
Hundredwater School for detention, and they were only
released from watching Mr Antibus's beard grow a whole hour
later.

Tycho chose the slow route home to Istanglia, a tower made of
shipping containers.

He lolloped down five storeys of spiral stairs and then took the zipwire from Amburg to Istanglia, whizzing over the water that surrounded the towers. After several more storeys of trudging, Tycho reached home. He pushed the rusty front door open, its creaking a reminder that he'd forgotten to oil the frame (and that a repaint was well overdue).

As he stepped inside, he was enveloped in a hug from his diminutive grandmother, Nonna, and given kisses. Two on each cheek.

'So, Tycho, how was the... um...'

'Raspberry?'

'Yes! The raspberry, what was it like?'

'Small, knobbly and the colour of beetroot juice.'

'And the smell?'

Tycho tried to conjure up the berry's aroma but the fruit's fleeting sweetness was a memory rapidly being overtaken by the fug of vegetable fumes coming from the kitchen, and he guessed they were having cabbage, potato and broccoli pie for dinner. Then he heard Grundi's voice, asking how big the crop had been. (His grandfather was hanging about outside their container-home, dangling off a rope eighteen storeys up, inspecting the gutters.)

'Just the one,' Tycho called out.

'Did they raffle it off at the end?'

'Yes, Jadri got it.'

'OooOooh! Her grandmother will be pleased.' His grandmother's smile lit up the room. And just when Tycho thought he'd got away with it, Nonna asked why he was so late home.

'I *tried* to explain to Mr Antibus...' he mumbled.

'I'm sorry?'

'It wasn't *my* fault.'

Nonna's eyebrows were threatening to take flight. 'Fault? Whose fault?'

'IT WAS JADRI WHO STARTED IT!'

'Started what?'

'The... fight.'

'But Jadri wouldn't hurt a — OH!' Nonna had noticed his

swollen eye.

'She'd do more than hurt a fly if she'd won the only raspberry in the Quadmos and it had been dropped and she thought that the fly had knocked it off a saucer and trampled on it.'

'It's been squished?'

'Walf stepped in to help, and —'

'That was sweet of him.'

'Actually, he was the one who bumped into Jadri and made her so cross, and she really went into overdrive when he skidded on it.' His shoulders drooped as he recalled the fragrant pink smudge on the Great Hall's stone floor.

Their silent contemplation of the sad end to Vispa's raspberry was brought to a smelly conclusion by a cloud of sprout steam rising from the kitchen of their downstairs neighbour.

Tycho coughed violently, Nonna wiped her hands on her apron and enveloped him in another warm hug, which squashed his bruised eye and threatened to suffocate him. 'Go. Catch up with Walf and see if you can rustle up something a bit more interesting to go with the pie. A handful of sea-fungus perhaps? I can hold supper back for twenty minutes.'

'Thanks, Nonna.'

'You'll go by the stairs, won't you, Tycho? It's too late to go abseiling down the building!'

He nodded, waited for her to put the radio on, then walked over to the inner door and opened and closed it, allowing its unoiled squeak to be heard. Creeping back inside, he went to the balcony where, toes curled over the edge, Tycho felt a fizz in the pit of his stomach as he looked down at the waves of Thames Sea below. He turned, flexed his knees and felt his way over the side until he was the right angle. He leaned a bit more, then hopped, skipped and jumped his way off the balcony and down the tower's side.

TYCHO!' The rope twanged and he looked up to see his grandmother, shaking her head.

'But the stairs take too long!'

Three containers down, Tycho knocked on a kitchen shutter,

which was opened by his friend's elder sister and her face was a picture of joy and expectancy – until she saw who it was.

'I just wondered if Walf was free for a bit of fossicking?'
'WAAAAALLLFF, it's Ty!' She dropped the shutter and left Tycho hanging until it opened again and his friend's mop of hair appeared. Walf jumped up and their gaze met briefly before he disappeared below the shuttersill again and was hidden by netting.

(Despite his height, Walf was by far the fastest and most agile in their class. A water-polo striker, he was also a world champion at doodling and armpit squelches.)

'What are we looking for, Ty?'

'We've got cabbage, potato and broccoli pie for dinner, so anything we can get.'

'We're having red cabbage and broccoli soup,' his friend replied, (which just goes to show there's always someone worse off than yourself). 'Sea-earwigs, I reckon, if we can find them.'

'Mm, only Nonna doesn't want me going too far down. Not after what happened last time.' There was silence and only the slow up and down of his friend's nodding blonde hair showed Walf was still there, keeping a respectful silence. The incident with the bag of earwigs and Mrs Bartlebot's flowerbox hadn't been forgotten.

'I don't mind where we go, Ty,' said Walf, 'We don't need to go down more than ten floors to get something tasty. There are always whirligigs and jellicopter beetles to be had.' He paused. 'Sorry about your eye. How is it?'

'Colourful!' came the reply.

Walf jumped up, grinning, and then resurfaced at the balcony gate and clipped himself onto a neighbouring line. Tycho slid around next to him and they sauntered down the outside of the building, hanging off ropes suspended over a choppy sea.

After ten minutes of grubbing about, they'd gleaned an impressive selection of sea-insects. Dinner was beginning to look much more promising. One of the larger whirligigs they'd found had made a break for it but they were happy with their haul and it was time to make their way home.

Stuffing their collection of critters into their belt-bags, Walf and Tycho considered how they would get back up. They had three options:

1.   They could walk up the tower's inner stairs. Fifteen flights for Walf and an extra three for Tycho.

2.   They could take the pedalift up. Fairly hard work but not as bad as walking.

Or 3.   They could subject themselves to the counterbalance.

The quickest (or slowest) way up, the counterbalance was also known as "the scales" and was always the most terrifying way to travel. It was also the most exciting.

Decision made, Tycho and Walf strapped themselves to the counterbalance cable, gave it a tug and waited. Ten seconds, twenty... they felt an answering tug on the line and braced themselves.

(Last time Tycho had used it he'd been matched with Mr Drinkwater, a man known for his love of spuds. Despite their best efforts, Mr D had shot down in a blur and Tycho had risen so fast he'd thought either the rope was going to catch fire or he'd be launched into space.)

But Walf and Tycho's return journey was disappointingly sedate; Mrs Gentry was on the other end. She was brave, but a lightweight.

News!

The school gong tolled half past eight and Tycho tipped himself out of his hammock, rubbed his face with a stiff, dry flannel and scrambled into his top and shorts. It was a warm, hazy morning, and looking out of the window he could barely make out the outline of Amburg, the tower next door. Although he would never have admitted it to anyone, the glide over to school was always a bit nerve-wracking when you couldn't see where you were going.

While the uniform of Kodiak School (three towers away) was a green mohican, Hundredwater School students just added some blue and orange dye to their hair; blue and orange cornrows, blue and orange pigtails and ponytails, blue and orange stripes or a pair of braided horns sticking up — one in each colour? It was all fine by the headmaster, Mr Antibus, who had long since lost every strand of hair on his head and simply coloured his beard.

Tycho ran ink-dipped fingers through his hair, sat down and nibbled at a hunk of potato bread and sipped a cup of tea, but he almost dropped his mug when Nonna began banging pots and pans together. 'IT'S FIVE TO NINE! BRUSH YOUR TEETH! TIME TO GO!' She was louder than the gong for school.

'It only takes seventeen seconds to get to sssscccchhhhooo—' The toothbrush she'd jammed into his mouth made complaining difficult.

'Not if you go by the stairs, Tycho.'

'I haven't got enough time before the gong sounds again. I promise I'll take the stairs tomorrow!'

'And it'll take longer than half a minute if you're clonked on the head by a basket of turnips. You know the zipwire on our floor is designed for deliveries, not school children — or indeed Mrs Goodacre! She really should know better, a lady of her size.' And on that note, she took Tycho's toothbrush, gave him a hug and relieved him of a small lump of cheese he'd taken from the larder. 'Grundi needs this for his lunch.'

'Ooooh, cheese?' Grundi squeezed his grandson's shoulder and pressed a couple of quintar into his hand, 'Get yourself some pumpkin crisps at break time.'

Tycho didn't have the heart to tell him the prices at the tuck shop had risen dramatically since the Fourth Formers had taken charge, and he'd be lucky to get half a sultana fritter for that money. They were an unruly year group, renowned throughout the school and there'd been a rise in rumbling tummies since they'd taken over.

The trip to school by zipwire was alarmingly quick and the warm, swirling mist added an extra dimension to a ride that was already fraught with baskets of speeding vegetables, twanging ropes and shrieking. Lots of shrieking. Almost as soon as Tycho let go of Istanglia, the neighbouring tower loomed into view through the haze.

Unlike Istanglia Tower's dented metal shipping containers, Amburg was built of stone. The tower had been dredged up from the seabed, a jumble of limestone, marble, quartz, brick and the occasional square of stained glass, and it was a mishmash of recycled ideas and materials.

Each floor had been fashioned into a different style of half-remembered architecture from the Old World; memories from before the Great Remove and The Even Bigger Bang, when the four planets of the Quadmos had been a distant hope.

Shouting 'sorry' to the person zipping below him (whose ear he'd caught with his big toe), Tycho bent his legs to absorb the tower wall's impact a split-second before he made contact with the ledge of Hundredwater School. He landed with a skip and a jump over the balcony, before unclipping with seconds to spare. He was greeted by the ear-splitting sound of the school gong being hit by Mrs Hawtrey.

Although he had known her all his life, Tycho never failed to be struck by the impressive height of his teacher's silver hair, and her great orangeiness (a lot of the paler-skinned Amburgers were slightly orange-coloured, as a result of all the carrot and pumpkin they ate, but Mrs Hawtrey was exceptional). Tycho took his seat between Walf (who was fairly orange) and Addie, an Amburger whose skin was dark enough not to show the alarming signs of ECC ('*Excessive Carrot Consumption*'), or what Walf called CFDA *('Carrots For Dinner Again')*.

'Have you heard the news?' Addie was always the first to find out what was 'up', so why she ever asked them what they knew was a mystery.

'Why do you even ask?' said Walf. 'Just spill the beans!'

'Do NOT talk to me about beans. Amburg must have done a trade recently because we've all had BEANS up to HERE,' Addie said, indicating a level somewhere around ear-height. 'My neighbour's room smells like a blobfish's bottom.'

'Just tell us the news, Addie!'

'Oh right! There's going to be a new boy at school.'

There was quite a lot of movement between the towers. Engineers and architects came and went, and gardeners were traded for their horticultural knowledge as much as beans, broccoli and tea were, so there had to be more to it than that. The mood in the room was electric; Addie may have been the school reporter but she wasn't the only one with this nugget of information.

'He's come from Delft Toren and he's got cocoa?' Tycho asked.

Addie crossed her arms and harrumphed.

'No, I know! He's got honey!' said Walf.

Addie rolled her eyes. 'Far too local!'

(Walf and Tycho's home tower produced the Quadmos's finest honey. Every Istanglian household maintained a flowerbox of poppies, lavender, honeysuckle, oregano and mint, grown to tempt the bees which were housed in floating hives attached to enormous helium balloons. Once the towers had had their fill, the rest was exported beyond the Thames Sea, to the far shores of Vispa, and then on to the four other planets — and further. Out into space. If this boy had honey, he definitely wasn't newsworthy.)

'Does he come from Tower Bakossi and have beetroot?' asked Walf.

'Why would I be telling you about someone from Bakossi? I can see it out of my bedroom window and we've all got beetroot coming out of our ears!' Walf quickly glanced around but couldn't see anything of the sort, in fact the only place on any of the towers not sprouting leaves was the tower-dwellers' ears.

They tried a few more place and produce combinations but their enthusiasm was beginning to wane.

'It's better than that!' Addie insisted, bobbing about on her seat, desperate to be the one to share the news, but the boys were saved by the gong and Mrs Hawtrey telling the class to quiet down. They ignored Addie's wide eyes and hand signals. She had missed her chance.

The preliminaries over with; present or absent? Broken bones or black eyes from the zipwire? Packed lunch or school dinners? Mrs H settled herself on an upturned plant pot and addressed the class. 'We have a bit of excitement, something I'm sure you'll all be interested to hear.' Addie's shoulders slumped.

'There is a new boy coming to the school in a matter of days and he'll need somewhere to stay for the rest of term. So I shall be sending you home with forms tonight to see which of your families has a spare hammock and would like to learn a little about where our visitor comes from.'

They'd had exchange students before and learning about dried fish or sultanas was just more homework. Sensing the anti-climactic mood in the hall, Mrs H went on.

'He's coming. From. One. Of. The. Space Arks —'

The class erupted.

An Other-Astral-Dweller! A SPACEBOY! And not only that, a Spaceboy who lived with the animals! Everyone's hand shot up. 'I'll take him — he can stay with me — we've got *loads* of room.' That was Sedge, who lived with five brothers and both sets of grandparents in a container designed for a family of four. The chance of him entertaining a guest was NIL.

With an awful lot of arm-folding, loud clapping and even louder trilling, Mrs Hawtrey eventually managed to quell their riot, but her clapping had developed into a strange dance, and it was the children's turn to wait patiently while Mrs H remembered what she was supposed to be doing and they had her full attention.

'It's a little out of the ordinary and, knowing how excited you'd be, the Headmaster and I have decided it might be best if we held another raffle. If you're interested in hosting our visitor you may take one of the forms home this afternoon, get your grandparents' signed permission and tomorrow morning we shall choose a household at random.' She turned to Addie who was trying desperately to get her attention. 'And NO, you may not interview him for the Hundredwater Herald!'

The rest of the day went by in a blur of raking, weeding, soil, weather-watching, carrot burgers and seed tipping. None of them learnt a thing.

And sleep was especially difficult that night. Usually the shipping forecast followed by a little light swaying in his hammock would send Tycho right off, but it was a particularly muggy night, his tummy felt like it was full of octopeds and no amount of counting earwigs would do the trick. So, he began counting satellites and meteors instead and by the time the Amburg gong tolled midnight he was asleep.

Arm Data?

The following morning, after inspecting the application slips, Mrs H carefully rolled them up and dropped the pieces of jellypaper into a small plant pot (there was always a plant pot handy). A little light shuffling later, she closed her eyes as twenty children leaned forward, their eyes wide open, waiting for the result. Her fingers approached the pot and —

'Before I do,' (there was a loud groan from the class) 'It might be an idea to consider for a moment what the differences between the Space Arks and our planet might be. Anybody? Ideas, anybody?'

Mrs H was confronted by a wall of sound, mostly the shouted names of animals that might live on the ark. The teacher acknowledged the class's interest in zoology and asked them for something else. Anything else? They all sat in silence until, as per usual, Addie's cousin, Suza reluctantly put her hand up and was picked (just as reluctantly) by Mrs Hawtrey.

'Yes Suza — it's always Suza, children! You might give her a break every now and again. Use your noggins!'

'Gravity.'

'I'm sorry Suza, I didn't catch that. You're speaking in your small voice again.'

'Gravity.'

'Yes, certainly, we shall have to ask about gravity or the lack of it. Anybody else? Habjema? Stirmatt? Addie, you might give your cousin a break … anyone?'

After a long, uncomfortable pause, a finger was timidly raised.

'Suza?'

'Living conditions.'

'Yes, I imagine they're going to be very different from what we know. Anything else? Anything at all? … Suza again?'

'Technology.'

'I didn't quite catch — IF WE COULD HAVE A BIT OF QUIET EVERYBODY. REALLY? I CAN'T HEAR A WORD THAT'S BEING SAID! I'm sorry, Suza, you were saying?'

'Umm. Tech. Technology.'

'Thank you Suza, yes. It's hard to believe but we were once all 'Technological' people. It's also hard to believe we are not a class of one.'

Eventually the silence was politely broken by Stirmatt, the only boy in class whose entire head was made up of blue, orange — and green peaks. (He was a fierce supporter of a local water polo team, the Amburg Sproutlobbers.) 'What does techno - … what does that mean, Mrs H?' he asked.

'Well,' she replied, looking around, 'It basically means we had *things*. Lots of things. We were a heavily 'thinged' people. For example, according to the history etchings, we all had miniature walking-around telepipes, the 'mobility telephonicles' you might have seen dredged up from the bay by the merchaeologists. And these things all worked all the time! Ringing, ringing, ringing! The Old World's atmosphere allowed for that, it must have been a very musical place.' She sighed. 'Of course, energy has been something of a problem since The Great Remove, which is why all the technological things we dredge up are checked for energy sources. Batteries are sent to the space station for the mathematics machine they have up there. Does anyone remember what it's called?'

They all shouted back 'The Babbage 652' '783' '528' and a variety of other numbers, that suggested that the Babbagian engineers were taking a while to get it right. *(It's the Babbage 821b at time of printing.)*

'So, we only have enough energy to cover our most basic needs, besides which, the transmissions wouldn't work here because of our atmosphere, but I believe the space station has all of those things.'

'Why does it have all those things we don't?' asked Devik, a boy whose brow was permanently furrowed and whose fingers were forever fidgeting.

'Well, the transmissions, as I mentioned ... and, with metals and crystals so rare and the air, you know, and we don't need — I mean, mathematics? Would we know what to do with it?'

Despite (or perhaps because of) Mrs Hawtrey's obvious confusion, Devik asked yet another 'Why?' He was a boy who spent a lot of time looking out of the shutters into space and was quite clearly living on the wrong galactic body.

The class looked to their teacher for another answer and, seeing no explanation forthcoming, they silently turned to Suza. She whispered, 'The space station uses that energy and technology to ensure the planets' biological security and safety.'

'Thank you, Suza. Yes, the space station makes sure the planets run smoothly. For example, it was space station laboratories that helped to create that raspberry you visited.'

Jadri began to sob and, despite Mrs H's best efforts to calm her down, in the end the teacher had to instruct the class to recite the Quadmos planets' names in order to drown out Jadri's terrible wailing.

'Fyel the Icy, Strom the Leafy, Aurinko the Sweaty — '

Mrs H glared at the children and they swiftly changed it to 'Aurinko the Arid'.

'And?'

They all looked confused, until the teacher supplied the missing information. '*Vispa the Watery.*'

'What's the space station known as?' asked Habjema.

'The Lucky,' muttered Devik.

'Now, now! I'm sure the Space Arks don't have a great many of the things we have, hence our space-friend's visit. Which is rather lovely, if you think about it. We shall learn from him and he'll learn from us.'

'What sort of techno stuff do they have?' Devik asked, his fingers skittering across his desk.

'Ooooh, I don't... Suza? What form does the technology take?'

By this time the girl's eyes were teary with embarrassment, but she dutifully answered. 'Um, data?'

'Arm data! Gosh! Of course, how exciting!' A whisper went around the room, quickly hushed by the teacher, until Devik loudly complained, 'I wish I had arm data.'

'You usually do have arm data, Devik. Let's have a look at your arm right now. Oh dear, oh dear, oh dear, who drew these? Is that your artwork, Walf?' She lowered her glasses to get a better look and then held up his wrist so they could all see the random assortment of Morpheo characters and rude words painted onto his skin with squid-ink. Mrs Hawtrey swiftly lowered it as the class roared with laughter, and he was sent out of the room to sift soil.

Mrs H settled back into her seat and began stirring the jelly-papers. 'Well, I hope for our space-friend's sake that Devik's name isn't the first one picked from the pot,' she muttered. She unfolded a ticket and they all held their breath.

'And the lucky host is … Fox Flintlo!'

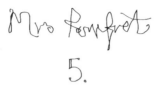

5.

The Chosen One

Although his name suggested otherwise, Fox was a mousy-haired boy without an ounce of cunning, who liked nothing more than to tend his seedlings. Everyone turned to look at the lucky boy, whose complexion had faded from rosey-orange to pale yellow. By the time he'd joined Mrs H at the front of the classroom, his face was a light green.

The boy put his hands to his mouth, made a disturbing gulping sound, a second even more disturbing gulping sound, and at the third — and most disturbing — gulping sound, he was sick all over the waxboard.

Chunks of carrot and pumpkin were caught in the letters Mrs H had scratched into the beeswax and goo dripped onto the rocky floor. YUK!

'Looks like Fox isn't quite as keen to have a visitor as the rest of us,' said Addie.

'Settle down!' Mrs Hawtrey, caught the eye of a number of Istanglians and said 'I would be most grateful for a jar of fresh wax tomorrow. However carefully I scrape this off and resurface it I don't think I'll be able to avoid the bits of breakfast and my teaching board is already rather smelly… Off you go Fox, go and clean yourself up. Right, well one down, nineteen to go…'

Tycho glanced at Walf and was surprised to see a level of determination he'd only ever shown at the beginning of a zip-slalom course. 'Tell me you didn't put your name in! But your grandmother, she —'

'I didn't do anything, don't look at me like that! I just want to be host.'

Walf's grandmother was EXTREMELY container-proud;

weirdly so, given Walf's love of a nasty smell. 'I can't believe your Gran would be very happy about having a visitor, let alone one who comes from an ark full of animals?'

'She'll be fine with it.' But being organised was not one of Walf's strengths, and school forms tended to return home several times before they were eventually completed.

'You haven't *told* her about this, have you Walf? How did you get her to sign it?'

'I may have forgotten to do that … but it's all right, I've sorted it out.' He showed Tycho his waxpad. In amongst a dozen animals he'd drawn (real and imagined), was his grandmother's name, written over and over again, criss-crossing the pad in his best joined-up handwriting. It looked like an anxious spider had been let loose in a puddle of ink. Added to which, Walf had written his grandmother's signature 'Mrs Pomfret'.

'Is that really how your gran signs her name? As Mrs Pomfret?'

'And how much tea does she get through before she starts writing?' said Addie, leaning in. 'Looks like she'd had at least six pots of Formosa Gunpowder before signing that.'

Walf ran to Mrs H and began a long story about how they probably didn't have room for another hammock in their container after all, and their pots and pans weren't big enough to make the extra food.

Mrs Hawtrey bent down and extracted his form from the bin under her desk (another plant pot).

'You might want to carry on practising your handwriting, Walf, and in the meantime I'll have 273 lines with a waxboard and stylus at lunchtime, and NOT of your grandmother's signature! This is what we call 'forgery' and it is not allowed.'

By the time Harrietta had admitted she didn't want a boy staying with her, Stirmatt had realised he liked his room as it was, Jadri had decided they didn't have a spare hammock, Habjema had revealed she was scared stupid at the prospect of space germs — let alone space-animal germs — and five other classmates (with much better handwriting than Walf) had pleaded guilty to copying their grandparents' signatures, it was down to Tycho and a handful of others, the names of whom would have fitted into a teacup.

Mrs H reached into the pot and drew out another piece of paper and read out the name of the person picked to host their visitor from space.

Time stood still and Tycho felt like he was underwater, everything in slow motion. He could see his classmates talking and shouting, and could vaguely feel them prodding his arms. Bubbles of excitement ran up and down his body, time rejigged and everything was pandemonium. Devik was stomping about in the corner while Mrs H was comforting Suza (who had somehow misheard, thought she was the host and had dropped her desk lid onto her fingers) and Walf? He was jumping for joy.

A brother. He'd have a brother. Any brother would have done, even a turnip-growing one, but he was going to have a star-chasing brother who lived with animals! Was it possible to explode with happiness? When the gong sounded at the end of the school day Tycho raced home in record time, pedalling up twelve storeys before swinging across on a zipline down from Amburg's roof (the steepest and quickest one there was). He zoomed into his container home.

'Slow down Tycho!' Nonna was sitting on the bench sewing together an assortment of fabric odds and ends as he barrelled into their container. As soon as she'd finished the row of stitching, she smiled at her grandson who was bobbing from one foot to the other like a catfish on a hot container roof. 'How was your day?'

'I won! He's from the ark and he's staying with us! Fox was sick and the nastronaut is staying with us!'

'Someone was sick on a nastronaut?!' Tycho went over his news again, at half the speed. Twice.

'Well, that's marvellous.'

'Nonna, you should probably ask amongst your friends for a spare hammock.'

'Yes Tycho, but may I say, just because he's come from the space station doesn't make his parents nastronauts. They're almost certainly ordinary, run-of-the-mill OADs.' *

'S'pose so, but he isn't a normad, so we'll need to get him a bag and a belt, and a clip for getting to school.'

'Let me just make a note of that ... a belt, a beltbag and a set of the bigger beginner clips but, as I've said a thousand times, the zipwire, vegetable rope, fruit line — whatever you want to call it, is supposed to be for fruit, vegetables and PE classes under the careful eye of Mr Flintlo.' She smiled. 'I shall make a list. Gosh, life is very different on a space station. They don't live in towers surrounded by sea for a start. He might not be able to swim.'

Within a minute Tycho was laughing so hard he could barely stand, but before Nonna could say any more to convince him non-swimmers existed, he'd reclipped and was abseiling down Istanglia to the honey vault to tell Grundi the good news.

The rest of the week went by at a poopslug's pace. Unable to concentrate at school, Tycho (and the rest of the class) found seed identification (a taxing lesson at the best of times) actually painful.

Both Tycho and Walf spent the week alternating between terrible disappointment at the speed of the twin-suns and high excitement. Tycho had been sleeping so badly his grandmother was surprised to see his energy when he set off for school on the big day.

Finally, he would be part of a family. A proper family.

*Other-Astral-Dwellers

The New Arrival

The buzz in the classroom was as electric as the build-up to any storm.

Mrs Hawtrey had gone to collect the boy from South Utzeera Tower and the headmaster was taking the class. Not knowing what they'd been learning, Mr Antibus had decided the safest option, was to give everyone a paintbrush and a pot of paint, and (while they were busy) a lecture on the importance of keeping the metal on the towers freshly painted, to guard against rust. They painted their desks.

They then had a singsong ('The Animals went in thirty-two by thirty-two', an old favourite that told of the Great Remove to the Space Arks) and they were just beginning to sing '534 blue and orange beltbags standing on the wall' when they heard their teacher's dulcet tones — and waited for her to walk up the remaining three storeys.

Mrs Hawtrey eventually made it up to the classroom. 'Good morning children! Let us all say a big thank you to the headmaster, who has taught you all such a lot, I'm sure.' There was a moment of awkwardness when Mr Antibus offered to take the next lesson too, and in the end Mrs H had to usher him out. ('He's got the Fourth Form now,' she remarked, which might have explained his reluctance to leave.)

Once Mr Antibus had gone, Mrs H stood aside to give the class a clearer view of the new arrival. 'And let us welcome our newest pupil, Sea … Fart?' A giggle made its way around the classroom. 'He's a nastronaut fresh from the Space Ark! … it's all right, you can take your nose peg off now, Sea…'

'No, no, I -'

'Really, the fish smell has gone now.'

'It's not that, I —'

But the new boy's protests were drowned out in a sea of excitement until, his voice rising with every attempt, Seyfert shouted out 'SPACE PARK, NOT ARK! … It's the name of my … school.'

The class sat silent, staring at the newcomer who, it turned out, didn't feed floating tigers, tend weightless walruses or play with bobbing baboons.

'And my name's pronounced Zay-furt … Mostly people just call me Zafe.'

'Right. Thank you. Sooooo … *Sey-fert* hasn't actually come from the Space Ark, but from SPACE PARK with a 'p', my mistake. Am I right in understanding that's part of the space station?' The visitor's cheeks were crimson and his eyes were filled with tears; a reaction to the stunned silence and air of disappointment hanging over the class.

He nodded his head and mumbled to her that it was indeed the name of his school. Then, from the back of the class, there came a chorus of questions.

'Oi! Zafe! Are you a nastronaut?'

'Do you know the zookeepers from the radio?'

'When you're on the space station, how do you go to the…'

'QUIET EVERYBODY!' Mrs Hawtrey glared at the back row.

'Yeah! Do you fly through the Quadmos wrangling animals with Milla and Flan Carrot?'

'Now, now Devik! Just because someone comes from the Space Ar — Park doesn't make them a nastronaut — or a zookeeper. Nor does it mean that they watch over the animals with *Meena* and *Ffang Garret*.'

A reverent silence befell the class as they considered the Quadmos-famous couple who broadcast from the Space Arks, until Devik yelled 'But EVERYONE knows *them*!'

'Knowing of them Devik, isn't the same as having breakfast with them, is it?' Zafe was, by now, the colour of Jadri's squashed raspberry.

'Okay! Well children, I think you'll all agree that Space Park, the name of Seyfert's school, sounds very like 'Space Arks' over a telepipe and is still **INCREDIBLY** exciting! Seyfert has come to stay with us, or more specifically, with the Gillhews,' (she nodded at Tycho), 'To learn a little of what it means to be a Vispan.' She scanned the room for signs of obvious enthusiasm and, as her eyebrows raised in a pointed manner, the class began to politely snap their desktops up and down.

So, he didn't live with space gibbons, and it sounded like he probably wasn't a rocket-rider, but he was still a Spaceboy, which was a lot better than being a nomad from one of the other towers ... or coming from the third floor.

One of the first things the Hundredwater children tended to notice about visitors was how wild their hair was. Many non-tower-dwellers had no idea about hair wax, headbands, hats or plaits and they often looked like they'd been dragged through a meteor storm backwards. And Zafe's hair was suitably mad, but hair aside, the boy was medium height, a bit more solid than the Vispish children and he was wearing a wide, white collar.

It looked uncomfortably like his head was nestling in a shallow bowl. Was it something to do with gravity? It was broad enough to cover his shoulders and Mrs H remarked that it might be best to keep the collar on until he got to Tycho's home. Seyfert was wearing a long-sleeved top, a pair of 'trousers' — shorts that went all the way down to the floor. Or rather, all the way down to the shoes he was wearing. Shoes?

Tycho also noticed that the only adornment on Zafe's top was buttons — they wouldn't last long. Any fanciness of that sort was reduced to a shattered nubbin of bone after being washed and *mangled*.

A couple of pupils bent down to examine Zafe's lower leg region and were dispersed by Mrs H. If his covered feet, legs and arms were surprising enough, the fabric was something else. Blue. Plain blue all over. Looking around at his fellow classmates, Tycho noticed they were clad in a rainbow of polka dots, stripes, tweed, tartan, florals and scraps.

Vispish clothes were a mishmash of any fabric their families could get their hands on and no single piece of clothing was made of any one pattern, let alone a single colour. Many of them also appeared to be splattered with paint.

The only person whose outfit wasn't covered in paint or made out of scraps was Mrs H's. She wore a feathered hat with a wide brim, a fluorescent hooded top and a monochrome kilt.

(One of Amburg's founding tower-dwellers had unearthed a couple of containers of theatre costumes which, given the urgency of the 'Great Remove' seemed a bit cheeky, but it had turned out to be a joyous find. Older residents of Amburg often modeled strange and exotic outfits for special occasions. At last year's end of term school festival, Mrs Hawtrey had worn a rara skirt — and the year before that, a three-piece suit.)

But if Zafe's appearance alarmed the Vispans, their surroundings were no less surprising to the newcomer. Their classroom was small and cave-like. So small that the children half-sat, half-stood at tall, but miniature desks. Each desktop was the size of the wax tablet it held; not dissimilar to the etch-o-pad Zafe used at home, and clipped to the side was a pot of correcting wax and a pointy stylus.

The desk's rear legs projected down into a small nodule, which formed the seat on which the pupil in front perched, whose desk legs made up the seat for the next student, and so on.

To ensure the class's stability, the row of desks was bolted to the floor and although a range of heights was catered for, someone inevitably spent the year sitting uncomfortably high or low.

Just across from Tycho, there was one desk spare. Directed over to it by Mrs H, Zafe hitched himself onto the small seat and promptly slid to the floor. He got up, but the mood had changed;

the class had become strangely silent and still.

Mrs H brushed the stone-dust from his trousers. 'This used to be Benitt's seat. I think the children find it strange having someone else sitting here,' she said, and he slid to the floor again but this time the silence broke with a wave of sniggering. After a couple more attempts, the newcomer was strapped to the *bum-rack* (Walf's expression) for his safety.

'Now Seyfert, I must add you to the register, can you tell me your family name?'

The boy mumbled something few of them heard.

'Sorry, I ... could you repeat that?'

He hesitated and spoke again, and Tycho could have sworn it wasn't the name he'd first said.

'Gallant?' repeated Mrs H, for all the class to hear.

'Gallant? Like Torres Gallant?' Walf asked.

'Like *The Chronicles of Captain Torres Gallant, Quad-King of DoomMonger*?' asked Jared, who was addicted to the cartoons, which were painted outside his home and frequently played on the radio. Zafe's pale, freckly face blushed sunset-red again and he nodded.

'Do you listen to the radio plays too?' asked Walf.

Zafe replied that he'd read the Torres Gallant comic books on file.

A big 'WAAAH' went up from the class, with various children saying '*on file*' in a way that suggested to Zafe, that files weren't a thing on Vispa.

When the class had calmed down, Mrs H asked Tycho to come to the front to meet his new roommate and, without giving it a moment's thought, Zafe reached up to flick his fringe. There was a loud 'WOOOOH', suggesting his classmates thought he'd done something extraordinary.

He shoved his hands in his pockets but the room seemed to have made up its mind that he'd been *scanning* them.

One of the boys referred to him as a 'Genius, far removed from the technologically-bereft and soggy clod of dirt spinning in space that they had to live on'. *(No prizes for guessing which of the boys said that.)* So Zafe nodded to Tycho as he strode

26

over, rather than shake his hand and cause any more disruption.

But Devik was right about it being *far removed*; the atmosphere on Vispa was very different to the space station. For a start, the place smelled so different from home. There was an odour of living, rotting 'green' mixed with a note of saltiness.

The space station didn't smell like this; it didn't smell of anything much at all. It was clean, for a start, and nothing unexpected grew anywhere outside the laboratories. No crumbs, no flakes of paint, no puddles of paint, nothing to fly around and get into your eyes, up your nose or into your ears when you weren't paying attention.

For the rest of the school day, Zafe was bothered by small bits of floating 'stuff' and every time he brushed his arms or face, he heard someone whisper something about his "bionic arm data" telling him when dinner would be ready.

There were legends about how advanced telepipe technology had been before the Great Remove, but Zafe could see that his classmates were impressed and, anxious to make friends, he didn't bother to correct them. When Devik had wanted to examine the data on his arm, he'd simply said that this atmosphere didn't support that level of information, which was true. But not exactly honest.

The mole on his arm was not exactly 'data'.

7.

Hot and Bothered

'Never... been... so... tired. And my legs!' Looking slightly green, Zafe's knees buckled and Mrs H hurriedly unstrapped him from his perch and got him an upturned plant pot to sit on. He let out another groan as his knees bent. Tycho gave them a brief poke and was surprised to find how soft his legs were.

'Miss, he doesn't seem to have any muscles!'

'Don't prod him Tycho! Remember, children, Zafe is used to a lot less gravity than we are. I imagine just standing up is an effort.'

'But they DO have gravity on the space station, Mrs H, gravity generators. My uncle Danbar worked on them,' Addie called out. 'And I wrote an article about it in The Herald.'

'So, you did, Addie, well done. Zafe, why are you so tired?'

'We don't have the up and down like you do here. It's all flat on the space station and then there are lifts if you want to transfer to another deck,' he rasped, 'and they only turn the generator on three times a week. I'm the Kneeball captain though,' he said forcefully, which only made his breathing more laboured.

The class was asked to return to their desks and begin Nature Study, giving Zafe a break from the inferno of interest he'd wandered into, and while they examined leaves and twigs his attention turned to the 'great outdoors'. He'd heard about the sky and seen pictures, but to see the real thing was something else entirely.

Long, thin clouds gathered in clusters of fluffy pink, only emphasising the blueness surrounding them. They came in all shapes and sizes, skidding across the sky, so soft *and* solid-looking at the same time.

It was a captivating sight and he found it hard to drag his eyes away from it, until a miniature drone buzzed through the window frame into the room, and a child yelped and jumped under a desk.

The spaceboy couldn't understand the commotion; here at last was some technology, and impressively small technology at that. Zafe leaned forwards and put his hand out, expecting the tiny transport to stop, which it did of course, although he wasn't expecting it to land on his nose.

It was an unfamiliar model, much smaller than anything he'd ever seen on the space station, and it obviously needed to have its fan seen to, as it was buzzing loudly.

He squinted at the miniature machine and then looked up to see the class, stunned. Tycho, his new roommate, was the only one to speak. He told Zafe to stand quite still otherwise it might sting.

'Sting?'

Zafe reached up to retrieve the small craft, but a searing pain at the end of his nose gave him something else to think about. It was as if someone had taken a kneeball bat and whacked him with it.

'AAAAAAAAAARRRGghhhhhhhhhhhhhhhhhhhhh!!!! It's short-circuited!' It was a pain, the like of which, he'd never felt before — until he stumbled over a rivet in the floor and bashed his knee on a desk. 'OUCH! What was that thing?'

'It was a bee,' said Tycho.

'B class? They haven't been used for years! And you can't get them this small, can you?' he asked, his eyes watering with the increasing pain.

'A honey bee, Zafe. An insect.' But the visitor's expression suggested something unfathomable to the Hundredwater class. *Surely* they had insects on the space station?

After his brief introduction to the school and the local wildlife,

Mrs H invited Zafe to sit quietly in the corner, away from the others, for 'a little peace', although it wasn't clear whether she was talking about Zafe's or her own.

Reflecting on the morning he'd had, Zafe began to go over all the children he'd met; more than lived on the whole space station in this class alone! He'd have to jot down their names. If only he could have pulled back his sleeve and tapped on his *data arm* for a list of names and faces.

His parents hadn't said much but they had warned him that the people of Vispa lived in a mechanical age, although Zafe hadn't anticipated his Vispish classmates thinking that he lived in a bio-nano-technical one with body data. Those days were long gone.

Zafe wracked his brains for his classmates' names but without his etch-o-pad in his pocket, he was forced to try 'remembering'. With a monumental effort he finally made sense of all his classmates.

Tyro Mildew was the boy he was staying with — friendly, skinny, not much of a listener, had a black eye and weird spikes of blue and orange in his hair. In fact, didn't they all have weirdly coloured hair? And paint on their bottoms? And who had Tyro been sitting next to? Suma was it? She was the one who didn't speak all that often but didn't miss much. Abbie was loud and had a brother who ate too many beans, but if Zafe needed to know what he was doing next, she was his go-to.

There was Ralf too, the boy who was always twirling a stylus and whose hair looked like a slightly mossy guinea pig. Or was his name Woof? Then there was Stirrup, Derveek, Chedderi and… Habmej? Hafjipep? Habjebob!

Easy! Who needs arm data?

Settling In

Zafe's legs were still shaking when the school day came to an end and he put on the belt Tycho had given him — heavy clips at his thighs and waist, all of them at least four times bigger than those of his classmates. Mrs H complained she would be able to hear Zafe coming 'a mile off' because of his clanking.

'So how do we get to your place?' he asked Tycho.

'If you like going really fast we can pedal up to Suza's on the 21st floor and then we get a good glide over to Istanglia, or we can take the zipwire from here for a slower ride across and then pedal back up. I reckon the best way to go —'

'Might I suggest you walk down to the third floor and take the sky-sedan across, as you're supposed to, and then walk up to your grandparents' container. It would be easier, given that it's Seyfert's first day.' And with that, Mrs H firmly closed the classroom shutters, barring their escape route.

'What's the sky-sedan?'

'They're closed chairs that are carried along wires that go straight across from Amburg to Istanglia.' Zafe still looked confused. 'They're people-sized boxes you sit in and then trundle across. No swinging or sliding and not much pedalling. And they're very, very slow. Sooooooooo slow.'

Feeling frazzled from an afternoon of climbing and gardening (not to mention his introduction to insects), the sky-sedan sounded appealing and Zafe was grateful to be taking the easy route back to Tycho's home.

They traipsed down to the sedan stop and while they waited, Zafe read an episode of *SuperBlobBoy, the Misfit Blobfish*, the story of a boy with a large, blobby head who was able to stun people with his weird, blobby smile.

Carved into the stone tower, the cartoon jostled for position alongside the sedan timetable, an article on fish migration and a recipe for turnip cake.

The ride was relaxing, Tycho did a bit of pedalling while Zafe admired the drifting clouds – he was under strict instructions from Mrs Hawtrey NOT to look down.

Arriving on Istanglia, they plodded up the tower's inner stairs and Zafe's many questions reminded Tycho how different their lives were.

Tycho explained how the huge pipes running up the centre of the building were flooded with light from large crystals fixed into the roof, which filtered the water, making it safe to drink. He said it was a process that used up most of the planet's energy.

The trip to the 18th floor, which Tycho usually cycled in five minutes, took over half an hour, but just when the new boy was beginning to think he'd never stop walking upwards, Tycho announced they were home. Zafe slumped against the door as it opened and fell at Nonna's feet. She helped him up and gave him an awkward hug — holding him at arm's length because of his collar. She offered to remove it.

'I thought it was a space thing!' said Tycho.

'The collar? No, Mrs Hawtrey put it on me when I landed.' Nonna stood on tiptoes and fiddled with the fastening at the back of his neck. 'They said it was for my safety.'

Nonna invited Tycho to help as she was getting nowhere, and when Grundi arrived all three of them were tugging at Zafe's collar. By the time they'd unclipped it, the boy's face was faintly blue.

In a slightly rasping voice, Seyfert thanked them, and remarked on the colours of the evening sky. 'I'd been told about it, of course, but it's all so vivid and —'

Tycho turned from the view towards his new roommate, but he'd disappeared. Where could he have gone?

There was a strangled cry a couple of storeys down. 'HEY Zafe!

You're supposed to use the stairs to get down!' The look on Nonna's face suggested now was not the time for one of Tycho's jokes. Grundi swung through the hole in the netting Zafe had disappeared down and brought him back up (via the stairs), after profuse apologies to the lady two floors below.

Zafe's face was chalk white. 'I FELL THROUGH THE FLOOR!'

'Actually, you fell through two floors.'

'Tycho! I am sorry. Seyfert, are you all right?' Nonna gathered him up in one of her rib-tingling hugs. 'You're probably used to a slightly more solid arrangement on the space station, and Istanglia has rather less flooring than Tower Amburg. You'll get used to it.'

[Built out of metal shipping containers, with holes cut for windows, Istanglia Tower had originally been fairly solid, but as the need for homes increased, so the planet's early settlers had realised that a solid metal box was a waste of resources. Leaving the containers' strong frame behind, they'd peeled the corrugated metal away from the sides; all the better to make furniture, utensils, tools and Bakossi Tower.

So, Istanglia's floors were a series of metal beams covered with thin reed netting, that prevented Young Istanglians (and frying pans) from falling too far. And the tower's walls were little more than thin fabric sheets, ruffled by the wind, tied onto metal-framed 'windows'.]

Tycho released Zafe from Nonna's firm hug and attached him to a doorframe while they waited for Grundi to fix a perch-stick (a stick with a small saddle on the top), into one of the few container beams.

The seat was surprisingly sturdy and Seyfert was safe, as long as he didn't allow his eyes to wander down to the sea that surrounded the tower and covered most of Vispa; *hundreds* of storeys below. *(Eighteen storeys actually, but who's counting?)*

Zafe had sipped a fair bit of water, of course, but he'd never seen more than a bowl of it on the space station, so being surrounded by it was frightening and strange. Writing waves peaking and troughing, up and down, around and around, blue, green, foamy white. It looked like it was alive.

When Zafe began to lean dangerously from his perch-stick, it was Grundi who suggested they put the collar back on for a while, so he could get used to his new surroundings. And so Zafe's gaze moved from the tantalising sea below to the faces of his new family.

Grundi was a tall, slim gentleman whose honey-coloured skin indicated a lifetime spent in the sun, worlds away from the moonlit-tinged complexions of the space station-dwellers.

Nonna was much shorter, just as tanned and wrinkly but it was her cloud of pinky-white hair that caught Zafe's attention. The gentle breeze blowing through the container made it sway gently and it was only when his name was called very loudly that Zafe realised he'd been swaying himself, hypnotised by the gentle movement of the fluffy floss.

When his collar was removed again, Zafe held on tight to his seat and, being careful not to look down, he looked up. Four storeys above the Gillhew home, he noticed a couple of little girls playing hopscotch on the beams of their kitchen.

How he'd managed to make it this far without falling to his death, he couldn't understand, and he redoubled his grip on the perch-seat, until Tycho invited him in to the container's kitchen. He reluctantly let go and was led from post to door frame into the kitchen, which was a collection of metal beams, crossbars and a sink. There was a larder filled, for the most part, with small metal cannisters with names on them like 'Orange Pekoe', 'Earl Grey', 'Darjeeling' Assam, Oolong and Irish Breakfast.

'What are those?' Zafe asked.

'Different types of tea.'

The cannisters were opened and the various scents were wafted Zafe's way. The boy didn't look impressed, but he was going to have to be. There was nothing else to drink.

While Tycho prepared the Oolongs, (using hot water dripped from a copper pipe), Nonna took down a waxed bag hanging in the room's shadiest corner. As she opened it, Zafe was hit by a wall of smell, odour, stink … whatever it was, it was the slimiest, most disturbing sensation. A smell of rotting *everything*.

Zafe screwed his mouth shut but was aware that his nostrils had flared so much that he imagined they'd doubled or tripled in size — huge great nostrils the size of his ears, wrenched open wide by the stench. His eyes watered, his lungs shrivelled and he fell to his knees, only avoiding falling onto the netting by blindly gripping onto Tycho.

He couldn't possibly breathe with that smell in the air, both sharp and sour, fatty and globulous… he couldn't let that smell into his mouth. He was going to have to scrub his nostrils! Could nostrils be scrubbed?

And then the worst of it was over. Nonna had closed the bag and, with a slight blush to her cheeks, she muttered something about them 'not having smoked mackerel for dinner tonight'.

Now, about that tea?

Tales of Destruction

Tycho's grandparents had added half a dozen more bed hooks into the ceiling so the boys could decide exactly where they wanted to sleep and Zafe's things were waiting for him when he arrived. The bag lay on a hammock rocking gently in the breeze. It was the most substantial thing in the room, which would have been better described as a 'cage' there was so little to it.

There was a knock on the shutter and Walf appeared, swinging outside, and he climbed in. They returned to the living area and, once Walf had been given permission, he began doodling on the wall with a sharp metal stick.

The cups of tea were surprisingly enjoyable (the parsnip cake less so), but Nonna had traded honey for some raisin biscuits and beetroot crisps which, along with her cheese straws, made for a party atmosphere. While everyone ate, Zafe presented his hosts with a gift.

It was a piece of pottery his teacher had made for him in the rocketbooster-kiln. Zafe knew deep down that his parents should have given him something to present to the family he was staying with, and so it was that he uncovered a muddy-green glazed ceramic bowl in the shape of a mammal with chunky ears, a big nose and a long, thick tail.

Zafe wasn't sure whether the details had been made bigger than they needed to be (for fear of them snapping off?) but the effect was puzzling and they spent a moment trying to identify it. Was it an over-sized mouse, an under-sized lion or a badly-made moose?

But a gift was a gift, and Zafe gingerly leaned over to pass it to Nonna, when he heard a loud CLICK — CLACK — CLACK come from Walf's direction and thought he saw a pair of large eyeballs curl their way around the shutter frame.

Eyeballs. Looking at him. Eyeballs on curling stalks?

Before Zafe could make a sound, the eyeballs had gone – and so had his gift. The ceramic lump dropped from his limp hands, and fell through the hole he'd fallen through earlier.

Plink

(Ooh!)

Clink

(Oi!)

CRASH

(Ow!)

SMASH

Drawing his eyes from the ragged tear in the netting (that revealed the watery abyss below) Zafe clutched his seat and focused on the door frame. And in amongst trying not to fall through the netting (again) and reflecting on the loss of his gift, he tried not to think about whatever it was that he'd seen.

Nobody else seemed to have noticed anything, but Zafe could

have sworn that before he'd dropped the mammal-bowl, he'd heard Walf say the words 'funny to see them so high' about *something*.

'Might it be time for you to get home now, Walf dear? I think you've probably done enough drawing, thank you,' said Nonna, 'And Seyfert, what a kind thought.' She leaned over and gave him a quick hug. 'Don't worry, I'm sure the aqua-tango ladies will find it tomorrow, during their class.' It was doubtful. The bowl hadn't squeaked, roared or mooed as it dropped. They'd definitely heard it smash, along with the occasional yelp of someone living lower down.

'It was very good of your parents and it would have been just the thing for...' Grundi glanced around the container while Nonna tried hard to think of a purpose for the figure. It wasn't clear where the thing could have been put as most of their few belongings were kitchen utensils and pans that hung from hooks, gently swinging in the warm breeze blowing through the container.

Grundi asked Zafe if he'd seen such a creature in the space zoo and, for the fifth time that day, Tycho and Walf were forced to clarify their visitor's origins. And the new boy revealed that his parents had originally come from Vispa.

'And they were keen for you to experience life in a tower?' asked Nonna.

'No, yes! I mean, it's just that my school closed down... There was a problem with the window seals and it was ... sucked out into space.'

'YOU DIDN'T TELL US THAT!' Walf shouldn't have been as excited as he was, after all, the loss of a school was not something with which he was unfamiliar. 'Did you do it?'

'I thought you'd gone home Walf!' hissed Nonna, hoping Zafe *wasn't* going to give Walf the answer he wanted.

'No, no, it wasn't me. They think it was down to wear and tear from space debris.'

'It's still brilliant.'

'I was waiting outside, ready to go in and one minute it was there, the next it was gone. BANG! No classroom! Except it wasn't a bang, it was more of a hiss, and my Morpheo cards went with it, I'd left them behind and —'

'Morpheo cards?' said Tycho. 'We have Morpheo too! They're painted onto buildings and we swing around finding them.'

'There's a Furry Fangdog on Bakossi at the moment,' said Walf.

Tycho grinned at his friend, and told Zafe, 'He's usually the first to find them and add his initials,' and he grabbed Walf's arm and proudly showed off the tally of 'first finds', drawn on with squid ink. The marks reached all the way up to his shoulder. (Now THIS was a boy with arm data!)

Zafe told them he'd lost the Doomcat Meister MVX, one of the rarest in the collection and the boys sympathised with their new friend — and then cooed with pleasure when he took, out of his pocket, an actual card. It was small, the size of his palm, and showed a Flint Frog Warrior holding a spear. The card was a bit bent and rough around the edges, but the colours still shone.

It looked like a small jewel in his hand, and was treated with the same reverence.

Over a second plateful of biscuits and another large cup of tea, Walf explained how their previous school, Ninetywater, had been built onto the side of Istanglia Tower (after the previous school — Eightywater — had dissolved during a particularly bad storm).

One night during the holidays a great crrreeeeaaaaakkkkkk was heard, followed by a CRASH and a BOOOM! Ninetywater had fallen off the building (hooray!) taking the badminton court with it (boo!) The Year Threes had been responsible for the school's anti-rust painting and they were roundly congratulated / blamed for what had occurred. The spring holidays went on and on that year.

So the plans for Amburg's long-awaited 'Museum of Jam' were changed and the rocky outcrop that protruded from floor 13 was transformed into a school which required no painting. Hundredwater.

Walf left, and it was time for dinner, and Tycho recalled that, before they'd left school that afternoon Mrs H had told him that she wasn't sure Zafe would be all that keen on the idea of eating sea-insects and she had suggested that, when they eat dinner, he tell the boy that they were eating bits of something called *baykon*.

The other problem that became apparent as they sat down to their bowls of broccoli stroganoff that evening, was that, used to eating foodcubes on the space station, Zafe wasn't particularly good at chewing.

Also, he'd begun the meal by saying he'd never eaten a green food cube and didn't intend to start.

Nonna had barely touched her food, when she weakly announced that Grundi wasn't to let either boy leave the table until they'd finished their vegetables and she muttered something about needing to be 'elsewhere'.

For the next half an hour Tycho and his grandfather waited for their new visitor to work out what his canines, incisors and molars were for. It also became clear that Zafe hadn't left the afternoon nibbles untouched because he'd been so entranced by Walf's story that afternoon. It began to look as if he might just have sucked the cake and biscuits.

Beltbagology

After dinner, Grundi found Seyfert a beltbag and Tycho introduced him to the science of 'beltbag-ology' by showing him what he carried around in his:

- two sharp stones (quartz and flint)
- a broken stylus
- the key of an unidentified lock, salvaged by his auntie
- a long piece of twine
- a small metal disk
- a button (uncrushed)
- a pin
- a clothes peg (yellow)
- a piece of chalk (white)
- a small piece of wax paper which held half a dozen morsels of 'baykon'

Zafe could see it was a pretty good haul and set to work thinking what he could put in his new beltbag. Tycho's bag was a treasure trove of *stuff* and Zafe scrabbled around in his luggage for his own small haul. Ten minutes later he had the following:

- a slender piece of bamboo (donated to him by Grundi)
- a small piece of soap
- a rubber band (from Nonna)
- a clothes peg (blue — also from Nonna)
- a lace he'd taken from one of his spare shoes
- a toggle from the pocket on his third pair of long trousers
- a coil of red wire (which he couldn't uncoil)

- the Morpheo card.
- a stylus (Nonna's)

They both agreed it was an excellent start. When Nonna had offered him her old 'stylus' and, he'd asked what it was, Zafe was told it was like a pen (without ink) or a pencil (without lead). And what he was given, was a short, sharp stick.

The boys got ready for bed and Zafe asked if he could use the washing room, and then had to be taught how to use the loo-chute (also known as 'the poo-chute'). Ten minutes and a lot of embarrassing questions later, Zafe had 'been' and was told to put his things away tidily, ready for school. There didn't appear to be anywhere to put them, but when Zafe hung his bag from a hook Nonna looked pleased enough.

Tycho lit a bug lantern, explaining that the mothquitos were less likely to bite if they had a light to flock to. (Walf had suggested that Vispa's insects might regard Zafe's intergalactic blood as exotic food and be more likely to attack him.)

Nonna said goodnight and told them it was time to turn in.

'But my parents don't mind when I go to sleep,' said Zafe.

'Seyfert, you go to sleep in this container, as soon as the shipping forecast is over. Besides, it'll be an early start and you've had a long day.' She gave him a hug.

He lay in the hammock (once he'd managed to get into it) and did his best to stay still; every one of his muscles doing its utmost not to do anything at all that might cause the string bed to move. Or flip.

Listening to the waves below and watching distant lights bobbing about, Zafe couldn't remember ever feeling so *alien*.

Tycho and his grandparents had been kind, if a little bossy (and really very huggy), and he knew it was a good idea to see what the worlds had to offer, but he felt very alone all the same. They listened to the forecast (storms coming in from the north-west) and Zafe fell out of his hammock three times (landing on the safety netting but shrieking nonetheless) but he must have eventually drifted off to sleep, because something woke him in the night. A flash of light?

He glanced over at Tycho, who was fast asleep, his limbs flung over the hammock's sides. He looked as solid as a rock and there was no question that Tycho was safe and secure, whereas Zafe felt like he might tip out at any moment and lay as still as he could, his arms locked by his sides, his legs poker-straight.

He wished he could have let his parents know how he was doing, although he doubted that they would have had the time to see anything he wrote. (If he'd been a rhinoceros he'd have had more luck.) He would have told them about the leaves invading the classroom's glassless windows. The flowers! So colourful, delicate and strange. He wished he could have told his parents how much his feet hurt.

He knew they'd have been proud to have heard that he'd been supporting his own weight for five hours straight (and that he felt heavier than he'd ever felt in his whole life). His teacher had warned him about that, of course.

And the children, so many children! He'd been assured they were his own age, but they were bigger. Stronger. Their clothes were a mixture of every colour and pattern he'd ever seen, sewn together any which way. He recalled the brightly painted toes of all the tower-dwellers he met. His heart dropped as he thought of the blisters he'd got from the two pairs of shoes his parents had insisted he wear on the planets.

He couldn't count the number of times in the month before he'd left that he'd been floating about and got told off for accidentally stepping on someone's head. He drifted back to sleep, lulled by the lapping sea.

Tycho also awoke for some reason. He rocked gently in his bed, wondering how the nastronauts managed to go to the loo if they weren't pointing their bottoms out of a hole in the wall? And as for the animals on the Space Arks, if they lived gravity-free what happened to all their poop? Was it floating around, free-range?

Milla and Flan had never mentioned anything about that in any of their radio reports.

A moment later he remembered that Zafe came from the space station, rather than the arks, and he wondered what they did there. And then he saw a flash of lightning, but must have fallen back to sleep before hearing the thunder of the clams.

Oolong or Formosa Gunpowder?

Still Alive!

If he hadn't been so tired from walking, pedalling, climbing, looking at clouds and dealing with gravity, this is what Zafe would have written in his etch-o-pad diary:

Day 2. Grundi saved me from walking off the container while looking at the sky. There was an incident with the hot water pipe, and I'm not allowed to make tea unaccompanied, until I've practised a bit longer.

I'm not a huge fan of Oolong, but Earl Grey is okay. And Nonna had to leave the room when I was eating beetroot.

Day 3. Nonna dyed a couple of orange and blue stripes into my hair and I feel like a proper Hundredwaterer now. Almost fell through the floor-netting getting out of bed and accidentally shut down the central pipes for two hours.

Nonna had to draw me a diagram to show me how to use the poo-chute correctly and I thought I would die of embarrassment.

Day 4. Nearly lost my life doing P.E. with Addie and then nearly lost my life eating dinner. Chewing is TRICKY!

Suza taught me the official Vispan days of the week —
Moonday, Tunaday, Wavesday, Thursday, Fishday,
Swimmerday and Sunsday.

I haven't heard anyone use them yet.

Day 5. WONDERFULLY boring. Nonna only had to tell me to
make my hammock three times, we had potato and bacon soup
for dinner and I'm still alive.

a Hercules?

12.

Haiku Confusion

Zafe reckoned he was getting the hang of life on Vispa; perching at his desk, learning the names of all the vegetables and fruit, helping Grundi and Mr Pomfret with the constant pruning, and identifying bits of metal that needed painting to protect them from the 'elements' (although no-one ever stipulated which ones).

But what he wasn't getting the hang of was getting to and from school, and sleeping at night. Zafe and Tycho took the sky-sedan across the divide between home and school, and they used the stairs and the pedalift back — which left Zafe exhausted, but he was still finding it hard to relax at night. However, a week of poor sleep finally took its toll, and Zafe retired to his hammock early.

He slept soundly and never heard the storm; but then, neither did his roommate.

Tycho had enjoyed the storms when he was younger. The drama of the electric stingrays agitating the giant clams, their clash and rumble, lightning and thunder could be heard all the way from the middle of the Midlantic Ocean. The rays would fight to exhaustion point or until dawn broke, when their current could no longer be seen zig-zagging across the sky.

But he didn't enjoy the storms so much anymore. They felt closer. Too close for comfort.

Unable to sleep, Tycho opened his shutter and poked his head out. It was a clear night and he watched the crackles of light tear across the sky. He listened for the giant clams lolloping across the seafloor, clacking their shells at each other, but tonight the only sounds were those of netting being torn and pans jangling in the wind. The storm itself, was silent.

In the morning, the entire class was yawning, except Zafe who'd rested his head on his desk and begun to snore. He was still catching up on his sleep.

'Mrs Hawtrey is due back any minute, you can't let him sleep!' said Addie, but Walf suggested Mrs H was unlikely to tell off the new boy.

'And what would you know about *not* being told off, Walf?'

'He knows a lot about being told off, so I suppose in theory he must know a bit about the opposite,' Habjeb suggested.

'Exactly!' said Walf.

While Addie, Walf and Habjeb discussed the ins and outs of whether knowing one thing meant you knew the opposite, Suza asked Tycho how the trips home from school were going.

'The sky-sedan attendant says the only person who needs more help is Great Great Great Aunt Nineveh. Although she's quicker getting in, because she doesn't read all the 'SuperBlobBoy' stories on the wall.'

'Yeah, but you can't blame him for that,' said Suza.

'Zafe says they don't have stairs in space, so his legs aren't up to it. He can't get over us all living stacked on top of one another like this. He's tripped over every single step in the container. It's a good job we've kept our netting and that he's got those shoes, although the smell when he takes them off is like a hundred blobfish burps rolled into one.'

Walf confirmed that he'd been able to smell the spaceboy's feet three storeys down and asked whose wise idea it had been EVER to take them off? (And then asked whether he could borrow one of them.)

'Nonna's given him strict orders to take the shoes off regularly to air them *and* his feet, but he stubs his toes so often.' Addie and Habjeb giggled, Zafe let out a particularly loud snore and Tycho blushed, the colour of a squashed raspberry. He patted his roommate on the shoulder. 'He's good fun though. He'll be all right. It's just his feet...'

'Ty, perhaps we ought to wake him up now,' said Walf.

'Gonzales will do it!' said Addie. 'I love it when he wakes me up, it's so soothing.'

'Gonzales is back?' said Walf, looking around the classroom.

'He wandered into our container yesterday. He'd been gone for ages, but you always come home, don't you boy? Aren't you clever!' Addie leaned under her desk to make appropriate cooing noises and entice her part-time pet over.

Of course, if any of them had known quite how Zafe would react to being woken by a Giant African Snail caressing his neck, they would just have given him a prod. The blood-curdling scream certainly got the attention of Mrs H who extracted the snail from the gibbering boy, wiped his neck dry and gave him ten lines to do at lunch time.

'Ten lines? For that noise? I told you he was teacher's pet!' said Walf, who was ordered to put Gonzales outside the classroom, with a large piece of cuttlefish to munch on.

When they settled down to begin an hour of carrot identification, Zafe's only consolation was that Gonzales wasn't likely to slither up and scare him senseless as long as he could hear loud cuttlefish-munching coming from the school corridor. But the boy was still trembling, his stylus wobbling over his waxboard, as he sat, entirely unable to differentiate an Autumn King from a Hercules. They were both long, they were both orange and they were both leafy at the top.

Walf wasn't exactly gripped by the subject either, and he began to mime feeding a carrot into his ear — and it coming out the other side. Zafe smiled, leaned across and whispered, 'I was wondering, how do you spell the teacher's name? A I C H ?'

'No, it's H. The letter 'h'. Her real name is Hawtrey.'

'Why don't you call her that?'

'Well, do you know how to spell it?'

Fair enough, Mrs 'H' it was. 'H' for Hawtrey. 'H' for Hercules. 'H A T G' for Humongous And Terrifying Gastropod.

And 'H' for homesickness.

Because of the previous night's storm, Panjin Dray, the presenter of 'Pleasing Poetry', was unable to present his half hour radio-show lesson of odes, sonnets and limericks (he was busy renetting Bakossi Tower). It was just as well, because they had homework: to write a three-line poem about nature (called a *haiku*). Although Walf and Tycho knew the haiku's 5-7-5 syllables rule, Walf hadn't entirely grasped the difference between a word and a syllable.

From what he'd seen so far, Zafe wasn't entirely sure Tycho could count., and he knew for a fact Walf couldn't.

The topic they'd been asked to write about was 'the weather', but the title of Walf's haiku was 'The Quad-King of DoomMonger'. It was 8-14-17 syllables, and it went as follows:

The SpaceKing of DoomMonger is
A Metal-covered Defender of the Fifth Universe
Who wears the Strongest Armour.

Tycho's haiku was almost the right number of syllables, and it was similarly 'off topic':

Ugly SuperBlob friend
Fish of the galaxy floor
Deep sea fish so cuboid and squashy.

Their return home was even slower than usual. Zafe's legs ached, but he was finding it difficult to concentrate; every storm-following sunset was stunning. A florid mixture of purple, burnt orange, fiery red and vivid turquoise swam before his eyes. At night, the colours would mix together around the horizon, then fade to a steely grey and a familiar black, although often the odd streak of orange persisted for hours.

He asked Tycho about it, and the Vispan boy agreed how weird it was that a sky so busy the night before, should be so vivid.

Tycho said Nonna told him that the bright sunset was generated by the excess electrical charge that had built up during the night, but that he and Grundi had agreed that the sky was bruised. Zafe told Tycho he should have written that as his haiku. He shrugged, but looked pleased all the same.

Later that night, whilst brushing their teeth, Tycho said the leftover streaks of orange were brighter than he'd ever seen them and something about the look on his face suggested this wasn't necessarily a good thing.

They settled in their bunks and lay quiet in the darkening light, entranced by the sky's colours. Taking a deep breath, Zafe carefully turned and asked the question that had been bothering him ever since they'd met.

'So, where do your parents work?'

'They died not long after I was born.'

Zafe flipped out of his hammock, and Tycho leaped out of his and helped him up from the floor.

'I'm sorry, I mean, I just didn't know.'

'I hadn't told you,' he shrugged. 'They were wranglers off Kodiak. We moved to Istanglia afterwards.'

'I didn't ... know.'

'It's all right. There aren't many children who see much of their parents out of season. We like living with our grandparents. It's just that ... I don't see them out of season either.'

He reached for his beltbag and opened up a small metal locket that was pinned inside. It revealed a pair of squid-ink portraits. His father's face was like Tycho's; open and smiling, but the expression was tempered by dark, serious eyebrows. His mother wasn't obviously smiling, but her eyes were, and she reminded him of Nonna.

13.

In the Briny

The next morning at school was swimming, so after registration and assembly they began abseiling down to the bay. Grundi had lent Zafe his swimming shorts and Nonna had suggested that, since he was going swimming, he forget his shoes for the afternoon, and give his feet a 'breather'. But the boy had tripped over one of the beams as soon as he'd taken them off, so she'd reluctantly allowed him to put them back on.

The class jostled in line at the Hundredwater balcony, impatiently awaiting their turn on the rope, and as Tycho was pushed into Zafe he felt the boy shaking.

'Zafe, what's wrong?'

'N-n-nothing.'

'Really? Because the abseiling is fine. We've practised this, haven't we?'

'It's not that. Not just that. It's ... it's the sharks.'

'Oh, don't worry about the Great Whites, Medium Reds or Small Yellows,' said Walf, and a weak smile lit up the newcomer's face. 'They were all eaten by the Double Stingrays, the Megalodon Maximi and the Ultra-ultrapikes.' And the light of hope that had briefly illuminated Zafe's eyes, went out.

Mrs H overheard Walf's remark and quickly got to grips with the situation. 'Walf, that is neither helpful nor kind. The bay is perfectly safe and Fox's grandfather will be in charge!

Mr Flintlo is a very good teacher, you're in the best hands.'

Zafe noticed that, aside from her shepherdess bonnet, Mrs H was wearing a judo suit with a heavy wrestling belt. He didn't know much about swimming but assumed (correctly) she wouldn't be joining them in that outfit.

Tycho clipped the two of them together and they followed the rest of the class down the tower at a slower pace; Zafe's abseiling was louder than everyone else's due to his clunky shoes.

The broad stone steps built into the tower's foundations, were known as the Amburg Ghats. Twenty metres from the far end of the ghats there rose two stone columns, a couple of storeys high, from which were tied nets to cordon off a swimming pool.

Usually, the children who lived on the lowest three floors of their blocks were allowed to get changed and into the water early (forming a human reef) while the less-able swimmers sat on the ghats, waiting for instruction from Mr Flintlo. But the current was strong that morning so they were asked to gather round and listen to his instructions before they'd got into their swimming togs.

And Mr Flintlo's instructions were that, as he was on honey duty, the rest of the lesson would be taken by Mr Drinkwater.

As Fox's grandfather pedalled up and away, cheerily whistling, the Mayor's husband stepped out of the shadows (although none of the class could believe there had been sufficient shadow to hide the man). He was wearing his usual, rather flappy attire and so, was, presumably, not intending to swim either. They were not 'in the best hands' after all.

A hot breeze blew across as the large man read out instructions written in squid ink on his arm, stumbling over any sentence that included a freckle or mole. Listening to very little of what Mr Drinkwater said, Year Seven were anxious to jump in the sea and cool down, and so they began fidgeting.

Stirmatt was dancing, Habjema, Jadri and Fox were catching beetles, and Walf and Tycho were playing 'chopsticks', until Suza gave Tycho a nudge and he caught sight of Zafe. The boy was listening to the teacher even less than the rest of them, and he had wandered away. Standing closer to the water. Zafe's eyes were like saucers and his body was stiff and anxious: until he moved. Taking one step and then another, before Tycho could shout a word of warning, Zafe had thrown himself into the water, shoes and all!

It was obvious as soon as the offworlder hit the waves that he couldn't swim. He smacked the Thames Sea with a loud crack, flailed for a moment and then sank like a stone.

Mr Drinkwater moved faster than anyone could recall him ever having moved before, shoving children aside, many of whom were pushed into the Thames themselves. He leapt into the sea like a magnificent walrus and hit the water with a much louder CRACK than Zafe had managed. In fact, the force of his entry into the water caused a small tidal wave which slammed Zafe back towards the tower and onto the lower ghats, where he was grabbed by Addie and Walf.

Tycho jumped in to check on Mr Drinkwater, who appeared to have got confused and was *doggy-paddling* towards the nets. The rate he was going, it would have taken him days, but still, it was very much the wrong direction. He turned in a slow, lumbering manner, made his way back to the class and dragged himself up the steps on his hands and knees.

Zafe and the teacher lay on the sun-warmed stone, coughing up salty water and the lesson was abandoned. Mr Drinkwater suggested that Mrs Hawtrey's class had learnt enough for one day.

Moving at the speed of flotsam, Zafe was accompanied up the stairs by Tycho and Walf, while the others took the pedalift.

By the time they got back to school Zafe and Tycho's clothes were no longer dripping wet, although over the course of the afternoon a small pool gathered under their desks.

Walf nudged Tycho and whispered, 'Should we put that collar back on him, do you think?'

Tycho agreed that Walf had a point, but suggested that teaching Zafe to swim might be less embarrassing and more useful. Zafe said nothing, but he appreciated the thought. He got his Flint Frog Warrior Morpheo card out of his beltbag, and put it in the sun to dry.

Tidying the classroom at the end of the day, Suza tapped Zafe's arm. 'How are you feeling after the swimming lesson?'

'Everyone said it was like being in space. You just float around. When we're not holding onto something and the gravity's off we do space-crawl. Arm-waving and leg-moving, just like swimming.'

'If you just plop in like a BLOBFISH dropped from a GREAT HEIGHT it's never going to end well, is it!' said Addie, as she passed. She was still fuming: swimming was her favourite lesson.

'It just looked so ... nice. So soft. And that breeze was so hot.'

'Don't worry. If you hadn't fallen in, I would have done.' She put a gentle arm round his shoulders. 'You're a long way from home. And on Vispa, sometimes it feels like we've got nothing but water.' Seeing the crestfallen look on his face she added, 'Don't worry. This planet takes a bit of getting used to and we don't expect OAD's to get it overnight.'

'But *you're* an Other-Astral-Dweller, not me!'

'Oh!' She laughed. 'I am an OAD aren't I? Or at least, if I went to Space Park School, I would be. I'd just never thought about it like that. We're all OADs, it just depends on where you're looking from.'

'Mm, I suppose so.' Zafe offered her a soggy beetroot snap. 'Mrs H said about swimming inside the reef, but how dangerous is it outside?'

Her smile evaporated and she took a couple of deep breaths and told him about Benitt, the boy whose desk he now had, and one of the best swimmers the tower had ever seen. 'He was invited to swim with the grown-ups, when they did the Sunset Swim. It was to the reef and back, the longest swim they did. A couple of people said they noticed Benitt near the reef, so he got that far, and then he disappeared.'

'He drowned?'

Suza shook her head.

'Did he cross the reef?'

She shrugged.

'Did something get him?'

'Nobody knows. He was never found.'

As soon as Nonna heard about Mr Drinkwater's lesson she got on the telepipe to Addie and Suza's grandma (another aquatango enthusiast) and they returned to the ghats that very afternoon to teach Zafe some water-sense. Despite his narrow escape during the lesson, when the suns were high and glinting off the waves Zafe had a tendency to simply wander off the steps of the ghat.

His senses were engulfed by the water's beauty until his body was — and someone had to dive in after him.

After a couple of hours of splashing about, they all agreed that floating was absolutely fine.

14. Hello? Over.

Talk and Walk Where?

Pedalifting home after a day of school, they were a floor away from the balcony gate when Tycho froze, listened carefully to something, and whirled around to Zafe with a look of utter joy on his face. 'Aunt Mirrah!'

Tycho's aunt was a merchaeologist who dredged the seabed for items dropped during the Great Remove (the period when some of the people of Earth had transferred to the four planets). She usually visited with something interesting to show her nephew, although Tycho tried hard not to look too expectant whenever she arrived. Nonna said it wasn't polite.

The last time she'd visited, she'd brought half a bike and Tycho, Walf, Addie and a group of grandparents had made a new pedalift from it, for the tower's south side.

His grandparents were out, so Tycho made the introductions and Zafe noticed how much Mirrah looked like Tycho's mother — and realised how few people of her age he'd met on Vispa.

Tycho asked Mirrah whether she'd recognised their new pedalift? (A subtle reminder of her last gift.) He was trying not to look too keen, but at the same time, anxious to get the waiting over and done with. Had she brought him something, or hadn't she?

Mirrah smiled and told him not to worry. 'I've found you something a little different, which might or might not work. Close your eyes, both of you, and hold out your hands.'

They did as they were asked and assessed what they'd been given. It was a smooth light object, the size of, well, of a mobile telepipe. Tycho turned his over and felt buttons — and a wave of disappointment. 'It's a mobile telepipe,' he mumbled. They were interesting to look at but completely useless of course and Mirrah had given him almost as many mobile telepipes, as she had the dvd disks she was forever hauling up. But his aunt told them they could open their eyes and guess again.

Tycho wrinkled his brow in confusion, it certainly looked like a telepipe.

'Is it a cackulator?'

'No. And it's pronounced "call-cyoo-llar-torr". We're not entirely sure of the name of these things, but think they're called 'Talk-and-Walkies.'

'Oh! You mean walkie-talkies?' said Zafe.

'Is one of them for walking and the other for talking?' Tycho looked a lot more excited than he had been.

'With some help from Walf's grandfather you might be able to hook them up to the radio signal. I gather Mr Pomfret has a radiophone and access to the solar recharging station.'

'Has it been released for use?' Tycho asked.

Auntie Mirrah explained to Zafe that batteries were in high demand but that occasionally they released technology that they hadn't found a space station use for, had too many of or just couldn't work out. So, the Talk and Walkies were theirs, batteries and all.

'And, I've got the walking one, right?' said Tycho.

'They're for communicating,' Zafe blurted out, 'like, you know —' and he inadvertently tapped his arm.

'Ah.' Mirrah nodded. 'I'd heard about your amazing "arm data" from Mrs Hawtrey.' Auntie Mirrah's eyebrows suggested she wasn't fooled for a moment. 'You might find these more helpful down here, once they've been dried.'

'It's like a mobile telepipe that actually works? Superb! Can we go and tell Walf?'

'After supper.'

'What are we having?' asked Tycho, anxiously. They

usually had something that wasn't potato and broccoli-based when Mirrah was over, but it wasn't a given.

'Nonna will be back up any minute now, with the prawn I brought. She's downstairs, roasting it in the ovens.'

'Great. It's all right, Zafe, you'll enjoy that. We'll cut it up for you.'

And as if by magic, Nonna and Grundi appeared with a plate, which was whisked into the kitchen and covered with a colander before he could get a good look at it. Nonna called over her shoulder that she would cut it into cubes for him but Zafe could have sworn he'd seen something bright pink with a dozen or more long, thin legs. (Little did Nonna know that the pink cubes he ate on the space station were a dessert, not a creepy-crawly.)

Zafe was about to ask if it was a kind of fish, when it struck him that, since living with the Istanglians, he hadn't seen them eat any. He asked Aunt Mirrah and Tycho about it.

'It's Vispa's contribution. We eat a bit on Fishdays of course, but most of it goes to the other planets where protein isn't as easy to get, and in return we get crystals for our filtration systems, metal for potato mashers —'

'And butter!' said Tycho.

So that explained Nonna's reaction when Zafe had eaten that chunk of yellow stuff the day after he'd arrived. He'd mistaken it for a mango cube.

Dinner was ... interesting, and as soon as it was over Nonna and Grundi went upstairs to negotiate for some dried fruit from a neighbour. Auntie Mirrah said she had a call to make, so the boys took the stairs down to Walf's. Mr Pomfret kept a large bag of rice in his toolkit, which he used to dry out technology that was brought up from the ocean bed by merchaeologists. He would know what to do with the walk and talking devices.

When they got to Walf's grandfather's workshop, Mr Pomfret told them that their new acquisitions should be dry in a few days. Tycho and Zafe thanked him and sedately pedalifted the three storeys back home, for dessert.

As they neared the 18th floor, they heard Auntie Mirrah on the telepipe. She was obviously talking to someone from work, which wasn't unusual, but what made them stop was the tone of her voice. She was speaking, whispering really, but she sounded worried. They stopped just below the balcony and dangled quietly, listening.

'What were? … I'm not sure it is a fairy story … I know it's just a little above average for the time of year, but it's getting worse. You'll keep an eye on it for me? … I know he doesn't believe me, I'm not sure I believe it myself, but I'm worried and I think there's more we could learn from the old stories about what were … The pantomime? … Well exactly, but it doesn't tell the whole story and he insists it's ancient history, and I hope for our sake he's right. Anyway, I'll pack up tonight and see you in a couple of days time.'

Zafe readjusted his grip and Mirrah must have seen the rope move because they suddenly heard their names, in a tone brighter and louder than before, asking them to join her for a cup of tea.

Auntie Mirrah quickly (too quickly?) explained that she was off to the Southern Hemisphere on a diving trip and would be away for at least a month. She'd never been worried about a trip away before, so why did she seem so concerned now?

Nonna and Grundi came in with a pot of honey and a handful of sultanas and the meal ended with honey-dipped, sultana-scattered beetroot chips. Auntie Mirrah said goodnight, leaped out of the shutters and abseiled away.

As the boys lay in their hammocks that night, Zafe felt unexpectedly tired and let out a long yawn. Waiting to hear Tycho's yawn in return, he was surprised at the silence that followed, until the boy whispered through the darkness the words, 'You wanted to know more about my parents.'

Before Zafe said anything, Tycho carried on speaking and everything became clear. 'They worked with weaver eels mostly. They were caught in a storm and taken down by the creature while they were trying to stop it from getting too close to the towers. It had got inside the reef, which doesn't happen often.'

'There are gaps in the reef?'

'Yes.'

'And they died … together?'

'I was only young and they've changed the rules now so parents aren't allowed to do those jobs together any more. I've lived with Nonna and Grundi ever since. And Auntie Mirrah of course.'

Zafe didn't know what to say. He thought about his own parents and the stomach-churning worry he felt every time they went away for work; a job they always did together.

'Sometimes I just miss having what everyone else has got,' said Tycho.

'Mm,' said Zafe, whose parents, alive, made him feel like that too. They listened to the waves hitting the reef.

'Do many children on Vispa live with their parents?'

'There are a couple in our class who aren't nomads. And the ones who work on the cocoa and coffee fields and the wasabi groves down south, they live together. Walf's parents are on Aurinko the next one along, he'll see them next term.' Tycho turned to face him, leaning on his elbow, a move Zafe would love to have tried but didn't for fear of landing on the netting. 'What about your family?'

'Well … it's just the three of us, but they work long hours and aren't about much.' There was an uncomfortable moment of silence which Zafe quickly filled, for fear of Tycho asking any more questions. 'I was really surprised when I got here and had to go to school every day. It's a couple of days a week on the space station.'

'Really?'

'And there's no soil sifting there, that's for sure. And Jimbib, you'd like him, he's a hoot. And we get to meet our teacher face-to-face sometimes. She's really nice. Mrs Oval. Luckily she wasn't at her desk when the school was sucked away into space.'

They laughed and Tycho was happy to see Zafe's expression relax into something less concerned.

'So, when you're not at space school, do you have to do any homework?'

'It's a bit like radio school you have here. We're on telepipe relays. There's a bit of interrupting, especially when it's maths. Less so for poetry.'

'You have poetry too?'

'Limericks mostly. We've never done a haiku, that's for sure.'

'School finishes early tomorrow, because of the Pantomime, so I was thinking, perhaps we'll pop down to Auntie Mirrah's in the afternoon, before she goes?'

Tycho had drifted off to sleep before Zafe thought to ask what a 'pantomime' was.

15. A Day at the Panto

Once a year the families of Hundredwater School went to the Great Hall for the Grand Pantomime, the poetic story-telling of their history and the feats performed in the interests of survival. (And attempting to thrive.)

The Great Hall in Amburg Towers was made up of lumps of rock, brick and glass and was located about halfway up, only four storeys from their balcony school. It was a traditional gathering designed to impress upon the audience just how important it was to water their flowerbeds, feed their bees, tend their broccoli, carrots and potatoes and generally keep the machinery of modern life going.

Nonna joined her friends at the back of the hall, along with the youngest children on Vispa, who did all the actions required during the performance. Grundi tended to avoid these occasions with a vague wave of his hand, saying it 'wasn't his cup of tea' and generally went out early on a fishing trip (he never caught anything).

The performance began at sunrise. When Zafe should have been listening more carefully to Tycho's instructions about what to do during the pantomime, he was grumbling that half past four was the middle of the night and no time for a school trip. He decided he'd just copy what everyone else did.

Mrs Hawtrey's class sat cross-legged on the floor alongside the other tower children, crammed into an enormous hall that was still quite dark, so dark in fact, that many of them were sitting on Mrs H's dress. She was wearing an outfit she liked to call her 'Victorian ensemble' which involved a voluminous tartan dress with a sequin-covered bodice, a waistcoat and a top hat, all of which, when rustled, released a generous helping of dust. As Stirmatt lowered himself he sneezed violently and Tycho followed suit, even more loudly.

Much of the ensuing chorus of body noises was copied by Zafe, before being shushed by Mrs Hawtrey, who attempted to rise to quell the riot, but was brought to her knees by the small crowd sitting on her skirt.

Despite the intervention of several other teachers, the excitement in the room had risen to a loud, squirmy chatter but the audience was stilled and silenced as the thick curtains opened and they turned to look out at the reflection of the sky behind them.

The twin-suns crept over the horizon, a streak of warmth, light and hope. Everyone sat in silence; the solar rays on their backs and their faces lit up in rainbows of purple and pink. Just as the suns became confident, the outside world was shut away with a swish of material and the room descended into darkness.

The only light now was from a hole in the fabric. A circle of warm yellowy-white light shone onto the wall, turning the smooth stone a watery red.

An elderly man wearing a long ginger beard and matching eyebrows hobbled across the stage with the aid of a gnarly, metal stick, and with a voice reminiscent of clam-thunder, *The Venerable Poet* stood to the side of the disk of light and began to tell:

A History of the Great Remove, The Even Bigger Bang and the Beginnings of a Courageous and Very Wet, Alternative World.

16.

Manatee Matinée

THE TIME TO LEAVE THE OLD WORLD HAD COME (he boomed).

'The people of Ancient Earth, had known the time was near and stories had foretold of the catastrophe for year upon year. Forests were dying, water was polluted and species of animals were disappearing at a rate never before seen on the Old Planet. The noble fruit bat was no more. The —'

'THE NASTRONAUTS!' came a shout. (Was that Mrs Hawtrey?) A cheer went up from Tycho's group and a number of his classmates gave Zafe a smile and a thumbs up, which he returned with a look of bewilderment. It appeared that a lot of the class still believed he either worked on rockets or tended flying giraffes.

'Yes. The nastronauts after years of searching had located a system of planets to sustain us, and a PAIR of suns, where we'd previously made do with just the one. And we'd had to live with a single shadow.'

[BOOOO!]

'The planets the nastronauts found for us could support life: our life. Planets with water. Although, of course, we had no idea just how much water we were headed towards when we came to Vispa'

'BUCKETS OF THE STUFF,' chorused the crowd.

'Each of the four new worlds represented a challenge. Where Vispa is warm and watery, Aurinko is a hot desert, Strom is mild and forested and a little dull, possibly, and Fyel is a cold and mountainous rock we're lucky to be able to see from a great, great distance. Oxygen cultures were planted on the four worlds, Ragnar the Beast cleaned the seas [a great cheer went up] and just two hundred years after their discovery the four planets of the Quadmos were deemed safe to populate.

'The key to our survival had been found and a great cheer went up around the Ancient Earth.

[Silence]

'Humans were to be scattered to the four worlds and the people knew they'd been saved. Only of course a lot of them hadn't.'

The disk of light went dark and there was a minute of silence, as was the way at this point in the telling. Tycho and his friends bowed their heads, and some older grown-ups in the hall could be heard sobbing (along with Suza's voice, trying to calm Mrs H down).

The curtain was lifted and the disk shone again, now a vivid turquoise, and silhouettes of puppet animals paraded across the illuminated planet, along with a host of choreographed hands, swaying in time to a distant drum beat.

'The first to leave the dying husk were the marine creatures. The dugongs, the marlin, the narwhals, the plankton, the jellyfish, the seahorses and sharks were amongst the multitude. And for some of them, Vispa became their home.'

Someone in the crowd meekly said, 'Tell us about the —'

'GOATS! GOATS! GOATS!' cried the crowd (led by Mrs Hawtrey).

'A precious herd of goats was brought to this beautiful planet, to clear the Vispish knotweed from the few plains we are so fortunate to have, so that we might grow energy with which to listen to our radios and learn from the shipping forecast. And leave, of course, when we feel the season shift.'

'GOATS! MORE ABOUT THE GOATS!'

They heard the VP sigh, wearily. 'And they cleared the vegetation from the rocks on which our towers were built; the mighty Amburg, the noble Istanglia, brilliant Bakossi, adamant Adamant, industrious Kodiak, fragrant South Utzeera (at which point a great screech of EUGH! went up from the crowd) and brave Helsingor, which stood alone and is no more.'

'RUST IS THE ENEMY — LET US NEVER FORGET TO PAINT!'

A lone voice sounded from the back of the room 'TELL US ABOUT THE BIRDS!' and the Poet raised his hand in acknowledgment. Story-time was often quite lively. By this time the illumination had changed from brilliant turquoise to soft orange with white cloud cut-outs and the performing children's hands began to flap, framing the puppet birds that were whisked across the disk as the Venerable Poet began to orate again.

'The puffins, the keas, the magpies, the lapwings, the budgerigars, the blue footed boobies —' A great cry went up amongst the crowd and for a moment the Venerable Poet looked flustered. 'Where was I?'

Someone shouted back, 'THE BLUE FOOTED WHATS?' (Mrs Hawtrey again?)

'Ah yes, the boobies. And then the peewits and the robins. Then came the animals. The pandas, horses, cows, sausage dogs, the dugongs, quokkas and pangolins were among the creatures shared between the other planets according to their needs. But of course, a lot of the animals were not saved either,' he said (adding 'Although a great many were!' before the mood changed).

'And when it was found we had not enough vegetation to support the mammals and birds, they were sent to the next worlds along — or the Space Arks — where they live to this day, in harmony, or so I understand.' [Zafe was nudged mightily at this point.]

'And our oceans were filled with a bounty of clown fish, catfish, dogfish, lion fish, tunny fish, fish fish, mahi mahi, mola mola, haddock haddock, tuna, salmon, flounder, herring, bloater -'

[GET ON WITH IT! As far as Zafe could tell this was a Fourth Former.] The Poet cleared his throat and got on with it.

'And much of this bounty we send away. And we gain in our turn the crystals and textiles our beloved Vispa cannot provide us with.'

[There was a brief but embarrassed silence before he spoke again.]

'Of course, a lot of insects and sea-insects joined us in Vispa too, uninvited and, hard as it is to imagine, the early Vispans were wary of such a feast. Wary I say!'

'NEVER!' came the chorus, as was the way at such an event. One child asked what the word 'wary' meant, but the rest of the crowd duly rubbed their tummies and chanted 'Yum-yum-yum' until they were silenced by their teachers.

'And I say it again, they were WARY!' (More yum-yum-yumming…). 'But they soon came round and many-legged sea-protein became our friend. The succulent whirligig, the crunchy water-beetle, the unctuous grub, the *umami* pond-earwig, all carefully chosen and examined before eating, of course.'

It was at this point that Tycho leaned over and whispered into Zafe's ear, 'It's all right, you've been eating baykon,' but before Zafe could ask what Tycho meant, someone had shouted 'TELL US ABOUT VISPA', which was met with a great roar of appreciation. In previous pantomimes, the Venerable Poet had been known to begin a lecture on the correct identification of edible sea-insects, a topic that could take him off course for an hour or more.

'Now, there's a story!' The light shining in from the back of the hall had turned a pale green and silhouettes of people walked across the lit-up globe. 'We humans were left till last, and enjoying, as so many of us do, the thought of a sunny day, Arid Aurinko was the preferred destination. The first settlers were chosen at random, to people the four planets; sent away long before the end of Old Earth, they suffered miserably that we might prosper as we do today. The early Vispans worked hard to build the towers we now inhabit and farm the few peaks, reefs and plains available to us. Years went by, more settlers were sent, towers began to rise and still the meteorite came closer to Old Earth.

'The journey was arduous and the shuttles that brought our ancestors to the family system of planets here were many and mighty, but the meteor arrived earlier than the NASArians had predicted. The date was wrong and a great many were lost.' At which point an embarrassed silence struck the room while the audience considered this, and many of his new classmates looked askance at Zafe whose maths ability was, by this time, well known.

'The meteor struck and there was a Bang, even bigger than the Original One. Where the first brought life, the second extinguished it. Just. Like. That.'

And the room dutifully shouted a mournful **BOOM!** at the tops of their voices, stamping their feet and waving their hands. There was the odd scream which was swiftly quelled by teachers. Or pupils.

'And so we began our life on the new Earths; Vispa, Aurinko, Fyel and Strom. Their fast-paced ecosystems present something of a challenge and we must not become complacent. Remember, pruning shears are our friends. Our space station continues to look beyond these shores for alternative homes when the time comes, but in the meantime, let us all agree how lucky we are to have these homes.'

'AND LET US NEVER FORGET IT!' roared the crowd.

The black curtain was pulled aside and the twin suns shone in, fully risen, bathing the room in light. The children, grandparents and many of the teachers joined in a riot of movement, dance and general frivolity, led by the HundredWater Fourth Form. There was a scuffle and they were escorted out by a group of goat herders.

The last class to actually leave was Mrs H's, who stood around watching their teacher as she carried on swaying to a song that only she could hear.

Bobbing Babout

Mrs Hawtrey aside, they returned to school a little tired after the general excitement of the occasion (and having to get up so early).

In a spirited mood, their teacher performed a loud, long-winded re-enactment of the dawn performance, and while some watched, some joined in and others slept, it was Zafe's turn to be Stylus Monitor, so he didn't get a chance to ask any more questions about the planet's history. He understood that The Pantomime was held to show them the ways of Vispa, to educate and entertain them, but he also understood there was a lot more to Vispa than the strange stories and weird dances he'd witnessed in the Great Hall.

Despite the theatrics of the Pantomime (and Mrs H), the underlying message was serious; telling of the planet's fragility and the need to protect it.

As his classmates made the appropriate actions and familiar calls to the mini-pantomime, Zafe looked out of the window. His attention was caught by Walf's sister and the rest of her class, who were dancing in mid-air — suspended from long lines hung from zipwires. Twirling and swinging like dropping leaves, their backs arched and their toes pointed; Zafe watched, awestruck, his mouth hanging open.

[GOATS, GOATS, GOATS —]

Tycho joined him at the window. 'Yeah, they're not that good.'

'They're incredible!' said Zafe.

He'd never seen anything like it. Such athleticism and grace. He turned to look out of the other window, tripped over a stone in the floor and hit the doorframe. As Tycho helped to mop his bleeding nose (using Zafe's pristine top) he asked 'Don't you have any dancing on the space station?'

'Bhell, bhe've bot bance but bithout bravity, bit's bore bike beople bust bobbing babout,' Zafe unpinched his nose for a moment and dripped onto his t-shirt. 'They bropel themselves off the walls and bloat about a bit. It's nothing like bhat.'

'Walf's pretty good at it — that and pedalift sprinting. Zip-slalom is the best thing ever, but they've banned that until further notice. They're rethinking the rules.'

The rest of the school day was a pleasant shambles during which a mud fight broke out and a box of carrot seedlings was trampled underfoot. They returned home early for lunch; the setting suns cast a golden glow over the calm waters and the air was unusually still.

'You know the goats they mentioned in the pantomime, do they still live here?'

'Yep, quite a few. We used to have hordes of them, too many, but Grundi says we wouldn't have been able to build the towers without them.'

'What happened to them all?'

Tycho shrugged. 'They're still about. Goat Curry Day is a really big deal for the Bakossians.'

When they returned home, Zafe asked Nonna some of the questions he hadn't had a chance to ask at school. She explained that, despite the lack of great white sharks (they had in fact been finished off by the electric stringrays), it was only the reef surrounding the towers within the Thames Sea that prevented the bigger, more dangerous creatures from coming closer than they did. Occasionally something did break through small gaps in the coral, but it happened rarely and was always swiftly dealt with by the wranglers.

As had been mentioned in the pantomime, many people hadn't survived the Great Remove due to the early arrival of the meteorite. Nonna told Tycho that among the space station's many functions was its continual appraisal of the four planets in the Quadmos (something Zafe, with much nodding, pretended to have known). It also sent out parties searching for other habitable planets (something he did know!) and new sources of metal and energy.

There was always a chance the energy sources of Vispa would run out again. The Coffee Crisis of '73 was still talked about: when the space station's flashing lights had dimmed and the giant machine had simply bobbed about for a year, doing nothing.

Tycho also had questions. As far as he was concerned, the plight of the dozens of animals brought to Vispa that hadn't survived wasn't covered in enough depth and he wanted to know more. While much was made of the huge numbers of Red Pandas living on Strom for example, the majestic Naked Mole Rat hadn't thrived on Vispa and he wanted to know why.

Zafe suggested it might have drowned, but his friend wasn't paying attention. How Tycho wished he could visit the animals on the Arks!

He was truly delighted to have an offworld brother but Zafe was no chimpanzee, hedgehog or lemur.

The Pantomime had also failed to mention the many sea creatures already on Vispa when the earthlings had arrived, and the species that had developed since they'd claimed the planet. The boys ate a late lunch with more questions than answers; unfortunately, Nonna's knowledge of Vispan animal life hadn't met their expectations.

After they'd eaten, Tycho and Zafe got ready to descend. They were keen to see Aunt Mirrah before she set off on her mission (and to ask her about that telepipe call). They had told the others about it, and Addie in particular, wanted to know more.

Mirrah lived on a submersible, a massive submarine moored on a jetty linked by a long zipwire to the fifth floor of Istanglia. Her home was one of a community of barges and boats that was mostly made up of merchaeologists and the scientists who recorded the cleanliness of Vispan water.

Tycho had already clipped Zafe on and was clipping himself alongside, when he realised Addie would pummel him if he didn't invite her along too. He unclipped (leaving Zafe dangling) and called her on the telepipe. In fact, he could hear her clipping onto a zipline even as he put the handset down and undialled the number.

Skylubbers, AHOY!

Despite living surrounded by sea, a large number of tower-dwellers were *skylubbers* with nothing in the way of sea-legs. Opinion was divided: was it better to eat a lot before getting on a boat (so you had something to bring up when you felt sick) or board with an empty stomach?

Tycho was a firm believer in the former, so the three of them scoffed some baked seaweed and a bag of pumpkin noodles before zigzagging down the last line to Aunt Mirrah's floating home.

Unfortunately, as they neared the jetty it became apparent that a herd of dog-crabs was visiting the dock too. They were scuttling across the jetty and up the zipwires and netting while Zafe dangled overhead, whimpering. His eyes were out on stalks (much like those of the crabs) as Tycho and Addie helped round them up, prodding them with long bamboo poles, back into the sea.

When a crab got hold of the bottom of Zafe's cable and glared at him beadily, he was not in the least bit reassured by what the others told him about the knee-high crabs not being dangerous. Besides, the sound of their vicious snapping suggested otherwise.

If it climbed up, Zafe reckoned he'd have to let go and hope he squashed a couple of beasts as he fell to his death. Addie told Zafe to calm down and picked a crab up with her bare hands before chucking it into the water, to join the others.

When Zafe finally descended his legs were shaking so much he looked like he was already sailing.

Addie led the way to Mirrah's sub and had already knocked on her porthole before Zafe managed to totter over. The hatch flipped open and Tycho's aunt popped up.

'It's great to see you, I've just finished packing for my trip,' and seeing the look on Zafe's face, she asked what was wrong. 'Oh, those pesky crabs, you mustn't mind them. It's Old Man Geoff-Bert's herd. He ought to have them on leads but sometimes he lets them have a run around by themselves.' Addie clambered up, climbed into the hatch and down into the submarine's hull, followed by the boys.

Auntie Mirrah explained that her sub had been turned into a home after being found on the ocean floor. She and the other merchaeologists weren't sure whether it had been brought over with the original settlers or had been built by them after the Great Remove. She also said it was no longer sea-worthy (although Zafe was sure he could feel it 'bobbing').

Apart from small portholes on each side, light entered the sub from its top, which was made up of a series of glass hatches. As soon as they'd safely boarded, she twisted the hatch shut, pressed a button and they submerged just enough to cover the glass with water — and little fish.

Waves of rippling green light flooded the interior, dancing across their faces. The effect was magical.

One end of the submarine was Auntie Mirrah's hammock room and the other end was an enclosed area which Addie referred to as the 'head' (she explained it was the sailors' name for a loo-chute). And the sub's middle was crammed with more stuff than Zafe had seen since arriving on the planet. There were bicycle wheels, frames and chains, a couple of brass instruments, a ladder, a sack of metal bits and bobs and the usual kitchen sink, in addition to the actual elements of Mirrah's home (and her own kitchen sink).

And all of these finds were covered in a thin layer of green algae giving off a distinctly fishy odour. The swirling light made things feel distinctly … *sub-marine.*

There was something called a 'periscope' hanging down from the ceiling (and up and out through the top of the sub) and Mirrah invited Zafe to take a look at the environment above water, even as they lurked below. Her neighbour on one side was another submarine, complete with curtains and flower pots (although Tycho was fairly sure the bees didn't bother coming this low) and on the other side, a tug boat that had seen better days. Beyond the neighbouring vessels, Zafe looked across at Amburg and then on to Bakossi and the other towers curving round in the distance.

All so different in style, the towers' one point of similarity was their foundations — great pillars of golden stone poking out of the waves, onto which the towers had been plonked. He looked closer at Istanglia's limestone base and was about to step away when he thought he saw something move. A shadow perhaps? No, he saw it again. An opening that came and went with the lapping waves.

Zafe scrunched his eyes, looked hard at the stone and noticed it was a swinging door. It opened momentarily as the wind blew, revealing a set of stairs leading up into the heart of Istanglia Tower. He was about to ask about it, when he found himself being examined by a pair of beady eyes on stalks and heard the clack-click-clack of a giant crab on the loose. It began scratching at the glass and the sound of its friends cantering over the submersible's hub was deafening — that and his own yelping.

Mirrah shooed them away with the clang of a bamboo brush against the hull, and Zafe swiftly joined the others, if only so that Tycho could protect him. He'd fend them off.

After another round of vigorous brush-whacking, Mirrah returned to them and told Addie what she'd found on her last dive. 'Nothing of interest to any of you, I'm sure. Some masonry, which may or may not be added to Amburg and a couple more containers, which may or may not be added to Istanglia. On the smaller side, we found something one of my colleagues identified from catalogue records as an 'ironing board' ...' They all made (appropriately impressed) wooOoo sounds. 'Knowing its name is one thing, but we've got no idea what it's good for. Still, it's metal and that's the main thing. Now, who would like a cup of Orange Pekoe?'

She pulled a copper gas pipe from amongst a tangle of bits and pieces attached to the wall, put the kettle on and managed to find some perches for her guests. Addie positively enjoyed submarine life and Zafe was getting used to the faint smell but the slight motion of the sub was always difficult for Tycho, whose face was beginning to blend into its green surroundings.

Auntie Mirrah fished a small crab out of a bucket she handed to her nephew — just in case. Unfortunately, the inhabitant landed on Zafe's shoulder and there was a bit of a to-do while they ejected the crab and Tycho threw up half his lunch.

When things had calmed down again, Auntie Mirrah carried on telling them about her latest finds.

'Lots of dvd disks, of course, and we dredged up a machine called a printer. We don't know how this differs from a typewriter, or whether it's the same as a printing press and we've no idea how a coil of jellypaper would fit in or how we'd apply the squid-ink. What we do know is that without knowing either of those two things, it's useless and will either be put in the museum archives or have the metal bits melted down and turned into a potato masher, but I'm hopeful one of my colleagues will find the time to make it work.'

Addie jumped up and down, waving her hand in the air, 'I've got the time! I've got the time!'

'Well, if you're interested, Addie? I'll see if we can get it up to you. Ah, Tycho, back in the land of the living? Have some tea, it'll settle your insides.'

While Addie, Zafe and Mirrah perched, Tycho stood, flexing his knees, bobbing about as he sipped his drink, trying to counteract the sub's swaying.

'Aunt Mirrah?'

'Yes Tycho.'

'I was wondering about something I heard the other day ...'

'Ye-es?'

Without actually admitting to eavesdropping on his aunt's conversation, this was going to be difficult. Fortunately, Addie stepped in. 'Tycho heard you on the telepipe, and we wanted to know more about what was —'

His aunt's face flushed. 'You heard about the ... Wotwa?'

The what?

Eavesdroppers

Auntie Mirrah hooked the teapot and her mug back onto a rack and got up. Each time the vessel swayed, luke-warm tea leaked onto the floor, only adding to the submarine's general sogginess. She paced back and forth and it was Addie, again, who broke the silence.

'When you were on the telepipe the other day, you were saying something about the old stories and how they're still important. We wanted to know what it was about. And, you know, about the *Wotwa*.'

Tycho couldn't help but be impressed by Addie's canny use of a word that, until the last ten seconds, they'd never heard before.

'I was fairly sure I'd been overheard when the two of you popped up so suddenly at the end of my call,' she glanced at Tycho and Zafe, 'I probably shouldn't have been discussing it on a civilian line, anyway.'

'Are you not a civilian then?' Addie asked, her eyes open wide. Tycho had always suspected his aunt was something official but had never had the guts to ask.

'So! You heard about the 'Wotwa,'' she reminded them, changing the subject back again.

'Um…'

'Yes, yes, the Wotwa!' Addie butted in, nodding her head and glancing at Tycho, willing him to be quiet.

Mirrah paused, preparing her words carefully, but it was Zafe who spoke. 'Wait a minute, are you talking about the Wotwot?' Addie and Tycho stared at him, their eyes like saucers. 'Like the fairy tale?' Aunt Mirrah's eyebrows shot up. 'Do you mean to say it's … *real*?' he asked, looking at each of them in turn.

'How do **you** know about it?' asked Auntie Mirrah, sounding quite put out!

He shrugged. 'It's something we say on the space station, you know, "if you don't go to sleep the Wotwot will get you. If you don't eat your green foodcubes or learn your times tables the Wotwot will eat you." You know, stuff like that. I didn't know it came from here. It's supposed to be diabolical, but not, you know … not real!'

'I'm sure it's just a coincidence. And what we're supposedly dealing with is something that lives in the sea, after all,' Mirrah replied, before Addie said 'Wotwot and Wotwa?'

Zafe went on. 'Yes, a sea creature. In the story, the story the Wotwot was defeated by the Ginormous Sea Gherkin of Doomvillia, although that might just have been my Uncle Ferdinand trying to cheer me up. I love the word "gherkin". Gherrrrkin!'

His simple smile evaporated when he saw the expression on Mirrah's face.

She walked over to the sink and began washing up, while Addie idly tinkered with bicycle gears and Tycho picked up the bucket again, just in case. When the cups were clean, Mirrah spoke, her hands resting on the sink, her gaze looking out to the sea.

'The storms used to be three times a year at most but they're becoming more regular, as I'm sure you've noticed. But have you also noticed that the giant clams aren't making as much noise as they were?'

Addie and Tycho nodded.

'Well, we think they're being picked off. The electric stingers haven't increased their numbers, so we don't think they're the culprit. We just don't know what's taking the clams.

I mean they're … HUGE, and as far as we can tell they're being laid to waste. Two thousand years old, destroyed in a single storm. Nothing else is being singled out and water pollution hasn't got any worse. It hasn't of course got any better, but it certainly hasn't got worse. We send our samples to the space station and they monitor them for us, and it seems there's been no change.'

'And the Wotwa?'

'Well, something's not right. One of my colleagues is convinced it's the Wotwa, Wotwot, whatever it's called! But surely it's just a legend! He thinks it's got something to do with Ragnar.' She shrugged.

'THE MAN IN THE PANTOMIME?' Addie yelled. Finally something they recognised! The story of Ragnar the Beast was taught at kindergarten. He was one of the first people to arrive on the planet and, as the pantomime reminded them, he'd cleaned the seas making Vispa safe for habitation.

Addie's excitement was short-lived. Was Aunt Mirrah saying there was was something BIGGER than a giant clam lurking in the water? Swimming lessons would never be the same again and they definitely would have remembered a ghatkeeper's report mentioning anything about giant sea-gherkins.

A second pot of tea was made and some dry potato crackers laid out. Mirrah told them what they wanted to know, while Tycho poured out the Earl Grey.

'A submersible went out two weeks ago to the middle of the Midlantic, looking for something entirely different, patterns of seaweed movement and colonies of blobfish. My colleague joined them on the off chance a couple of containers had gone down nearby because there'd been a disturbance in the wave patterns. Bits of clam were found, enormous shards of shell strewn all over the seabed, and they're a truly formidable animal. I wouldn't want to fight one and I don't know anything that would.'

'Perhaps they're tasty?' Addie suggested.

'You may be right, but whatever's eating it must be huge.'

'Did the crew see something in the dark sea?' asked Zafe,

his eyes open wide. 'Something scaly with a long tail that was bigger than anything they'd ever encountered, with teeth like daggers and —'

Mirrah let out a long sigh and looked at her guests, unsure whether she should carry on. 'I don't know what to believe, but you mustn't tell anyone about this wotwa-wotwot-I don't' know what! There would be mayhem.'

The three of them nodded their heads and, seeing Aunt Mirrah's expression, began shaking them instead, until Tycho spoke up. 'Apart from Walf! We have to tell him.'

'And Gonzales and Suza, obviously,' said Addie.

Aunt Mirrah rolled her eyes. 'The main thing is that we don't need everyone to get into a great panic.' And with that, she gave them each a seaweed bar for the trip home, the sub bobbed up to the surface and they clambered out.

The hatch closed and Tycho stood on the jetty, his hands on his hips, looking out to sea. 'If there's any chance the Wotwa is real, the scientists are going to need all the help they can get.'

'Just as well we're here,' Addie replied, to which there came a muffled 'I HEARD THAT!' from within the sub.

With two of the three of them excited about what they'd learnt, and the other one muttering about how he'd preferred it when the Wotwa was just a way to make him eat his greens, they sprinted to the pedalift (Zafe thought he'd heard some more crabs). They pedalled pensively up and across to Addie's container, where they argued over just how few (or how many) people they'd agreed they could tell.

The only thing Addie and Tycho did agree on was that there was no question of talking to any other grown-ups about it. They had made a promise to Mirrah — which Addie then revised.

'I'll keep *schtum* as long as the Hundredwater Herald can have the exclusive when the story breaks.' Tycho knew this was something to do with her reporting, agreed to whatever it was and skipped all the way down the stairs to the sky-sedan. Zafe followed at a slower, more thoughtful, speed.

By the time Zafe and Tycho got back home it was dinner and the *cabbage con carne* wasn't as spicy as they'd hoped, added to which, the apple surprise had curdled. Tycho listened in horror as Zafe discussed the interesting knobbly nature of the pudding they were eating and asked Nonna how she'd managed to create such an effect. They were sent to bed early.

They brushed their teeth, slunk off to their hammocks and lay in the dark, listening to the waves.

Tycho?'
    'Yes?'
    'Is there going to be a storm tonight?'
    'Nope. It's too quiet.'

'Zafe?'
    'Yes, Ty?'
    'What are times tables?'
    'What?'
    "The thing you had to do or the monster would get you."

Not knowing about the Wotwot was one thing. Not knowing your times tables, let alone never having *heard* of them, was quite another.

Adventure!

Hunched over a pile of seeds the next day at school, Tycho whispered to his table-mates about his aunt's forthcoming trip to the Southern Hemisphere. He recounted the conversation he and Zafe had overheard, the discussion they'd had and what they'd learnt about the 'Wotwa'.

'You what?' Walf asked him.

'You know, the 'Wotwa'. It was what Mirrah was talking about on the telepipe when I pedalled up with Zafe.'

Walf turned it into a tongue-twister and spent the next couple of minutes wittering about '*what a Wotwa was when a Wotwa wasn't*', which wasn't getting Tycho anywhere, and he was only made crosser when Walf asked 'So what is it then?' and he was unable to answer.

Zafe tried to explain. 'It's what they say when you're mucking about at bedtime. "If you don't brush your teeth the Wotwot will get them! If you don't stop mucking about the Wotwot will eat you." Stuff like that.'

'So, it's a Wotwot now?'

'What?'

'Not a Wotwa then?'

'Um.'

'Zafe! What-what-what are you talking about?' It was Mrs H. The boys quickly looked down at their seed trays and Suza had the good grace to drop a pot of lavender on her foot, as a distraction. Maybe.

With Mrs H otherwise engaged, the boys knelt behind a row of plant pots and Zafe waited until Addie had joined them. 'On the space station we call it the Wotwot. It's the Worst Of The Worst, a giant … thing. It's a nightmare. I mean it used to be a nightmare … when I was small.'

'Mine is cabbage,' said Walf.

Addie added, 'Mine is an afternoon with my neighbour.'

Walf shivered, 'Cabbage is frightening, it keeps me awake at night.'

'When my neighbour eats cabbage it keeps me awake at night.'

'All right, think about your worst, most nightmarish *monster*,' said Zafe, in a tone that suggested none of their nighttime horrors were quite what he'd had in mind.

'Ooooh. A blobfish, no question about it,' said Walf.

'Bigger than that.'

'A shark-octopus?' said Addie.

'More frightening,' although the tone of Zafe's voice suggested he desperately wanted to know whether such a thing was real but was afraid to ask.

'A giant shark-octopus with claws and big teeth?' said Walf.

'It's … it's even worse than that and a bit more like a sea serpent. A monstrous serpent with loads of teeth, rows and rows of them. FANGS. Rows of fangs.'

While Addie and Walf were adding diabolical and dangerous elements to the Wotwot, Zafe noticed that Tycho had fallen silent. The boy's face was chalky-white. 'What's wrong?'

'What I saw was real —' They turned to look at him. 'The thing I told you about, Walf. It was a year ago. It was late, there was a storm, not a very bad one, but my ears were aching and I needed some fresh air.' Zafe made a face. 'Okay, I needed some *more* fresh air, so I went up to the roof, by the hive anchors and I was sitting under a tarpaulin to keep dry. Anyway, I was looking out to sea and I saw something, beyond the reef. Just for a second or two, lit up by the lightning. A huge, dark shape in the water. Bigger than anything I've ever seen before.'

Tycho looked at each of his friends in turn, willing them to speak. They sat in silence until he blurted out, 'No wait! There was someone else there too, they must have seen it!'

'Who?' asked Addie.

'I don't know, they were a long way off. On Amburg's roof, I think.'

They could have done without Walf's next question. 'Did it breathe fire?'

Tycho punched Walf's shoulder and stomped off with his arms crossed, and Zafe was annoyed that Walf had thought of the one thing which, according to the stories, the monster didn't have. It was Addie who suggested that seeing as the Wotwa had all the other stuff they'd mentioned (horns, poisonous fangs, claws, scales, an electric prodder and acid shooting out of its nostrils) AND Tycho had actually seen it, they ought to have been grateful for the lack of fire.

They hadn't realised that Suza had joined them. 'So that's the way they make you brush your teeth on the space station?' she asked. The boy nodded.

'Zafe does have nice teeth,' said Walf.

They agreed that they'd promised not to mention anything to anyone; Auntie Mirrah didn't want people to panic. They also all agreed that although a diabolical sea creature threatening to eat towers was worrying, they could handle it themselves. All but Zafe.

'Don't you think we should tell your grandparents about this?'

'*Enid Blyton*, remember!' Tycho's expression had changed from worried and frightened to excited. Very excited.

'I don't understand.'

'We can handle this ourselves! There are FIVE of us! It's a Book at Bedtime thing, you wouldn't understand. We can do this, I know we can.'

'BUT IF THIS THING IS REAL —'

'Shhhhhhhhhh!'

'But you promise you'll keep it secret, for Tycho?' said Walf, 'This is our adventure, and there are five of us, like he said.'

After much cajoling Zafe agreed to say nothing but he was worried by the tone Tycho's aunt had taken AND the possibility that Tycho had actually seen the thing. Not to mention the fact that he said he'd seen it but was still thrilled about it.

There was more to this than an idle, hygiene-related bedtime threat.

They were tidying up the seed packets and sweeping the floor, when Suza whispered, 'We could go to a library and find out about it.'

Tycho's brow was as furrowed as Walf and Addie's. 'A what?'

'A library?'

Zafe looked just as confused until his expression suddenly cleared and he piped up 'It's a room of books isn't it?'

They all looked at him, confused, apart from Suza who gave him a confident *thumbs up*.

'Who, on Vispa, would have a room *full* of them?' Tycho asked. 'I mean, who'd ever need more than one or two?'

'They've got the answers to questions.'

'Like what we're having for dinner tonight?' Walf asked.

'No, not that sort of question,' said Zafe.

'Like why Mrs H always tells Walf off when Devik is being an idiot too?' said Tycho.

'No, no, more like questions about subjects like history, geology, marine biology, horror, crime, you know — fiction stuff ...'

'Wait a minute, biology-horror? Is that a subject?' asked Addie, grimacing.

'It is now!' Walf was grinning ear to ear.

'And you think we might find the Wotwa in a library?' Tycho shrugged. 'Okay, lead the way!'

Suza came to with a start. 'Um. I don't know where one is, I just know we need one.'

'There's a library on the space station,' said Zafe. 'It's enormous. Four million books at least.'

'*Million*! What does that even mean?'

'As many as there are fish on South Utzeera,' said Tycho.

'Too many to count,' said Walf, 'So how big is the space station then?'

'Well, you know … they're on file.'

'Ooooh, technology!' The children all shook their heads and "swiped" each other's faces before clipping onto their zipwires.

Tycho checked Zafe's clips and clapped him on the back. 'Okay, after school we'll ask Grundi if we've got a library.'

The school gong DANGED, Mrs H shouted something and Tycho leaped off the side of the building, forgetting he was going home with Zafe. He climbed back up the tower and they took the sky-sedan, together. Sedately.

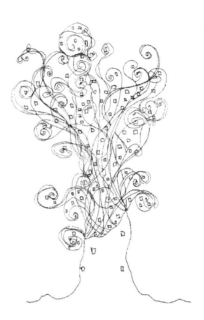

21. Bakossi TWANG

Although Vispans were able to read and write, books were a rarity. Paper was difficult to make and expensive to import, and the quality of the re-re-recycled paper was low, so whenever documents were required (swimming certificates and so forth) they were printed onto dried, rolled jellyfish tentacles. But the production of jellypaper was so time-consuming that books were no longer produced and stories were told by pantomime or radio, or around the warm glow of a candle with a beetleburger in your hand.

Vispan schools had the curriculum painted onto walls, and the classrooms were covered with lists of spelling words, and brightly painted animals, birds and fish (mostly drawn by Walf).

News was spread by graffiti (much of it done by Addie) and the floors with zipwires and sky-sedans were a font of information; articles from the Herald, details about tea mornings, gardening tips, ferry timetables, local elections and weather reports, all scratched into the paint until there was so much going on none of it made sense anymore – at which point the area was repainted and the scrawling began again.

Sometimes the elder Vispans had a bit of a grumble about the lack of books and falling standards in education, and Tycho recounted an afternoon tea he'd spent with an uncle of Nonna's who'd said that when he was a child, they'd learnt all about "the Agyptians and how they conquered the dinosaurs". (And he remembered his grandmother shaking her head.)

What he did not recall, was any mention of a library.

They found Grundi in the lower quarter, bottling honey. Taking care not to spill a drop, he raised his eyebrows at them.

'We've got a question. Do you know of a —' Tycho had forgotten the word. He looked at the floor, the ceiling, Zafe, and then Walf who muttered 'Wotw-' before Addie quickly yelled 'LIBRARY!'

The old man's eyes lit up. 'Excellent! What is it you want to look up?' As Walf and Tycho's gaze swung to the ceiling, Suza that they wanted to know more about Vispan history, the first people to arrive – and the creatures they found.

'Vispan creatures eh? Interesting. Give me five minutes, I know someone who may be able to help.' Grundi finished the jar he was working on, squirting honey through a long tube that wound its way down the tower's centre, filtering the golden goo as it dripped.

He made a quick call on the telepipe and they were off — to meet a lady who worked at the Thames Library and Broadcasting Service.

'Where does your friend live?' asked Addie.

'I don't know her terribly well; she's a neighbour of a Bakossian friend of mine, but I have known librarians in the past, and they're lovely people. Happy to answer any questions you have — if they can, and if they can't, they'll always help you find an answer. So helpful, they really do live for knowledge.' Grundi got a bit day-dreamy at this point, until Tycho told him that the others had swung off and that they may have already arrived at Bakossi, not knowing where they were actually supposed to be going. Tycho, Zafe and Grundi made their way to the sedan stop.

'A little patience wouldn't go amiss, Tycho. It just so happens they live right next door to the sedan stop on the other side, so there's a chance we'll beat your friends over there.'

While Istanglia Tower was a medley of colourful metal containers dotted with flower-boxes, and Amburg was a mixture of salvaged stone, brick and glass, even in the late afternoon light it was clear Tower Bakossi was something different again. Crafted from metal strips salvaged from Istanglia, it had been welded together to make something that resembled a broccoli floret, its stalk firmly held in the tower's stone foundations.

Aside from its broadcasting, Bakossi was famous for its grapes and runner beans, and vines wound around every metallic frond. From a distance, the tower appeared to be covered in a lush green fuzz.

'What's that smell? It's…' Zafe's nostrils were twitching, but his usual expression of horror was replaced with one of confusion. It looked like broccoli, but …

Where Istanglia's gutters were full of flowers for the bees, Bakossi's were full of sultanas, raisins and currants. 'Bakossi is famous for its dried fruit. It's nice isn't it? I understand that Mrs Altvassa, the lady whose house we're going to visit, makes a particularly toothsome sultana bread and —'

TWANG.

The noise was unexpected and they made the little craft lurch when they leaned out of the sedan windows, trying to see what had happened.

TWING.

It was coming from the direction in which they'd come.

Zafe alone turned to Bakossi as they arrived — and he was the first to get out and battle his way through the leaves and vines, while Grundi and Tycho scanned the horizon.

Cast in a faintly green light, Mrs Altvassa's home felt subterranean, as if they'd arrived at an underground burrow, although Zafe was relieved to feel metal beams, rather than branches, under his feet. He could hear the hiss of a kettle of water coming to the boil, obscured by a rack of dented pans, long ladles and curling fronds.

DOY-YOY-YOING.

'It's zipwires snapping,' said Grundi.

Intrigued, Zafe turned and realised from the expressions on everyone's faces, that this wasn't one of those things unknown only to offworlders. The Vispans looked just as bewildered as he did. This was definitely something out of the ordinary, un-run of the mill and totally anti-normal.

There was a sound of splintering glass. And a couple of seconds later, a smell from hell.

'THAT'LL BE THE POO-PIPES!' It was Walf, swinging beside them, still clipped on.

'I'd better go back,' said Grundi, 'Make sure everything's ...' Then his head tilted to the right.

KKRRRIIIIIIIIIIIIIIIIIIIIIIIIIIIIIIIKKKKKKKKKKKKKKKKKKK
KKKKKKKKKKKKK.

Istanglia was at an angle.

Not Visiting the Library

The tower was broken. The water was high, lapping Istanglia's metal foundations, but below the waves something had snapped and the entire tower was tilting towards the reef. Teetering.

'It looks like it's stopped drooping for now,' said Grundi, 'but I'd better go. Nonna will be gathering a team together to stabilise the tower with cables.' He managed a brief smile before adding, 'We'll fly the black flag if it isn't safe, in which case you lot will be sleeping at school tonight.'

And with that he began climbing up the metal branches hidden within the tower's greenery and a moment later they watched him zipping sedately towards their mangled home.

They all entered the container to which they'd been invited, but there was no sign of a host. Should they make themselves comfortable? Were they even in the right place?

'This is weird,' said Tycho, 'Not much of a welcome.' He was biting his lip, and it seemed to Zafe he was trying his hardest not to look in the direction of home.

'I wish Grundi hadn't gone,' said Addie.

'Well *I* wish our tower wasn't falling down!' pointed out Walf.

'IT'LL BE FINE!' They all stared at Tycho, whose eyes were blazing.

'Yes, I'm sure it'll be fine,' said Addie. 'Nonna will sort it out.' She flicked some foliage, studiously avoiding his gaze. 'Anyway, we're here to do a job. We've got to find out about the Wotwa.'

'Quiet,' said Suza, 'We're not even supposed to be mentioning it.'

'Mentioning what?' said Walf, 'The Wotw- '

And then they heard a voice: smooth and dreadful. Reminiscent of a writhing eel, it oozed from somewhere beyond the pans.

'Well, well, well, what an interesting incident. And a slightly tardy pleasure, I notice. Won't you sit down?'

A young man entered the room, holding a slice of turnip and raisin cake in one hand and a large knife in the other. Dumbstruck, the five of them were hypnotised by the shining blade and it took an arched eyebrow from their host for them to react. Tycho stepped forward and proffered a hand, before realising it looked like he either wanted to take the cake, disarm the man or be stabbed. He took a step back. 'We've come to visit the library. My grandfather is a friend of a neighbour of Mrs … Antwater.'

'My great-aunt conveyed the message and was unable to make it, so I shall be entertaining you instead,' he replied, 'And the name is Altvassa. Horst Altvassa.'

He invited them to make themselves comfortable, but as there was only one perch they had to make themselves uncomfortable, cross-legged on the floor. Their host left the room and returned with a tray laden with afternoon tea, but his hospitality was at odds with the look of boredom on his face.

Without the knife in his hand, it was easier to concentrate on the man. Or boy. He wasn't actually much older than they were, but old enough that he was out of place and of an age when he should have been working down-planet or off-world by now.

He wore long trousers and his dark hair was neither plaited, dyed nor shaved. He showed no allegiance to any tower or school. They introduced themselves, although Horst seemed to know who Zafe was, pronouncing his full name slowly, carefully — and correctly.

The turnip and raisin cakes (fresh from the Bakossi furnace) were the nicest thing Zafe had eaten since his arrival, but they ate in silence; with the exception of Walf who hummed cheerfully as he wolfed three slices. Zafe wondered whether he was trying to find some comfort in the food. Walf and their host seemed to be the only two whose faces were not ashen with worry. Or unease.

'I understand you are scholars, interested in Vispa's marine history and biology?' They nodded. 'We at Broadcasting House often visit schools for outside broadcasts. You all listen to the shipping forecast I hope?'

They nodded again. Addie mentioned the name of their teacher and asked when Hundredwater would be chosen for the Youth Broadcasting Competition. For the first time since they'd arrived, their host stumbled over his words, saying something about their calendar being booked up.

'I wonder what that was about?' Zafe whispered to Walf.

'You know what Mrs H is like when she goes to the Pantomime. Imagine what she'd be like on the radio. LIVE radio.'

'Much as I'd love to tell her we've been to a library, it might be just as well to keep this trip under our hats,' said Addie, in what she imagined was a whisper.

'And I'm happy to tell you we won't have to go to the library,' said the young Altvassa. 'I have everything you need to know right here.' He picked up a bag, from under his perch, and extracted from it a book. A single book. 'Our collection is diminishing at a fierce rate of knots so some of the more important items are … held elsewhere. There's little we can do about crumblage, cack-handedness, mildew and bookworms.' (Zafe noticed Tycho wondering what bookworms did, while the look on Walf's face suggested he was wondering what they tasted like.)

'In fact, the problem is so acute, that in the time I've been watching you eat, we've lost another book.' And for a split-second, the young man's "smile" was replaced by an expression that suggested they'd taken that book and lobbed it off the tower themselves.

Beaming her brightest (actual) smile, Addie tried to win their host round, by telling him that Zafe came from a place with *millions* of books *on file,* but her attempt to win favour couldn't have been less successful. The look that Horst gave Zafe was almost as hostile as the tone with which he spat out the words, '*Spaceboy*'.

He said nothing more and turned to the book on his lap. It was loosely bound within a cover of rough, seed-splattered paper; its thickness due to the coarseness of its pages, rather than their number. He held it close, leaving smudges of dust and cobwebs on his shirt, and the title (which appeared to be handwritten), was 'Hand Picked: An Early History of Vispa.'

The librarian stared at each of them in turn. The effect was unsettling, and his pale blue eyes were suggestive of an animal Zafe had read about but could not recall. When he was sure he had their full attention, their host began to recite the history of Vispa, and it was clear this was a book Altvassa had read many times as he barely referred to the written page.

'The first people to arrive on Vispa were scattered to the four winds, building towers, finding and settling land in a way that is hard to imagine today. People were arranged according to their interests and abilities, their love of vegetables and their knowledge of a particular terrain, but squabbles arose between people who did not want a sea view and those who wished to live in metal containers or bamboo boxes. It was a time of great turmoil.

'Amongst the many tribes were one particular people; the wild and wondrous Uiskers. Much-misunderstood, they were famed for their farming and their music, and they were renowned for their sweet-tooth and their height. But the islanders of Uisk were lumped in with folk with whom they'd been lumped before and promises were made and forgotten.

'Famed for their herding prowess, they turned instead to piracy and were known throughout Vispa as 'the Worst of the Worst' for that very reason.' His eyes shone — and at the mention of '*the worst*' all five of them gasped (wishing very much they hadn't). The historian surveyed them, one by one, and returned to his lecture.

'The Worst of the Worst were the scourge of the spice territories, controlling mustard, wasabi, paprika, cinnamon and chilli trade routes, and they were determined to chase others from land they considered their own.'

'But Vispa's made up of sea!' whispered Zafe (a little too loudly as it turned out).

'There's land in the south,' hissed Tycho, 'Plantations where they grow coffee —'

'What did you say?' Horst's voice was hard, agitated. This man was a world away from the helpful book-finding people Grundi had raved about.

'Zafe just wanted to know about the south.'

'Did he? And what is it *you* want to know?'

The others felt the young man's piercing gaze boring into Tycho and they paled in solidarity. It was Addie who broke the awful silence by blurting out 'SEA WORMS.'

'Sea worms? That's what keeps you awake at night?' Horst closed the book, a smile playing on his lips. 'I can assure you worms are real. I'm surprised you haven't covered them in school. Is this part of a project?'

The children carried on telling fibs, babbling about how Mrs Hawtrey hadn't taught them this, that and the other, and how they were studying this, that and the other, (so that they might get their hands on this, that and the other).

Addie told him they were particularly interested in anything of a marine nature. Horst sat silent, listening. Very still.

'I'm afraid I have to disappoint you. I know the library's books like the back of my hand and we have nothing about sea worms, giant or otherwise. You'd be better off studying the graffiti on your classroom walls.'

'What about the Ginormous Sea Gherkin of Doomvillia?' asked Zafe. Tycho's eyes opened wide; Horst was bound to suss out the reason they were there.

'Ah, now the *Humongous* Sea Gherkin of Doomvillia is fictional and won't be on any of your classroom walls, assuming your teacher knows what she's talking about.' His smile was the warmest one he'd managed since they'd met him; happy he could allay their fears with regard to another ridiculously enormous creature that was the stuff of nightmares. 'And there are no books on that either.' He continued reciting his history of Vispa.

Suza whispered what they were all thinking. 'So, the only thing that could save us from being eaten by the Wotwa is made-up, and all the terrible stuff we thought was just a story might still be true. And unless we find something to help us, our tower is going to be something's lunch.'

'At least you've got a tower to **be** lunch, ours might have fallen into the sea by now!' hissed Walf.

'… and so, for a good half of the history of our planet the Uisker have been silent, a forgotten threat we have forgotten again, to our cost. Stories were told of the most terrible sea creatures, created by the tribe from sea-dwellers which existed before the Great Remove and those we'd brought with us.

'Creatures that combined the size of the Indigo Whale, the predatory instincts of the Clownfish, the speed of the Tunny fish, the many tentacles of the Giant Squid, the poison of the Bag Jellyfish and the electrical charge of the Hammer Ray. Creatures more terrible than anything encountered before, that could only be wrangled by the Uisker.'

Tycho put up his hand and said, 'Excuse me, but what happened to the Uisker people?'

'And did they have whiskers?' asked Walf.

But before Horst could answer, there was a strange sucking sound, followed by a scream.

Bannabage

GONZALES IS ON MY FOOT!

Zafe leapt up and, after crashing into the foliage, he whipped round and knocked into the librarian, who tipped from his perch-stick. A dozen loose pages fell from the book and Suza rushed to gather them up while Walf attempted to coax the snaily, ankle-sucking fiend away from Zafe with a piece of cake. Gonzales' little eyes waved about in alarm when Tycho tried to pull him off Zafe's leg and Addie announced that there was only one thing that would shift Addie's friend and that was CUTTLEFISH.

The quiet intensity of Horst's lecture had been shattered by the giant gastropod, and their host marched into the kitchen with the book under his arm. By the time he'd returned (carrying a salt shaker) the snail had gone, leaving a long trail of slime up Zafe's leg. The boy muttered something about it being "the last time he'd wear shorts," and Walf telling Zafe that Gonzales obviously liked the way he smelled didn't help at all. Meanwhile, Addie put Gonzales on the sky-sedan, with strict instructions to be a brave snail and to behave.

Altvassa rearranged his seat, bristling with rage. 'Where were we, *Spaceboy*?'

Zafe had barely recovered from his run-in with Gonzales, and unable to speak, he blushed — all the way from his slime-ridden legs to the roots of his hair.

But Addie spoke up, 'WE were wondering if you know anything about Ragnar? Suza was thinking of doing a project on him.' Suza gulped. Loudly

'You're interested in Ragnar ... the Beast?'

'The engineer we learn about in the pantomime,' said Addie.

The young man slammed the book shut amid a shower of dust, and announced he had other more pressing matters to attend to but that he hoped they'd learned everything they needed to of Vispa's magnificent history. He ushered them out onto the balcony and closed the gate as they inched along the sedan stop. Meanwhile, Altvassa climbed a couple of floors up the building, his lanky legs eerily reminiscent of a crane fly, and fastened himself onto a zipwire. He whizzed across to Amburg. Was that where he lived?

Addie blew out her cheeks. 'I wonder what THAT was about?'

'And I wonder why the Worst of the Worst is called the Wotwa now, and not the Uisker?' said Zafe. 'And why the "Worst of the Worst" anyway?'

'It's like calling Kerrin, "Kerrin the Psycho", or "Kerrin who Kicks for No Good Reason" or "Kerrin the Boy with the Hardest Pinch in Hundredwater School" said Walf. 'It begins to get you down. So, I just call him "Kerrin". Or, when he's not too near, "Bottom burp" ... "BB" for short.'

'Mm, perhaps that's something you should talk to Mrs H about,' said Zafe.

Oblivious to Walf's problems, Addie stomped her feet and tugged at vines. 'This whole trip has been a complete waste of time., he didn't actually tell us anything. In fact, I think I know less than I did before.'

And then Suza retrieved a pair of pages from her sleeve; pages from the (Hand Picked) History of Vispa, that Horst had read from. 'I spotted they had the name "Ragnar" on them when I was helping to tidy up.'

'You STOLE them? Suza!' Her cheeks reddened, but Zafe thought he detected a streak of pride.

'I also noticed that what Horst Altvassa was reading, wasn't exactly what was written down,' she whispered.

Beaming at her cousin's ingenuity, Addie cleared her throat and began to read, '*Ragnar Best was a -*'

'The beast!' Walf corrected her, 'He's THE BEAST.'

'Perhaps this is a different Ragnar and he was just really good at what he did?' Zafe reasoned.

'It says "Best" here. Would you like me to continue? Right, so,

"Ragnar BEST was a Master of Celery Cultivation. The most competent athlete Vispa has ever known, he represented his tower five times in the Aqualympics. Trained as a sculptor and stonemason, BEST assisted in the building of the under-tower chambers that are still used today by naval services and was a leading light in the development of biovegetal-engineering."

She turned to the other page.

"One of the many tales told about the Uiskers is of their ways with farming. Such was their anger that they were driven to create a most terrible food, designed to increase their strength and stature tenfold, namely the dreaded banabbage –"

'Isn't that the maths machine?' asked Tycho.

"- that was originally created to feed the sea cows. It was a cross between —"

'Banana and cabbage?' suggested Walf, 'Doesn't sound very dreadful.'

Zafe nodded, muttering something about 'Not knowing how much longer he could manage on potato and broccoli.'

And that was where the story ended. It said nothing about what happened to the Wotwa and it looked like Ragnar Best was a dead end too.

'Wait a minute,' said Addie, 'There's more on the back of

this page. "*In his spare time BEST enjoyed building medieval siege equipment, and was working on a treebucket to ensure the safety of the waters, when he retired.*" Safety of the waters?'

'That's it! It must have been something to protect them from the Wotwot!' whispered Zafe.

'And why, if he defeated the Wotwa with a treebucket, don't we all know about it?' asked Tycho. Ragnar's Aqualympics record alone should have guaranteed him a place on the History Wall of Graffiti.

'Well, I don't know what a *treebucket* is.' Walf's declaration was met with a sea of blank and embarrassed faces. None of them did.

There was no black flag flying, but they stopped at Hundredwater School before returning home. Suza wanted to know more about this "treebucket" they'd read about, so Addie asked Mrs H whether she knew anyone who had a dictionary they could use. Their teacher caught her breath and she asked them to promise to stay where they were; then they heard her enter Mr Antibus's classroom, and then the sound of scraping, huffing and puffing.

When she re-emerged a minute later, Mrs Hawtrey looked rather ruffled around the edges, with a muddy trowel tucked into her jodhpurs, she was holding a soil-encrusted sack in her hands. 'Books prefer to be kept in the dark, much like potatoes. Or treasure. Knowledge is golden, after all.'

'Isn't that silence, Mrs H?'

The teacher ignored Suza's question, but did tell them quite categorically, 'There's no need for *any* of you to mention this to *anyone*.'

She withdrew a second, much cleaner bag from the sack, and from that she pulled out a 'Concise Cambridge Dictionary'. It was sun-faded black, covered with a bloom of mildew and its pages were curled, but there was, nonetheless, something magical about it, until Mrs H dropped the book and the spell was broken.

When everyone had recovered and Mrs H had retrieved the 'treasure' (she'd only torn a handful of pages) she offered Suza a pair of white gloves, and told her to 'take care'. Ignoring Walf's sniggering, Suza turned the oiled, slightly translucent pages until she found the *tre* page, and the definition of "treebucket" which, it said, was also known as a *trebuchet*.

"Medieval weaponry used for throwing stones etc.; tilting scales for weighing."

While Mrs H was replanting the book in its hiding place, Addie said, 'So, assuming Ragnar wasn't weighing things, he must have been throwing stones at something. Something big that needed stones thrown at it.'

'What are we going to do now?' Tycho asked.

'Go home, probably have broccoli for dinner,' Zafe replied with a sigh, savouring the memory of the sweet turnip cake and the smell of raisins. Walf nodded.

'I think he meant what are we going to do about the Wotwa,' said Addie,

'Oh that. I was trying not to think about tower-devouring monsters. It's a lot more fun when it isn't real and someone just wants you to go to sleep.'

'Unfortunately, I don't think not thinking about them will be enough to ward it off,' Addie said, 'But a treebucket might be.' And she suggested they talk to Mirrah again, having forgotten that Mirrah was deep undersea, hundreds of leagues away.

'What would Captain Torres Galllant do?' asked Walf.

'Good question!' Tycho looked at each of them in turn.

'He usually gets battered for a bit,' said Suza, 'And then remembers to summon up his DoomMongers and the story ends like it usually does.'

Walf jumped up, teetering on the balcony's edge. 'The Uisker! Can't we get *them* to wrangle the Wotwa away?'

'Good thinking, Walf!' said Addie, (which by the look on Walf's face, wasn't something he'd ever heard her say before).

'We need to find out about the Uiskers,' said Suza, furrowing her brow. 'What if they're still active?'

'We'd know about the "Whisker" people if they were!' said Tycho.

'The same way we knew about the Wotwa, you mean?' said Addie.

'Anyway,' said Suza, 'We should really find out what a trebuchet looks like.'

'But how are we going to get into the library when the librarian acts as if we're going to chuck all of his books into the sea?' asked Zafe.

'Or scribble on them,' said Walf, tucking his stylus behind his ear.

Addie nodded. 'I'm not sure evil old Altvassa necessarily wanted us to know more about the planet's history at all.'

A Ginger Mantis

When the others had dispersed, Zafe and Tycho took the stairs down to the sky-sedan, but they had to wait a couple of minutes for the Mayor's husband to complete his journey. Mr Drinkwater was large and he'd been involved in a couple of zipwire incidents. One where the zipwire had simply snapped and he'd fallen into the ghats (and interrupted an aqua-tango class) and another time when he'd taken the wrong line and had smashed a family's kitchen to 'smithereens' (*a technical term which means that none of the bits of kitchen recovered was bigger than a sea-giblet*).

While they politely waited for Mr Drinkwater to squeeze out of the small contraption, the mayor talked to the boys about the tower's jaunty new angle, and his wife clambered over the top of the sedan and was pushing him from behind.

But neither one of the boys was listening. Tycho was reading the latest episode of a SuperBlobBoy cartoon, and Zafe was gazing up at the sky. It was a crystal-clear afternoon and he looked beyond Amburg, to the beehives dancing in the breeze above wonky Istanglia.

And far, far away, in the depths of the soft blue sky, he caught sight of what might have been the space station's lights, blinking. His parents, winking at him, thousands of miles away perhaps? He felt a pang of guilt. A planet to discover, his new school and friends had taken his mind off the space station and for two weeks he'd forgotten what space felt like. He'd forgotten home.

It was all very well listening to Panjin Dray reading out space station reports, but he knew they didn't always reflect what was happening on the arks — and what his parents had been doing. He'd heard one a couple of days before that was at least two years out of date.

Zafe brushed his cheek against his arm. If only he could have tapped it and seen them, found out what they were doing. Despite Devik's daydreams, there was no flashing star on Zafe's arm to tell him he had a message. But the thought of that flashing star reminded him of morse code and the flashes of light the space station used to send a dot-dot-dash message in times of peril. (Or low battery.)

Sat at opposite ends of the little sedan carriage, the boys were half-way across to Amburg Tower when Tycho spotted a narwhal, which would have been exciting, had it not been swimming at twice its usual speed. There was a piercing AAARRK call, followed by another even higher NIKK-NIKK-NIKK. The sky-sedan juddered to a halt and Zafe looked up to the sky for signs of bird-life. But Tycho told him that NIKK-NIKK-NIKK was the call of a ginger mantis and he scanned the waves for its distinctive orange stripes and high fins. And then he saw it!

He pointed the mantis out to Zafe and the two boys scrunched their eyes, intently watching what unfolded.

The animal was thrashing near the coral reef and by the sound of its call it was distressed. It had scraped itself badly. Not only that, there was a small fishing boat nearby. Their net was caught on the reef, and if the mantis continued to thrash, the fishermen would be in serious trouble. The drumbeat and heave-ho of a wranglers' dragon boat could just about be heard above the creature's calls, along with the fishing vessel's foghorn booming across the water.

Tycho beat his fists on his seat. 'SOMEONE TELL THEM TO STOP!'

'Why? What's wrong?'

'The foghorn sounds too much like a tridecalobster and that's only going to make things worse.'

'They're not friendly?'

'They're tasty. And that's not good when you're a small fishing boat and a ginger mantis mistakes you for a bag of Turnip Bites.' The creature's antennae flickered above the water and it let out a deep rumbling THRUM that echoed off the towers. UM-UM-UM-UMMMMM.

They saw a fisherman drag something around the boat's prow, poking it with a long stick. There was a crackle in the air and a flash of light.

'He's got a sting-ray. A young one! YOU CAN'T DO THAT!'

The ginger mantis reared up and looked even more agitated, and dangerous than it had before. Avoiding the young ray's charge, it lunged at the boat and took a chunk out of the hull, and it was about to take another, when the crew of dragon boat rowers from the Bakossi squad swept up, their silvery oars flashing in the sunlight like fins.

They watched the captain pick up a long, thin horn made of loops of brass with which he mimicked the call of the mantis, or rather, he attempted to. His first try was badly off key, but his second attempt was good enough to capture the animal's attention and still its fins for a moment.

While all this was happening, the fishing vessel limped away as fast as it could (which wasn't very fast at all) until it was beyond the mantis's reach. Tycho clapped his hands as he spotted the young ray swimming away in the opposite direction.

As the lamentable BAG-BAG-BAG-BIRK-BIRRRRK of the horn carried on, the animal's long spiky antennae calmed and it stopped thrashing. The wranglers flicked their oars around and began gently slapping the water — the plip-plop of the sea was a diversion that continued until the animal appeared to have fallen asleep and lay, merely bobbing on the waves. While half of the team carried on with the plip-plopping, the other half rowed the boat closer to the floating animal, gently pushing it back towards the gap in the Atlas Reef.

The sky-sedan began to move again, the boys resumed their gentle pedalling, and by the time they'd reached Istanglia the ginger mantis was gone and the Bakossi wranglers were on their way back to base.

At home, Nonna and Grundi were acting as if they'd always lived askew. And when Tycho asked why the tower had leaned over, they admitted they weren't sure, but suggested it might be something to do with maintenance, although Nonna quickly added that Istanglia had been secured by cables pulling the tower from the other side. It wasn't straight, but it was safe.

Grundi asked about their library trip and was disappointed to hear they hadn't seen the books. 'Mmm, now I don't know his great aunt particularly well, but Horst Altvassa I have heard of. I had no idea he'd joined the library. He is an odd fish. Not the most approachable young man and certainly not representative of the librarian 'breed'. It's just they can be so helpful, so quick to answer your questions ...'

That night, Zafe asked Tycho if he wouldn't mind if they went up onto the roof. He wanted to send a morse code message to his parents, and he explained the dots and dashes alphabet to his friend.

'But how are you going to do it?'

'I just thought I'd use a torch.'

As he described the kind of torch he meant — a handheld light that could be turned on and off at the flick of a switch (rather than a fat wooden stick set on fire and held at arm's length) he realised there was no question of Nonna and Grundi having such a thing. Then Tycho offered him the mothquito lamp and suggested they cover and uncover it with a piece of waxed black-out fabric.

As soon as they heard Nonna turn on her radio, they sneaked out of the container and up the crooked stairs to the top of the tower. The lamp was weak and Zafe wasn't sure it would work, but if he could see his parents' space station winking in the distance, perhaps they could see him? But what to say?

That his new home was teetering at a precarious angle and no-one knew why? That he wasn't sure what he was eating ... or perhaps that he was eating vegetables? He knew they'd be impressed by that, although they'd never really insisted that he eat his green cubes like Nonna did. That he was doing well at school? (With the exception of Suza, the standard of maths among the Vispans was poor. The answer to any sum of more than two hundred was generally "lots".)

No need for his parents to know that where the topics that mattered to Vispans were concerned (herbology, botany, knots, climbing, survival, etc.,) he was firmly at the bottom of the class. Zafe's attempts at pruning had been described as 'vicious' and 'an attack on the food chain'.

Should he mention his attempts at swimming? Or that his new home could be eaten at any moment?

Zafe considered all the things that would take too long to dot and dash in Morse Code, that he really wished he could tell them. About his new friends; adventurous Tycho, funny Walf, quiet, clever Suza and Addie, who knew everything that Suza didn't and was only too happy to share her knowledge. Nonna and Grundi grumbled and drove him a bit crazy but, in a funny way, they made everything better. Mrs H at the pantomime, the wranglers and the zipwires; so many different things.

He thought about the amazing towers and looked across at solid Amburg, writhing Bakossi, and the distant lights of Kodiak and Adamant.

He felt the breeze on his cheeks; a far cry from the space station's still, sterile air. If only they could see and feel how much he had experienced.

And so, after much umming and aahing about dotting and dashing, Zafe simply 'blinked' the following message to the night sky:

Wish you were here. Love Zafe x

Zafe?

Zafe could hear Nonna's voice loud and clear, and yet he could tell she wasn't singing in the kitchen or her bedroom. It was a school-free day and the offworlder's legs were aching from all the pedalling, abseiling, walking up and down stairs and gravity. Tycho's hammock was empty and Zafe was having a lie-in. Opening the shutter for a breath of fresh air, he leaned out and saw Nonna dangling three storeys down. 'What are you doing?'

'Harriet's set sail for the Wasabi Quarter to see her son and I said I'd look after her flowers while she was gone. I'll be back in a minute, but could you put the kettle on for some tea?'

Zafe dressed and slid into the kitchen where there was a note from Tycho scratched into a waxboard, along with one of the gadgets Auntie Mirrah had dredged up. Tycho had gone down to Walf's, and would Zafe let them know (ON THE TALK-and-WALKY!) when he was coming down? Zafe pushed a small red button on the device, and it screeched into life.

The three of them took it in turns to chat about the fact they could chat. A second call was about what they'd like to eat for lunch and what they were likely to actually get for lunch. A third call discussed whether the tower was leaning any more than it had the day before and then they rang off.

A minute later they were on it again with nothing more to discuss, except Walf suggesting Zafe might join them by abseiling down ON HIS OWN.

Tycho told him, 'Remember, you're a nastronaut. You've lived in space — you can do anything! It's easy ... I mean, even Suza can do it!' He also mentioned that the down-lines had been secured, so Zafe would be sliding down the tower, rather than dangling *from* the tower, and reassuring him that that made it much easier.

But did it?

Despite all the evidence to the contrary, Zafe was afraid, very afraid; not that he was going to tell Walf that. Walf who looked like he was actually flying whenever he zipped from one tower to the next, making even Tycho look like a slow-coach. Zafe didn't feel remotely safe about abseiling down, but the conviction in Walf's voice (and the mention of being a nastronaut) prompted him to say that he would. Of course, he would. Tycho asked him if he really would be fine but Zafe brushed off his concerns. If everyone else could do it, surely he could?

Turning the device off, he made Nonna's pot of Orange Pekoe tea and put his beltbag on, trying not to think too hard about what he'd just agreed to do. His first solo trip.

Zafe was beginning to get into the swing of things though. He could eat using his teeth. He'd learnt how to perch at a desk. He also knew it was unlikely that some element of that night's dinner would be mashed vegetables.

(Due to the lack of valuable metals on the planet, there were certain kitchen implements that were shared and tonight wasn't masher night. He'd also noticed that the people 'favoured' by the potato masher roster were noticeably bigger than everyone else. Likewise, the floors shared washing buckets, mangles, fish knives and toasting forks. The only items every household had as standard were a radio and a kitchen sink.)

In fact, the one thing he hadn't got into the swing of, was swinging up, down and between the towers. It was time to take the plunge and become a proper tower-dweller.

Adjusting his clips, Zafe hesitated at the balcony edge and his tummy lurched as he looked down. He'd promised himself he wouldn't do that, otherwise he'd be taking the stairs. He counted and checked his three clips and then, just for good measure, he stepped back from the edge and unclipped and reclipped them a couple of times, just to be sure.

Approaching the edge again he thought about the number of times he'd stood a floor above the school's balcony and practised this one move. Walf lived three floors down on the 15th. If Zafe didn't managed to get it right he'd scrape his face, knees and chest all the way down to the jetty. Or Mrs Bartlebot's. Ending up at her place wasn't, of course, the worst thing that could happen to someone dangling precariously from a tower, but still … he'd heard about the earwig incident. DON'T LOOK DOWN.

He looked up at the beautiful blue sky, took a deep breath and eased himself out, leaning back as he did so. He was at a safe angle, he'd done well. Good. But his legs wouldn't go anywhere. He willed them to move. He even went so far as to glance down at them, careful not to look any further. They were still there but they were as solid as a rock.

Rather than panic he decided to take his time and wait for them to work. He took another deep breath and had another look around.

There was always something to look at in Istanglia: so many households, boats and people; vegetables and children zipwiring from tower to tower, not to mention the clouds, the sky and the sea. BREATHE, Zafe, BREATHE.

There was a squawk and he saw a flock of seabirds pecking at one of the beehives suspended from balloons that flew above the tower. When it was time to harvest the honey the balloons were pulled down, along with the attached hives, and the residents of Istanglia were asked to close their shutters and fix their netting, for fear of a swarm finding their way inside. He'd been told that having a few bees visit your flower-box was one thing but having a swarm of them enter your kitchen was quite another.

Grundi said that when there was a really severe storm the hives were pulled in, piled precariously on top of each other and lashed down until the wind died down. WHY DO MY LEGS FEEL LIKE THIS?

He listened to clothes whipping in the wind, crunchy from being washed in salt water. The laundry was beaten to relieve it of some of the salt crystals, but a newly-washed garment was still unpleasant to wear, not that anyone else seemed to notice the constant scrunching sound and scratches. He flexed his knees very slightly. It felt like his legs were being held prisoner by his trousers (fresh from the clothesline this morning). The Vispans had no idea how soft fabric should be.

He let out a long sigh and was just allowing his legs to relax when he felt a stiff breeze tug at his top, realised afresh that he was stuck to the underside of the tower and his legs refroze.

Nonna was watering her friend's flowerboxes and nowhere to be seen, Grundi and Mr Pomfret were doing something with the filtration system and Walf and Tycho were at Walf's container, just three storeys down, although they might as well have been a world away. He tried to speak but could say nothing, the effort of breathing taking every ounce of concentration he had.

As far as the tower-dwellers were concerned, Zafe was doing the most natural thing in the world. He was one of dozens of children pedalling up, abseiling down, zipping across, just … hanging about.

This act of trying to blend in had rendered him invisible. This act of grand bravery had been mistaken for something very ordinary.

Why had he ever left the space station? Why couldn't he have stayed? His parents would never know what he'd done, how courageous he'd been. Would they question why he hadn't taken the stairs (which were in themselves, something of a trial for a space-dweller)? Dangling from a thin cable, $17\frac{1}{2}$ storeys up, over water. Nice, soft, yielding water.

Only Zafe knew that if he hit the Thames Sea from this height it would be like hitting stone.

26.

Chocolate

Clenching his fists, Zafe locked and unlocked his knees again. His heart was thumping at a fearsome rate. 'Safe?' He was anything but safe. Then he realised it was a distant voice, calling.

Zafe?

With a lot of bumping and scraping Tycho and Walf managed to pull the stricken boy up from the side of the building. The three of them lay panting on the kitchen floor beams as Nonna arrived and cheerfully put the kettle on again, oblivious to the drama that had just unfolded (and the pot of tea Zafe had made).

'Well done Zafe, you did well. Try again next week eh? After a few more goes on the school balcony,' Tycho patted him on the shoulder. Walf nodded in agreement, before crawling back to his container. Via the stairs.

'How did you know I needed help?'

'I think you must have left the talk-and-walky on because we heard you clip on, and then a bit more clipping and some scuffling, and Walf was worried about how long you were taking, and we heard you mumbling about trousers.'

A couple of days had passed and they had no new knowledge about the mysterious 'treebuckets'. The library was off-limits and, given that the Wotwa had been created so long ago, there was only one thing to be done. They had to find the oldest person they knew. They had to go up to the roof, to the great bungalow in the clouds. To Nineveh Puffbird.

Grundi had once remarked that Great-great-great Aunt Nineveh was 'as old as the hills', which Tycho had reinterpreted as 'being as old as the non-existent hills''. All in all, it would have been easier to just say she was really, really, REALLY old. He also said that, because of her great age, Aunt Nineveh slept a great deal and if you arrived mid-nap, you weren't allowed to wake her up, you simply had to leave her be. Nonna had told Tycho countless times that an unexpected wake-up had killed many a centenarian (although he wasn't sure that was true).

Nineveh Puffbird also had a tendency to be a bit grumpy if you arrived empty-handed. Famed for her sweet-tooth, if you didn't turn up with a small bag of raisins or a jar of honey, she'd simply pop her headphones on and carry on listening to the radio or drop off to sleep.

So, it was with this in mind that Tycho was turning the kitchen upside down looking for something sweet with which to bribe his elderly relative. 'We must have some honey in here.'

'In your first aid box?'

'Yes, Nonna says it's good for cuts and sore throats; she gets through enough of the stuff. She's as fit as a flea so maybe it works, but I reckon she just really likes it.'

Tycho searched high and low and was wondering whether they should swing over to Bakossi to ask if they might have some dried fruit in return for a bag of critters. Zafe's face went white, but Tycho couldn't tell whether it was the thought of bumping into Horst Altvassa or the long swing over there.

'You said she likes sweet stuff? Do you think she'd be okay with chocolate?'

Tycho dropped the first aid cabinet on his foot and in between yelping and hopping, he was frantically shushing Zafe.

'Tycho what's wrong?'

'SHhhh!' And then in a much quieter voice, 'You have chocolate?' Tycho eyed him, hungrily. 'You're not mucking about?'

'Um, nope. I have got some.'

'Are you sure?'

'You think your Auntie Puffbird would like it?'

'She'd go mad for it. How many pieces do you have?'

'Well let me see… I don't know, how many pieces in a bar?'

'You've got a whole bar?' he asked, wide-eyed.

'I've got three, I mean two. ONE!' Frightened by the look on Tycho's face, he whispered, 'Do you think she'll tell us what we need to know if take some … chocolate … up with us?'

Tycho sank to the floor and looked up at his new friend. 'One piece of chocolate? She'll sing like a canary. Two pieces and she'll sing like the Kodiak choir and we'll have to ask her to stop.'

Zafe fetched the bar, broke four pieces off by accident, halved them and was about to rewrap it with the two loose pieces when he glanced over at Tycho again. He reluctantly offered him the spare chunks and his friend tentatively reached for them. Tycho was about to take it when he snatched back his hand as if it had been burnt. 'No thanks. I've heard what it does to you. I think I'll leave it to Nineveh.'

Zafe shrugged, what was Tycho talking about? He popped the chocolate into his mouth and ate it thoughtfully. The squares of warm, unctuous, mellifluous perfection sat on his tongue before melting languidly and sliding down his throat. Yum. Yum. Yum.

Chocolate.

Warming his heart and soul, it embraced his stomach, singing its siren song loud and clear. It glided around his innards, an affectionate, silky yumminess calling his name.

Chocolate.

A sonnet of sweet, sweet loveliness that, as it faded, delivered an echo of strange sadness, but while it existed caressed his insides, hugging him with a smooth, milky, luscious love. It was a far cry from jellicopter beetles and broccoli and, just for a moment, Zafe was transported home.

CHOCOLATE.

What was there to fear?

He was about to break off another piece when he caught Tycho watching him. Strangely.

Zafe reluctantly returned his stash to his travel bag before they set off with Nonna's gift of critters. And the two chunks of cocoa-bliss.

Much as he would have liked to have taken the pedalift up, Tycho accepted that all the way to the top was quite a long way to cycle and they took the spiral staircase.

A journey up or down the core of Istanglia was truly a marvel. Much like Bakossi, the tower's core housed the filtration system, and a ceiling of small crystals fed light down the column in a way that was magical to behold. Rays of topaz-green, beryl-brown, sapphire-blue and ruby-red danced across the cylinders that ran up and down the tower, ensuring equal amounts of exposure to the light. The liquids the pipes carried were clear, opaque, amber-yellow, honey-golden … and brown.

Zafe carried on walking and tried not to think too hard about which tubes were and were not honey, and just hoped there wasn't a leak again. Repairs had been made to the poo-chute system since the tower had tilted, but the memory of that burst of smell would stay with him FOREVER.

Great-great-great Aunt Nineveh's home was a container known as 'The Bungalow', where she lived with her sister Battily who, although she was six years younger, must also have been at least a thousand years old. Tycho had no idea of the ladies' actual ages and was polite enough to know not to ask, but if appearances were anything to go by, they'd arrived with the first group of colonists and helped build the towers themselves. *(That's just silly!)*

Knocking on the door, they waited. They knocked again, and the door opened automatically with a creak. Zafe noticed cables and a series of pulleys which led to the two rocking chairs in which the sisters sat; as thin and wiry as the contraptions themselves. In fact, the dark room was filled with gadgetry designed to make the ladies' lives easier; levers that slid a sink towards their chairs, lowered and raised a hovering telepipe and even moved a hefty wooden chest. (Full of visitor's treats, perhaps?)

Zafe felt like he'd set foot inside one of the space station engine rooms, albeit on a slightly smaller scale. It had a floor, walls and a ceiling and was the safest, most secure container he'd set foot in on Istanglia.

Zafe and Tycho were invited to 'take a seat' (on the floor). Their aim was to find out as much as they could about the Wotwa without scaring the two ladies to death although, glancing at Battily, they couldn't be sure she hadn't already succumbed.

Bungalow Puffbird

Nineveh Puffbird had wrinkles on her wrinkles, especially as her nose was twitching as they walked in. Her hair hovered around her head like a cloud with a touch of rain in it and she looked like a gentle breeze would knock her over, although her nails and lips were painted a violent beetroot-pink which lent her a little weight. She was smoking an elaborate pipe and the small room was filled with purple smoke and a terrible smell of cabbage.

Battily appeared to be asleep and Zafe was surprised she wasn't woken by their violent coughing, but the boys wished her a "good morning" all the same. Just in case.

Tycho presented Triple-G with the bag of goodies Nonna had left for him to take and she thanked him effusively and kindly offered critters to the boys. They waited patiently for the kettle to boil; a giant samovar hovering over Mrs Puffbird's shoulder which looked so heavy that if it had fallen it would have crashed through the solid floor and at least another five storeys. And in answer to her question? Tycho was too polite to take one of the whirligigs offered and Zafe was too appalled.

Tycho made the introductions, and Auntie Puffbird said she'd known a nastronaut once. (Zafe didn't bother to correct her.) When the giant samovar whistled, the elderly lady turned a handle and it descended, along with a tray of teacups. Tycho made the drinks and they sat back down again, cross-legged on the floor.

'We've come to ask you some questions, Great-great-great Aunt Nineveh,' Tycho began.

'I'm not sure I've got time. It'll be one of my favourite radio programmes, '*Just a Moment*' on in a minute and I don't like to miss it. It's been lovely seeing you though.' And with that she picked up some large headphones and clamped them to her head, shut her eyes and started singing in an odd, jangly way.

'Is that it?' whispered Zafe.

'She's waiting for her offering!'

'Offering?'

'The c-h-o-c!' he whispered, 'I suspect she smelled it as we came in.'

Zafe passed it to Tycho, who got up and silently wafted it under Nineveh's nose. Her eyes flashed open and she gazed at the gift in her great-great-great nephew's hand. She smiled and took the offering, stealthily hiding it under her knitting (glancing over to check that her sister hadn't noticed). The headphones were promptly removed and the radio was switched off.

'Please, call me "Triple-G", everyone does. Well not Battily of course, but I can't have everyone your age calling me Puffbird this, great-great-great that, auntie whatever and a hundred other things. It takes up too long and at my age I simply can't afford the time.'

'What was the world like when you were a youngster, Great Great Great Auntie Puffbird?' asked Tycho, apparently ignoring everything she'd just explained.

'Shiny. Ever so shiny. We had more paint you see. And there was less time spent listening to the radio and chatting on the telepipe.' At which point the telepipe squeaked and the old lady's eyes lit up. 'Ooh, this will be Agapantha, I shan't be a tic.'

She spoke VERY LOUDLY on the telepipe for what seemed like a-g-e-s, while Zafe watched the hive-balloons bobbing above them and Tycho re-caught the whirligigs that had escaped from the bag he'd been holding.

Slamming the telepipe earpiece down in a surprisingly violent manner (despite what appeared to have been an entirely reasonable conversation) the old lady chirruped, 'You were asking about the old days? School was very different of course. We had twenty books or more in our classroom! And there were papers, newspapers. None of this graffiti on the sides of towers.' Neither Tycho nor Zafe said anything. The outside of her home was a feast for the eyes; stories, cartoons, shopping lists, histories, portraits, pictures of wildlife, still lives, landscapes and half a dozen Morpheo, if not more.

'If you wanted to know something you got a newsjelly! I don't hold with this painting and repainting the sides of the buildings all the time...'

'We wanted to know about something very particular,' Zafe prompted Tycho.

'We wanted to know about the Wotwa.' He gasped. 'I MEANT THE UISKERS! We want to know about the Uiskers!' Tycho's cheeks were scarlet.

Puffbird let out a high-pitched squeal and both boys leapt to their feet, until they realised it was laughter. 'Nobody has asked me about the WORST OF THE WORST for a very long time. It's come back hasn't it?' She looked at both boys intently but neither of them said a word. 'I'll take that as a YES,' she cackled. She reached for her cup of tea and downed it in one, before pouring herself another that was the colour of rust. She sat back in silence and looked out of her shutter window.

'Make yourselves comfortable, this might take a while.' It was a muggy morning but she wrapped her shawl around her shoulders, closed her eyes and sat silent for so long they thought she'd drifted off to sleep.

'IT CAME FROM THE SOUTH!' She suddenly boomed, her eyes opening wide.

'We heard it had come from the west,' said Tycho.

She dismissed his remark with a wave of her hand. 'My grandmother had heard stories about it of course and knew it must be on its way, but she said they weren't prepared for the Wotwa, not really. There was nothing keeping the creature in the south. It was set free by those wily Uiskers when they got the land they wanted, although they complained it was only good for raising dust, and wouldn't listen to anyone else's advice on what it would grow.' She coughed violently and they were enveloped in a cloud of smoke.

'After they'd let the creature go there were no wranglers

who could take it on. It was long before your dear, dear parents.' She leaned forwards, reached out and patted Tycho's hand; her touch so soft it was like being brushed by the wings of a shy moth.

'My grandmother said her mother had got her hands on all the books and every scrap of engineering that might be of use to fight the beast. And that they cut the school day too. The children spent every afternoon either terrorising the tower-dwellers — threatening to take their belongings away for scrap, or picking at the junk dredged up to get every speck of metal from it. They were fishing mobile telepipes out of the bay like there was no tomorrow, which in a sense, there wasn't. And out of it all they built the Guardiax to save all our tomorrows — and yours. Until now, anyhow.'

'What's the Guardiax?'

'My grandmother's grandmother, Hetti Puffbird, was one of the engineers who helped to design them and Hetti's husband, my great great grandfather, Norwich, was one of the workers who welded night and day to make the bally things. The space program was put on hold for years while the northern tower-dwellers worked together to devise something that would knock the Wotwa back, and that was when the four Guardiax were built.

'But the Wotwa was getting closer. Every day the shipping forecast included details of sightings but nothing could prepare them for its arrival. Such was the level of fear when the weather began to whip up, some people threw themselves off the towers. Scared to fight the thing. A horrifying waste.' She poured herself a new mug of tea and looked out of her window. A minute of silence.

'I shall never forget what my grandmother said about the day it arrived. The storm felt like the end of our new world. The sky cracked open, daggers of light spread across the heavens, the rumbling spread through your body like cold-fever and the crackle of electric made your hair stand on end. But they said it was amazing to watch. Amazing, until you saw the beast's tail lashing the waves.' The light faded from her eyes.

'The residents of Helsingor had been moved out for the most part, those who would leave. It was the outermost tower, built just beyond the safety of the reef, where the fishing was good but dangerous. It was the home of most of our fishing community. The Wotwa circled it, its barbed tail whipping at the base, sending shocks up the metal, cracking the foundations. Helsingor fell the second night. The Guardiax were too late to save it.'

So Helsingor hadn't fallen apart because of a lack of paint. It had been destroyed by the Wotwa.

The boys sat dumbstruck — and at an angle. Could the foundations of their tower have been nibbled too? Surely the Wotwa hadn't got close enough to do that without them seeing it?

More Puffbird

'Of course, the four Guardiax worked eventually and when they finally got them going it was a bloody mess, I can tell you – I mean it! Its blood was a dark sludgy green!' She shivered. 'And then the remains of the Wotwa sloshing around the bay were gathered up for food.'

'What did Wotwa taste like?' asked Zafe, although judging by the look on Nineveh's face, it wasn't a question that needed to be asked.

'It was awful stuff, but it was protein.' Triple-G took an intense sniff of her chocolate, and they waited patiently for the expression of cocoa-bliss to fade. 'You see the Wotwa had frightened the fish and the spiders away, so people were desperate. The tower-dwellers had Wotwa sausages, smoked Wotwa, Wotwa with custard, Wotwa chops and chilli con Wotwa for breakfast, lunch and dinner for weeks on end. They were still eating it when she returned.'

'When who returned?'

'My grandmother!'

'Where had she gone?'

'Oh, you see, the children were evacuated. Taken to the plains to keep safe when things began to look scary.' Auntie Puffbird's story up until this point had been so engaging, Zafe had forgotten that *she* hadn't been the one nibbling on cutlets of Wotwa, and when Tycho spoke up, it was evident he shared

Zafe's disappointment.

'So, your grandmother didn't actually see the Guardiax in action?'

'No, no she didn't, but she saw the drawings. They were like huge metal monkeys with flashing eyes and great bowed legs and arms. Enormous things the size of ten containers, glinting over the waves.'

Glinting? The more questions they asked, the clearer it became that Triple-G didn't know what these 'Guardiax' had been designed to do any more than they did.

'A lot of Vispans thought that was the end of the Wotwa but my great great grandfather Norwich reckoned they'd been eating stinkfish. He thought the Wotwa had just been driven away somewhere deep like the Kamchatka Depths.' She took a sip of tea and smiled. 'But Hetti wanted to know why the creature had come out from wherever it had been hiding in the first place.'

They pondered that for a moment but with no answers forthcoming, they returned to the subject of the Guardiax.

'The giant machines were dismantled. Metal was as precious then as it is now and the people who'd lived on Helsingor had to live somewhere, so they built Tower Adamant. As long as it wasn't around, the Wotwa's terrible ways were forgotten and anyway, there was rebuilding to be done.'

The elderly aunt pulled a long piece of string and the boys heard a faint scraping sound. They eventually noticed a small lump making its way under a narrow carpet, through the spokes of her chair and finally arriving in her wrinkly fingers. A box of matches. She relit her pipe.

Zafe joined Tycho at the shutters for some much-needed fresh air and when they'd stopped coughing, Zafe followed Tycho's gaze to a metal tower in the distance. Adamant was quite different from Istanglia.

Apart from the fact it was standing upright, it was the only tower with no obviously stony foundations and looked as if it were standing on legs. Six legs.

'Zafe, if there are six legs on Adamant and there were four Guardiax, how many legs did they have each?'

'What's six divided by four? One and a half legs each. Which is a funny number of legs for anything to have, really. There must be two more legs somewhere.'

Nineveh must have heard what he'd said, because she called over, 'My great great grandparents were nothing to do with Tower Adamant but my brother, Gilgabont always believed they used the left-over parts to make the tower's gubbins. He was fascinated by that tower's design.'

But what if they hadn't? What if there was actually a whole, spare Guardiax lying around somewhere, ready for action?

'Would it be possible to speak to your brother?'

'I'm afraid not, he's long gone.'

'Oh, I'm sorry,' said Zafe, 'He's passed on?'

'To Kodiak, yes. Gilgabont has lived there for a while now, spends his time fishing, but he enjoys a chat on the telepipe every now and again.'

Triple-G Aunt Nineveh let out a loud yawn, blinked her eyes and began making herself comfortable, reaching for her headphones. Tycho hastily rustled the bag of whirligigs and she obediently put the headphones back on her lap. Zafe reckoned they had two more questions at most and he kept them impressively short.

'Ragnar?'

'The Best? He was a peculiar man. Talented though.'

'And treebucket?'

'I haven't heard that word for a long, long time! Ha! Ragnar, Hettie and Norwich worked together on the treebucket but my great great grandmother said that the Wotwa crisis was over before they managed to find any suitable ammunition. A weapon like that's no good if you've nothing to throw. Ragnar believed his treebucket would finish the creature off, but the sea went still, the Wotwa was nowhere to be seen and in the end he was sent off-world, to … what's it called … the mountainous one?'

'Strom?' asked Zafe. Tycho rolled his eyes.

'Anyway, they didn't want 'it' mentioned again. And in the

tower-dwellers' defence, it has taken a while for the Wotwa to come back.'

She took a last sip of her drink, and looked into its murky dregs, watching the swirling tealeaves. When she spoke again her tone had changed; as if a cloud had passed over them. 'It will have grown since last time. If something isn't done soon, we shall lose a tower again, maybe two.' She tapped an errant earwig, which promptly rolled up into a ball, and she set it on her armrest. They watched it roll off, and trundle away.

It wouldn't take much to bring Istanglia down, given its current condition.

Nineveh popped her headphones on and flicked a switch. A small sink full of hot, bubbly water flowed and she washed their cups as she warbled along to a song on the radio.

Aside from the hideously creaky door, shrieking as it opened and moaning as it closed, they left in silence.

Halfway down the stairs, Zafe thought he'd lift their mood by asking about the 'stinkfish' Norwich thought they'd been eating. He soon wished he hadn't.

'It's a fish so famously vile it can't be exported to other worlds and if a fishing vessel catches one in its net, the captain has to take the entire catch to the smelting works at the base of South Utzeera to get rid of it.'

'It sounds like something I ate last week.'

'Mm, I wouldn't mention that to Nonna if I were you.

peas

sweetcorn

29.

Adamant

The boys decided they needed to take a closer look at Tower Adamant, agreeing that a trip to the tower's aquarium was as good an excuse as any.

'Woohoo! An aquarium! I've never seen one of them before! How do we get there?' But the look on Tycho's face told Zafe everything he needed to know – and that Tycho's stomach was already feeling the effects of the journey. And then Zafe's expression changed to match Tycho's and he asked how an aquarium worked.

'You know what my swimming is like. Will we have to wear wetsuits? Are we going to be swimming with stag sharks? Will we be surrounded by fish? Will they be able to touch me with their teeth?'

They popped home for a quick lunch. Zafe had soup and Tycho gloomily picked at a bag of kale crisps, hoping the sweetcorn porridge he'd had for breakfast wouldn't be troublesome on the boat trip over.

Their telepipe call with Walf had to be abandoned because critters had got onto the line and were crawling out of the mouthpiece, and they had to wait ten minutes for Nonna to get rid of them. When they finally got through to Walf, he said he'd be down in a minute; he'd heard that there were new Morpheo on Adamant and he was missing Juggernautix XI. Then they heard his grandmother tell him he was going *nowhere* until he'd finished his seed identification homework, so that was that.

As Zafe and Tycho gingerly abseiled together to the port, they heard Addie in the ferry queue and she joined them. Addie's grandfather, Mr Norris, was working at the Aquamarine Visitor Centre that day and she was going over with his lunch. While they waited together, the boys told her what they'd learnt from Auntie Puffbird.

Was it possible that Adamant had been made out of machines designed to fight the Wotwa?

They boarded the ferry (a decommissioned dragon boat) and took it in turns to row with the other passengers. Zafe did his best to take Tycho's mind off things, with almost constant chat about sea-creatures, navigation and rowing techniques, but his friend's face was looking distinctly murky by the time they arrived.

Tower Adamant was vast and shiny; much shinier and newer than any of the other towers. It crouched over the ocean on its six crab-like legs, with a small jetty attached to one *ankle*. The tower itself was a patchwork of bamboo, bits of containers and metal guttering, each material fighting for supremacy; metallic hands juggling bamboo balls.

The whole thing looked like a giant, robotic, mutant, mushroominous tree and they floated under the base of the trunk, looking up into the heavens, a ring of silver, a halo of leafy light, a canopy of golden baubles.

They were waiting to alight from the boat, when Addie mentioned something about the colour of Tycho's cheeks, but her face turned a similar colour as Tycho lent over and whispered something into her ear, something that made her head jerk back at speed. 'HE'S GOING TO CHUNDER!'

'Don't start dancing now,' said Zafe. 'In fact, you look like you're going to be —'

BUUAARRPPPPP

A great funnel of green erupted from him, covering Addie and Zafe. Miraculously, the two of them absorbed *all* the sweetcorn and kale chunks, preventing any sick from landing on the other passengers or the ferry floor. Despite being covered in Tycho's breakfast and lunch, Addie was over the moon that none of it had landed in her hair, but the same could not be said of Zafe who appeared to be wearing a yellow and green flecked wig, top and trousers. And Tycho? He was spotless.

They disembarked carefully. The captain had warned them against any sudden movements that might dislodge their mess onto his boat, saying something about them having to 'swab the decks' if they did. They were met (at arm's length) by Grandpa Norris and ten minutes later they emerged from the Visitor Centre, clean and wet, but smelling much the same.

Tycho, now on dry land and fully recovered, was full of beans.

Addie gave her grandfather his lunch and he promptly offered to get them each a cauliflower scone (which only Tycho accepted). They followed him into the café but were immediately ushered out by the staff, and Mr Norris suggested they eat on the walkway outside and enjoy the view. And the fresh air.

Adamant's middle was a network of metal walkways with handrails; the tower was a hollow trunk made up of slides and ladders, and an enormous cranking system that moved a series of small lifts. The water lapping between the six legs was particularly rough and Addie's grandfather explained that this was because the rocky base under the tower was so shallow and flat. He told them that the hydroelectricity generated by the waves supplied energy for the lifts.

Although Tycho had visited Adamant many times, the lifts' size (and noise) never failed to surprise him. Zafe was similarly entranced. It was like nothing he had seen on the planet so far and, unlike the other towers, this was clearly a machine with people living in it.

Despite Tower Adamant's shiny facade, as they drew nearer to the huge metal legs, untidy seams of welding told of shoddy work, and close-up the metal was knobbly. Either it had been built in a hurry (and badly), or the nodules were part of the design. A very strange design but, then again, compared to what?

On the way to the aquarium lift, Tycho briefly stopped Zafe to show him something far out to sea. Zafe scrunched his eyes to catch sight of some sea creature or vessel and realised he was looking at a small party of picnickers floating cross-legged on the water.

Zafe looked closer. The party of picknickers were seated on something, but what?

The Aquarium

The picnickers' feet were being lapped by waves and, listening very intently, Zafe heard shrieks of laughter.

Someone called their names and they heard Addie again. She and her grandfather were waiting for them at the aquarium lift, which was small and rounded like a metallic seedpod, with a couple of portholes. Once they were all inside, Grandpa Norris cranked the doors tightly shut, spoke on the telepipe and the lift began its slow descent. Having spent so many weeks on zipwires, Zafe enjoyed the slow journey down. They trundled at a snail's pace until something, some small change in the atmosphere or dampening of the sound of their voices, indicated they were under the waves. And finally, the lift stopped.

The lift door released, just a fraction, and a single drop of water seeped between the opening black rubber edges, before the doors opened fully to reveal a second set of doors which creaked open to reveal another room, twice the size of the lift. They stepped out and a family of grandparents and grandchildren hurried past them and into the lift before the two sets of doors abruptly closed. It rattled upwards and they were alone.

The aquarium was made out of countless small, irregular windows and was bathed in a strange green light which twinkled through the waves onto the floor, which was damp.

Addie had skipped out of the lift and appeared to be hugging the wall, her legs twitching with joy. Zafe looked out at the bluey-green rush of sea and fish surrounding them. So many fish. Great silvery shoals dodging and weaving their way past, ignored by colourful little individuals who tootled about pretending to mind their own business. A turtle glided past with its family, a sea snake looped the loop and a moray eel poked its head out from behind one of the girders.

Zafe was anxious to have someone identify some of what he'd seen but there was so much to see he couldn't drag his eyes from the glass and he hadn't noticed Tycho, frozen next to the lift entrance. He was holding onto a column in silence, with his eyes firmly closed. It was Mr Norris who eventually coaxed the boy away, all the while explaining how long he'd worked as a guide there, how thick the glass was and the strength of the tower's legs, adding that lots of tower-dwellers felt like this and it was all quite normal.

Tycho's eyes remained shut until Zafe shouted 'What was that?' and the boy's curiosity got the better of him. A great wave of white rushed at the windows, a column of swirling angry water followed by a huge mass of grey, and then another and another, and a crackling sound that bounced off the tower's metal foundations.

Mr Norris identified the animals as blue stingrays and peered through the glass. 'They're not often seen in these parts. It's quite unusual … and so many of them.'

The light on the aquarium floor evaporated and the room transformed from lilting green light to swirling brown shadows. The waves roiled outside and there were flashes of grey and more crackling noises. And booms.

'It's a storm!' said Addie, 'We should go back.'

'There wasn't one forecast, I'll just call the lift.' Mr Norris dialled but the line was dead: no line, no lift. 'We'll just have to stay put for a while, but don't worry, blue stingrays are actually very peaceful creatures, despite their appearance.'

The creatures circled them again and there was a thud as one of them hit a pane of glass with its tail which scratched it with a high-pitched squeal. 'They don't usually get this close,' muttered Addie's grandfather.

Then there was a noise none of them recognised until they

saw it with their own eyes. The sound of cracking glass. A pane had sprung a leak. And then another. And another. A cabinet in the ceiling opened and air-pipes fell down, just three of them. The other cabinet door had jammed and, try as they might, they couldn't get it open.

Water was beginning to gather around their feet and with each ear-splitting crack a new leak sprang and more water sprayed into the tiny space.

'HOW FAR ARE WE DOWN?' asked Addie, above the splashing and cracking that surrounded them.

'One storey,' Mr Norris yelled back. So it was swimmable or even floatable, as long as they could get out of the chamber. The windows were too small to get more than a leg out of, so their only option was to get out the way they'd got in. Zafe and Addie clawed at the doors, aware that each time they gouged the rubber edging more water dripped in. Without letting them out.

'We need a LEVER!' Addie shouted. They rifled through their beltbags but could find nothing that was long or strong enough to divide the doors, and a waxboard stylus wouldn't do. Zafe refastened his bag — and noticed his belt was different to the others'. His clips were twice the length of everyone else's and while they had just one small clip, he had three.

He undid his belt and unlooped two clips, handing one each to Addie and Tycho. The water was around their thighs, they were shivering with cold and for this to work their efforts were going to have to be done together and evenly spaced up the length of the doors.

Zafe also knew he was more frightened than he'd ever been in his life and that if he stopped for a split-second to think about the enormous creatures circling outside and the thought of joining them, he'd slide beneath the rapidly rising water and never recover.

Caught

Tycho took a deep breath, ducked his head under the water and, when Addie shouted 'Heave HO!', he jabbed the clip's flat end at the doors' rubber edges and pulled while the others did the same higher up. Their first attempt only let in more water. It was up to their chests now and Tycho could see Zafe losing his earlier confidence. Even if they did get out of this room, they still had to swim up, through the storm, to the ocean surface, and all they'd managed to do so far, was teach the offworlder to float.

Mr Norris passed them each a pipe and they took it in turns to breath the fresh air as the water reached their necks. The cold was beginning to take its toll. Addie's hands were shaking so much she fumbled and dropped her clip, but her grandfather caught it before it drifted down, out of sight. They tried again but the door still wouldn't budge.

They were all shivering and time was running out. With another deep breath, Tycho ducked down and Addie popped under the waves.

Holding their clips as tightly as they could in hands trembling with cold, they positioned them between the rubber edges and Mr Norris kicked the door three times, the signal to use their small, metal levers, and again they pulled, they rested, they pushed. And the door opened.

A wall of water slammed them back into the room. Addie was still clinging to her grandfather who, when they'd both had a gulp of air, put the pipes in the boys' hands. As Zafe and Tycho braced themselves for their escape, Mr Norris and his granddaughter swam out and up, together, into the stormy, surging darkness.

Tycho felt happier and more comfortable now than he had since getting into the lift's confines. Water and swimming were something he knew and he was confident that with a lungful of air he could get to the water's surface no problem, but Zafe was another matter.

When Tycho pointed to the door, the boy shook his head, holding tight to his air-pipe. Tycho gestured again, and again Zafe clung fast to his anchor. Tycho began to pick at Zafe's fingers, trying to prise them free from the pipe but the boy wouldn't let go, so he pointed to a small window. When he had Zafe's full attention, with a shaking finger he slowly and deliberately traced individual letters on the pane.

M   U   M   D   A   D

Hoping with each stroke of his finger that the boy could read what he was trying to write, he saw his friend's eyes close, open, close, open — and then widen for a second. They sucked a lungful of air from the pipe and Zafe tapped at the broad beam of metal above the patchwork window. There were letters scratched into the paintwork. What did it say? Tycho grabbed at his hand and he was pulled from the chamber.

Moving in the open water was even cooler than it had been in the chamber, each flap of an arm or leg a new blanket of searing cold. Zafe looked up at the light twinkling through the waves and, with a violent shiver, lost his grip on Tycho's fingers and was stolen away by a wave. His chest began to feel tight. Something large swam past but he didn't see what it was. All the small, colourful fish had gone.

He floated for a while, his hair like a halo around his head, watching shafts of light play on the currents. Debris drifted past and he watched a small rainbow disk — round, colourful, enchanting — wing its way past him, down into the depths, lolloping into the darkness. He stopped kicking his legs and realised he didn't feel so cold anymore.

A great grey thing whooshed past, but the light was beginning to fade. Zafe wanted to follow the rainbows but something pinched his arm and he felt himself being pulled along, through the cold.

'WE'VE GOT HIM! Here we go, wrap him up. You're all right now! CAN YOU HEAR ME? (What's his name? What?) Say Burt? Sayford! You're all right! We've got you.'

Big hands rubbing his arms and legs, the piercing ache of blood returning to his hands and feet. Teeth chattering so violently he thought they'd snap. Zafe's eyes began to focus and he saw two faces. Faces he didn't know. Shiny black spiders. No, too big. Sealions? No, too long and thin. They were wranglers in wetsuits. He'd been pulled from the depths. He was floating on a boat, he was back in the land of the living and he was safe.

The others were on the jetty, so wrapped up that all they could do was move their eyes. As soon as they saw Zafe they made shivery, chattering noises and their reunion consisted of bumping into each other, their arms pinned to their sides by the tightly wound blankets, which were only loosened when they began to warm up.

While the Zafe and the others looked relieved to be alive, Mr Norris looked perplexed, muttering every now and then about how there were "So many of them, so close to the towers".

Addie and her grandfather were ferried over to Amburg as Zafe and Tycho were helped off the boat at Istanglia jetty and met by Nonna and Grundi. After much hugging, they were strapped into a sky-sedan rigged to move upwards, a system usually reserved for invalids. Tycho began to protest but quieted down as soon as they began to ascend and Zafe tried his best to make his tired eyes convey his gratitude.

At home, the boys were unbundled and Nonna positioned them in the suns' full glare, safely tied to their hammocks, repositioned to get the last of the afternoon heat. It had been a long day. They learnt later there hadn't been a storm. The aquarium had strict rules about running the lift during bad weather and the flurry of sea-creatures (electric stingrays, stag sharks and weaver eels) had come out of nowhere.

Grundi explained that a stingray had clipped the lift line with its tail and that it was only when someone noticed the pump to the air-pipes was in use that they sent out the boat crew.

Potato and leak soup, cauliflower croquettes and a plate of beetroot biscuits and cheese later, the boys retired to their room and lay in the darkness. It was a warm, still night, but there was a tangy metallic taste in the air grating against their teeth, and a liveliness to the atmosphere that set their hair on end.

'Don't suppose you noticed a spare Guardiax while you were floating about?'

Zafe shook his head. 'Did you notice that Tower Adamant is covered in small nodules, like the suckers on an octopus?'

'Yeah, like little hooks.'

'What do you think they were for? Fishing nets?'

Tycho shifted in his hammock, in a way that would have landed Zafe on the netting. 'It's a lot of extra metal to use for no good reason. And I was thinking … just because we didn't see the Guardiax while we were at the aquarium, doesn't mean it isn't there.'

'You mean the nubbin those people were having their picnic on, just above the waves?' asked Zafe.

'Mm.'

'Thanks for the writing by the way.'

'Huh?'

Zafe readjusted the mothquito light. 'You know. Writing Mum and Dad on the glass.'

'Well I wasn't going to leave you down there.'

Zafe bolted upright in his hammock and almost flipped out but Tycho steadied him. 'There was something written on the metal!'

'What?'

He took a deep breath and gave it a second's thought. 'It said, "The threat may have gone but the whistlers are going nowhere".'

'They've got it wrong, it's the *Adamant Pipers*, not the *Whistlers*. They're one of the tower's best water polo teams.'

'Oh … right.'

Could the "Whistlers" be anything to do with the "Uiskers"? Zafe settled down to a night of troubled sleep.

Herd

Zafe dreamed of giant tentacles, crashing claws and monstrous waves. He dreamed of floating alone in gritty gloominess, his breath dwindling to nothing. The darkness became hotter, brighter, louder as he drifted toward the light and screamed for help but the waves pulled at his shoulders, shouting his name.

'Zafe, wake up!'

'Help me, HELP!'

'Zafe, CALM DOWN.'

It was morning.

'Oh. I was drowning and then there was this terrible sound. A terrible clunking sound, as if bits of the tower were being ripped away.' Tycho patted his shoulder and he attempted to sit up in his hammock but froze as he heard the sound again. He was awake in his own nightmare. The sun was shining and *something* was coming to get him. 'WHAT IS THAT?' He was as alarmed by Tycho's calm demeanour as he was by the terrible sound.

'What?'

CLUNK.

'THAT.'

'Oh, it's the goats.'

Zafe's expression suggested more information was needed. 'It's our turn for them to weed the tower, Grundi's working the winch.' Legs flapping, Nonna appeared out of nowhere, swinging back and forth, yodeling a goat-charming song. 'The towers looked like great weeds before and you had to prune just to look out of the window every morning. According to Nonna, we tried everything before the goats worked out.'

Zafe flinched at the sound of another CLUNK. 'Really? Everything?'

Tycho had never seen Zafe so cross, and answered limply, 'Yeah, everything.'

'Did you try otters?'

'Er, yes.'

'Did you try pandas?'

'… yep.'

Zafe yawned angrily. 'Did you try gamma rays?'

'Are they like stingrays?'

'I BET you didn't use Bolivian weed-crabs!'

'Of course, we did!'

'HA! They aren't a thing, I just made them up! And who invented goats anyway?' Zafe complained, knowing full well his anger was borne of embarrassment, tiredness and confusion and was nothing to do with Istanglia's policy for tackling weeds. He was still in shock after their escape from the aquarium.

'If Bolivian weed-crabs were real we would have used them,' Tycho said solemnly and heard a barely audible 'Sorry' in reply.

Zafe eased himself out of his hammock and joined Tycho at the window. Leaning out, he was confronted by the weirdly-upside-down eyes of a munching goat that appeared to be floating, until its feet neared the metal walls of their container and it *clanged* fast to the side with four loud DANGS before tramping up and down with yet more thunderous noise. It was patchy brown and greenish-white, the result of an algae growing on its fur which may have accounted for the smell.

'They wear magnetic goat-shoes so they can graze better. But you might want to be careful Zafe —'

And that was when goat poo fell on his head. Splip-splop. Without thinking Zafe held out his hands and caught the goat-trottles as they rolled off.

Goat poo. Poo of the goat. In his hair. Rolling off his fringe. In his hands.

'Sorry, I should probably have given you a hat. Hey, don't drop them, goat dung is good stuff!' Tycho said and, noticing the look of horror on Zafe's face, he added, 'It's all right, they'll be caught in the trottle net. There's plenty more where that came from.'

Zafes's body still stiff with shock from what had happened to his hands (hands used to the cleanliness of SPACE), he was led to the washing-room where Tycho washed his hands for him, before returning him to the kitchen, planting him on a perch far, far away from the window, and making him a nice cup of Earl Grey and some breakfast. When the boy had recovered his voice, he asked 'Why does Nonnna have to herd them?' She was still swinging around outside shouting a cheery 'hallooo' and waving around a mop.

'If you don't keep an eye on them, they'll eat anything they can get their teeth on. A couple of years ago, Nonna's friend had her kitchen eaten. This lot are looked after by Suza's great-uncle and they live on the roof of one of the subs, but they're kept pretty busy. There are a lot of weeds.'

BLEEEEET!

Trying to look casual, Tycho left Zafe in the kitchen and popped back into their bedroom to close the shutters. It would be a shame if their hammocks, or Zafe's smart blue clothes, were eaten. Besides, it was time for school; assuming the goats hadn't eaten the zipwires, Mrs H or the desks.

Despite Mrs Hawtrey's best efforts, Addie, Zafe and Tycho daydreamed their way through the day, barely able to focus on eating their lunch, let alone their lessons. It was clear from the trip to the aquarium that things in the water were changing and they'd decided that the Wotwa must be behind it. Nibbling seaweed sandwiches, they discussed what they should do next.

Tycho, Walf and Addie were hell-bent on keeping the Wotwa's existence to themselves. Was it worrying them? Yes, hugely. Was it frightening? Yes, incredibly. Could it hurt them? Yes, terribly. Would they be better off asking for help? Almost certainly, and yet still his friends insisted on keeping it to themselves.

But by the time Zafe's voice had risen two octaves and he'd started using expressions like 'the end is nigh', they reluctantly agreed to ask a select few grown-ups what they knew about the Guardiax (although nothing was to be said about the creature itself).

The first person they approached was Mrs H, who could tell them nothing, but asked them to work together to produce a mini-pantomime about these 'Guardians of the Deep' and present it to class at the end of term.

Mr Antibus said the Guardiax sounded like *bunkum and tomfoolery* and none of them had heard of Tom or Bunk, and they weren't prepared to ask the headmaster for further details. When Addie and Suza spoke to their grandparents about the Guardiax, they were asked whether this was a way of asking for more pocket-money, or if they'd been reading too many wall-comics.

The grown-ups agreed that the storms had increased but didn't appear overly concerned about why that should be; all except Grundi. He asked Zafe and Tycho to show him the plans for their 'Guardian' engineering project and then asked them more about the storms.

'Umm, well we don't really have any plans to show you, but we were hoping you might have an idea.'

'Keeping an eye on the weather is always beneficial,' he said. 'I'm off to the roof for a couple of hours. The hive masters only work until sunset, as I'm sure you know, and it's an amazing vantage point. Very quiet at night and you can see for miles and miles, well beyond the reef.'

Zafe left the kitchen feeling none-the-wiser, but Tycho came away looking thoughtful.

The two boys rolled out of their hammocks, bleary-eyed, at midnight. Zafe still wasn't very quiet or steady on his feet (especially given the tower's angle) and his pedalling wasn't all that quick so they crept to the front door, oiled it and walked up the stairs until they got to the roof.

They were wearing knitted goats-wool earmuffs to guard against the wind, and they sat on the hive anchor mounted on the roof of Istanglia. It rose against the skyline, a collaboration of rigging reaching up to the hives above them and ending with a prow looking over the sea and reef to the broad ocean beyond. An ocean filled with things that were no friend of this tower or any other.

They scanned the horizon, looking for an unfamiliar ripple, an approaching darkness, a hint of luminescence. After an hour of keeping watch, they'd eaten all of Tycho's bag of celery jellies and taken turns with the pair of binoculars from the beekeeper's shed. Getting bored, they began a game of chopsticks and Zafe was winning 746 to Tycho's 23 when their attention was caught by the sky and a crack of light that tore it in two.

They waited for the accompanying thunder-clap of a giant clam, but there was nothing.

Then it happened again. A knife of electricity sliced the sky and? Nothing. Not a sound, not a murmur. But there *was* something. A hint of something. A dark, metallic smudge under the waves, far beyond the reef, but bigger than anything Tycho had ever seen out there before — and that Zafe was unable to make out. What was it?

Stag sharks, tridecapods, globe lobsters and enormous schools of emerald mackerel were as big as it got, but this was on a different scale. It was colossal, and it appeared to be rippling.

Another silent crack of light across the sky. And whatever the large, ominous, flickering dark smudge had been, writhing under the waves, it rose again, broke the surface and dived, leaving a fingernail of white against the dark water.

They counted four more cracks of light that night, nine the next and ten two nights later. All of them storm-free nights, the sky silent with waves so calm they appeared to have frozen.

goat nav

33.
Sailing with Goats

It was Clean Sea Appreciation Day, a planetary holiday and they had the day off school. Walf, Zafe and Tycho decided to glide down to the jetty near Auntie Mirrah's sub where they were met by Suza, her great-uncle, Captain Darburt, and a herd of goats. When they weren't busy pruning, the captain generally hired the animals out to pull pleasure cruises around the bay but because it wasn't a particularly sunny day there weren't many takers, so he agreed to let them have a herd for free (which was just as well as they'd spent their last quintar on a bag of turnip sherbets).

Zafe was surprised that goats were used for anything requiring obedience or navigation, and Suza explained that because there was no way of controlling them, the pleasure cruises just tootled around wherever the goats chose to take them. The captain called the boats in by rustling a bag of sprouts at the end of the trip (although Suza admitted one cruise had lasted 13 hours, because the goats had eaten themselves silly on the day-trippers' picnic lunch).

Waiting for the goats to be assembled, Zafe looked at Tycho for any signs of him being 'green around the gills', and was surprised to see him whistling: Tycho was clearly much happier in a small boat than a big one.

As far as animals were concerned, Addie had the 'gift', and if she hadn't been busy, she'd have been in charge. And so it was Suza who, under Darburt's watchful eye, lashed the herd together and attached the rope to the dingy. They set sail, and the goats swam this way and that as usual and, only when the crew were sure Uncle Darburt no longer had them in his sights, did they employ their *secret weapon* and begin heading for the picnic platform that they hoped was the tip of the fourth Guardiax.

It had been Walf's idea to waft a pair of Zafe's shoes in front of the goats; they had been tied to a long cane and were being held aloft at the boat's prow. And the shoes did make the goats strangely biddable, and they drew near to the tiny island and their hearts leapt. It was metal. A heap of metal, just barely sticking out of the sea. The goats noisily scampered on board, magnetically stuck to it with a loud CLUNG and happily grazed on tufts of seaweed. Tycho tied the dinghy to a helpful rivet and they pulled themselves onto the wreck, alongside the goats.

Zafe had insisted on wearing his secondary shoes for the trip, which were more slippery than the first and they weren't surprised when he slid on the slimy weed, back into the sea. Once he'd been pulled back on board, he removed his shoes and added them to what they referred to as *the Goat Navigation Device* (also known as the 'goat-nav').

Tycho and Walf privately agreed that given Zafe's poor swimming he ought to have been lashed to the dingy too.

'How do you reckon they got the Guardiax to move?' Zafe asked, yanking his half-eaten sun-hat from one of the herd.

'Goats?'

'I don't think so Walf. They're good, but they're not that good,' Tycho replied.

'Energy,' said Suza holding up one of Nonna's courgette muffins, which they all agreed was a bad example of a source of energy. Even the goats wouldn't eat them. Walf suggested a mixture of manures might do it but Triple-Aunt Nineveh hadn't mentioned anything about the Guardiax having a smell. Zafe suggested crystals and they all looked confused until he mentioned that they used them on the space station to increase battery energy output. And they continued to look confused.

While Walf fitted his snorkel, Suza used a periscope to have a look around but said that the muffin crumbs brushed into the water meant all she could see were small, nibbling fish. It wasn't a particularly warm afternoon but Walf cheerfully slid into the water, swam about a bit and dipped beneath the waves to investigate. Zafe was glad he hadn't been asked to swim (or float) but was reminded that he was just as wet as Walf when there was a stiff breeze and he shivered.

Of course! Might the Guardiax have used wind power? But they agreed that Auntie Puffbird hadn't mentioned anything about the Guardiax being windmillish in design either.

'So, what's left? Solar energy, energy from the waves, energy from choc-'

Suza interrupted. 'What about energy from sea creatures. From the rays or the electric magna-eels?'

'But how could they be harnessed?' asked Tycho.

'The same way we harnessed the goats?' said Walf. 'Zafe's shoes. Both pairs.'

Suza ignored that suggestion. 'The captain says the magna-eels gather around Kodiak Tower at certain times of the year.'

'What does Kodiak have that the other towers don't?' asked Tycho.

'Pineapple, rambootan and chives,' said Zafe. The others stared at him and his cheeks turned a deep crimson as he shrugged and said 'First lesson I had at Hundredwater School, I listened. Thought napple pie sounded nice. It made a bit of an impression. We don't have any of that stuff up on the space station and I just … remembered the weirdness of the words. Piiiiiiiiiiiiiiiiiiiie of napple.'

Walf joined in with 'rambooooootaaan' but Tycho butted in before the two of them started chanting about 'chiiiiiiives'. 'So maybe there's something about those three things that they like?'

'Unless it's what that tower is made of?' said Suza.

They sat deep in thought, pondering the possible powers of bamboo, when Tycho remembered why they'd gone on a goatboat trip in the first place! 'WALF! You're back! What did you see?'

'Lobsters. The bit of metal we're sitting on is the nose of a submarine wreck that's being used to farm lobsters.'

'Poopslugs!' said Tycho dejectedly. 'Not a laser cannon then? No robot warrior under the water? No pirate ship?'

'Nope.' It was time to go home.

They were slowly steering the herd back when Walf let the stick drop and Zafe's shoes were dipped into the water, and the spell was broken. The goats, no longer mesmerised by the smell of sweaty feet, were now paddling randomly, in a bleating tangle. After ten minutes of mayhem they ended up on the rocks of Istanglia's foundations, a nature reserve no one was allowed to set foot on (and they wouldn't have done if the goats hadn't had their way).

The morning's gentle waves had become stronger and the goats scrambled up the steep bank, threatening to pull the dinghy behind them and puncture it on the rocks. They jumped into the water to lessen the weight on the boat's rubbery bottom, all except Zafe who followed the goats onto the sharp peaks and slid back into the water, only to be saved by Walf's quick-thinking and impressive backstroke.

By this time, they were all soaked to the skin and they dripped their way carefully around the boulders to a beach where Zafe was ordered to put his shoes back on, in an attempt to recharge them with smell.

Sheltered from the wind by a large rock, they lay for a little while, listening to the squawking birds whose home it was and Tycho opened up a small bag of 'goodies'.

Chewing on something rubbery that he didn't recognised, Zafe said 'I'd give anything for a sausage right now,' recalling the small brown foodcubes he'd enjoyed so much at home.

'We've got sausages,' said Walf.

'What, here?'

'Well, no, not here.'

'Are you talking about sausages made out of kidney beans and spinach.'

'I might be.'

'It's all right, I've changed my mind. A beetroot biscuit would be um … thank you.'

Suza wanted to get the goats back to Captain Darburt, but Walf said 'The goats aren't going to go where we want them to go unless Zafe's shoes are properly appealing, so we might as well relax for a bit. Better than getting in the boat and ending up at

South Utzeera. You know how much they like the smell of that place.'

A couple of minutes later, the goats had run off again and the group began trudging up the beach to retrieve them.

Slipping on pebbles, Zafe glanced up the tower's rock face and caught sight of a door; it was the door he'd seen from Auntie Mirrah's sub. He was just about to show Tycho what he'd seen, when Suza and Walf screamed. The herd of goats had done an abrupt u-turn, and they were being chased by a scuttling herd of enormous crabs. Cow-crabs.

Walf lobbed a couple of courgette muffins, which stopped the tussling crabs in their tracks, and gave them just enough time to retie the petrified goats to the boat and set sail. The cow-crabs clacked at them from the beach, their beady eyes on stalks.

'Don't worry Zafe, they're all right really.' But the tone of Tycho's voice didn't match his words, and neither did the speed at which he'd run.

'I can't believe they live at the bottom of Istanglia!' said Zafe, although there was something about their eyes that seemed familiar. Had he seen them before? Did they ever make it up the tower?

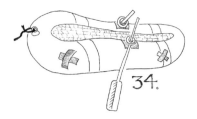

The Cave

They managed to sail back without Zafe falling in again, losing
his shoes or circling Istanglia any more than three times (when
the goats began following a shoal of mackerel). They returned
the herd to the jetty master who, with Tycho's help, took them
off to their pen (to prevent them from eating the barges or the
jetty) and they tied Auntie Mirrah's dinghy to her sub. Suza had
a sleep-over with her cousin and was anxious to get to Addie's
container in time for eel pie so she and Walf jumped on the
pedalift home.

Zafe was playing with the periscope again, zooming in on the
tower's rocky foundations when he remembered the cave he'd
caught sight of above the beach (before he'd been run down by
a couple of goats), the doorway he'd seen weeks before from
the window of Auntie Mirrah's sub. It was only once he and
Tycho had clipped themselves onto the pedalift that he finally
got a chance to ask about it.

Cave? What cave?

While the other towers had ghats for swimming and jetties for
fishing, Istanglia had glide lines straight out to the moorings
that surrounded the tower's bottom so its rocky base was
usually obscured by flocks of seabirds, and was a bit of a
mystery.

The two boys began pedalling and no more was said.

Tucked up in their hammocks that night, Tycho prompted
Zafe to put out his lantern early, and as soon as the shipping
forecast finished, he spoke.

'Ready?'

'Huh?'

'Come on!'

'What?'

'Down to the cave.'

'The cave?'

'The doorway in the rock. Your cave!'

'My cave? Now?'

'It's low tide and if we go during the day we'll be seen. You don't want to be seen, do you?'

'No, it's just … are we sailing there? What if I fall into the water?'

'We'll be fine. Together. Anyway, you *always* fall into the water.' Tycho gave him a gentle punch on the arm.

'And the cow-crabs?'

'Yeah, I'm not crazy about them either, we'll just have to keep our eyes peeled. I've lived here ages and never noticed a cave. Anyway, you found it, it's yours. You've got to go.' A glow of pride extinguished Zafe's concerns. He had a cave!

Pulling on their clothes, they reached for their belts. Zafe pulled his around his waist and in his haste, he dropped the buckle end. It swung and hit the floor beam sending a sharp clang of metal on metal. They froze, hearts in their mouths, waiting for Nonna and Grundi to discover them, confiscate their belts and prevent them from leaving their room. A loud sigh and a disgruntled 'GO TO SLEEP' from Nonna reminded them that she was listening to a rerun of '*Have You Got Enough Talent to Sing Me a Shanty*'.

Asking Zafe to wait, Tycho tiptoed into the kitchen, re-emerging with four bamboo plates, which he shoved down the back of his shorts.

'Are we having a picnic?'

'Nope. They're for paddling over; the oars will have been put away, and I don't fancy rounding up goats at this time of night.' They manoeuvred over to the balcony where Tycho tapped Zafe's arm and gave him the 'thumbs up'. They caught their breath, tightened their belts and slid over the edge and into the night.

Aside from the odd snatch of radio, the only sound they heard as they descended was the roar of waves crashing against the reef. The journey in the dark was quite different from the journey during the day, which was littered with snapshots of people's lives.

(People practising musical instruments, painting their nails, repainting their containers, planting flowers and vegetables, repairing hammocks, plaiting their netting, adding graffiti to their walls, reading other people's graffiti, fossicking, tending bees, fending off bees ... all sorts of things.)

But at night the blinds came down. Made out of loosely-woven raffia, the blinds protected the containers from a bit of the weather, but allowed wind to whistle through in case of storms. (Zafe had been told that if they used anything more wind-tight, a typhoon could bring the entire tower down.)

When they'd reached the fifth floor, they unclipped and reclipped themselves to the zipwire and whizzed down to the harbour and Mirrah's sub. Tycho untied the dingy while Zafe kept watch.

They set sail and lay flat on the dinghy's bottom, with their arms hanging over the side. Using the plates as bamboo paddles, the two boys wafted their way back towards the tower's foundations and the cave Zafe had seen in the afternoon.

The sea was choppy and the short journey to the tower's steep foundations was very different to the goat-powered trip they'd taken earlier in the day. By the time they'd reached the rocks and Zafe had identified the boulder he'd slid on earlier in the day, their arms felt like lead weights. Tycho crawled to the back of the boat and madly flapped the bamboo paddles in the water to keep the dinghy close enough to the foundations for Zafe to lasso a rock and pull them in but, at the mercy of the current, they tried and failed five times.

Zafe had never used a lasso before, and it wasn't as easy as it looked. 'I'm not sure we can make it without the goats,' said Tycho, but emboldened by the darkness, Zafe suggested they swap places.

'We have to make it to my cave, we've come all this way!'

He handed the rope to Tycho and they managed to swap places without either of them falling in. Using the bamboo plates, Zafe sculled for all he was worth. 'GOAT POWER!' he yelled, and with an almighty effort, he managed to keep the boat close enough to the rock for Tycho to hook it with the lasso.

Together they pulled the boat in and for five minutes, they lay like a couple of dead codfish on the sand.

35.

Inner Tubes

The limestone sides of the tower's foundations were pocked with small holes just the right size for a foothold, and Zafe was about to stick a shoe-less foot in, when a small rainbow beak poked out, squawked loudly and pecked.

'Agh!'

'It's only a puffin, Zafe. They're harmless, just try not to step on one or you'll get them all going. They're loud when they're angry and we don't want them to alert the you-know-whats.'

'Those enormous crabs with pincers the length of my arm?'

The boys scrambled along the holes, their hands attacked by angry little multi-coloured heads until they finally made it to the gouge in the rock that Zafe had seen from Mirrah's barge.

It was a cavernous doorway, and the rusty door swung open for them. They pulled themselves onto the stone lip and once they'd caught their breath, they crouched in the narrow passage.

'It's too dark, I can't see a thing,' said Zafe, although he could obviously see something, because he'd noticed that Tycho had his eyes firmly shut. 'What are you doing?'

'Just a bit longer ....' He opened his eyes and smiled. 'That's better! If you close your eyes and get them used to total darkness, when you open them again it's easier to see at night. Night's never as dark as your eyes being shut.'

So Zafe sat with his eyes closed until Tycho gave the word, and they were able to see a vaguely illuminated world. And a pair of monstrous eyes on stalks peering round the doorway. Fortunately, both boys were frozen with fear and it was their stillness that saved them from a nasty pinch. When the eyes (and their owner) had wandered away, they stood up and the first thing they saw was a small nook in the wall that Tycho, without thinking twice, shoved his hand into. He gasped and Zafe pulled him away.

'HEY! I nearly had it!'

'What?'

'There was something in there. See if you can reach it.'

Zafe was about to say 'what if' when it occurred to him that his hands were already puffin-pecked to pieces and a cow-crab would have been too big to lurk in that particular hole. He reached in and brought out half a dozen candles. That was *much* better than night vision. 'What do we do now?'

Getting handfuls of dry feathers from the puffins' burrows was easier said than done and both boys were covered in scratches by the time they'd collected enough feathers to make a 'fire-nest', at which point Tycho dug about in his beltbag, found one of his stones and unclipped his belt. He showed Zafe what to do and, after a few close-misses with the razor-sharp edge of the quartz, sparks began to fly as he struck the belt buckle and the tinder caught.

A small, precious fur of fire ran around the feathers and Tycho gently blew until the flame grew.

They lit their candles and set off, up the uneven stone steps into the tower, up the winding stairway, round and around, until their way was blocked by an ill-fitting door.

'Look, we're above the flood-line now,' said Tycho. 'There's no moss on these walls, no sign of damp. Whatever's in this cave was meant to be kept dry.'

'We've come so far, I wouldn't be at all surprised if Walf doesn't open the door!' said Zafe, trying to catch his breath. 'Should we knock?'

'I don't think so,' said Tycho, who, after heaving at the handle for a minute or two, slammed himself against the door and slid to the floor.

'Couldn't we try your key?'

Zafe held up both candles as Tycho scrabbled to open his beltbag and find the small, rusty key he'd been given by his Aunt Mirrah when he was a tot. In fact, it was the first thing he'd ever put in his bag. He inserted the key and turned it. Or rather, his wrist turned, but the key did not. It didn't fit.

Poopslugs!

The two boys sank, together to the floor, gazing at their candle-lit feet. Tycho offered Zafe a waterbeetle which the boy declined.

'Seems a shame to come so far, find this place and not be able to get in,' said Tycho. 'What have you got in your bag? Any screws or nails we could use to jemmy the lock?'

Zafe had been steadily adding to his bag since Tycho had introduced him to beltbag-ology; his collection of three buttons was of no use, but he did have the sliver of bamboo he'd been given by Grundi. He idly poked it into the keyhole and the two of them heard a 'clink' as something fell to the floor on the other side. Whipping his belt under the door, Tycho moved whatever it was close enough to the door's edge for Zafe to flick it out with the little stick.

A shiny key. A cared-for key. The right key.

'But, if there's a key on that side, there must be more to this … unless someone has locked themselves in.' And as soon as he'd said it, Zafe wished that he hadn't. He had visions of a skeleton clinging to the handle on the other side of the door. Or a hungry cow-crab and a pile of clothing.

'Wouldn't they just unlock the door and go fishing?' asked Tycho, 'Eat a puffin or two? Move into a container?'

'Yes, yes, of course,' said Zafe (not mentioning the cow-crab). He inserted the key into the hole, it turned, clicked and the door swung open.

A narrow chamber with shelves carved into the walls, it led to a door at the far end, on which was scratched the words 'ISTANGLIA TOWER'. If this led to the first storey, there was no question of them trying the key again and turning up, unannounced and uninvited, in Mrs Bartlebot's kitchen.

Besides, the shelves were lined with enough bits and bobs to save them any further exploration. Spanners, hammers and welding equipment were identified, along with first aid boxes and thousands of dusty tins of food. All of it arranged in a manner that suggested they were in safe-keeping for an emergency. (Unless it was Mrs Bartlebot's pantry.)

Pleased to have finally got in, they were both a little disheartened not to have found an army of miniature guardiax. A treebucket kit would also have been nice; the countless jars of honey, beans and beetroot were frankly disappointing. As they turned to leave, Zafe dropped his candle and it rolled into a dark corner. He knelt down to retrieve it from the folds of a large waxed-paper sack, which had been sealed along its edges with more wax. It was covered in sticky, aromatic dust.

The boys were relieved to have discovered something other than jarred food, but when they broke the seal, they found thick loops of black rubber. Dozens and dozens of them.

'Could they be useful?' Zafe asked.

'Don't know, but we've come a long way and we can't leave empty-handed.' Tycho read the writing on the sack. 'It says they're "inner tubes".'

'Is it something to do with the poo-chute, do you think?'

'No idea, but there are plenty here. I'm sure they wouldn't miss a few.'

Tycho slung a couple of them over his shoulder and passed a couple more to Zafe, but as he turned to leave, one of the inner tubes got caught on a hook. He tugged and there was a loud 'click'; they looked in its direction and saw a thin panel of metal jutting out of the highest shelf, just above their heads. Zafe reached up, felt around and retrieved a handful of rusting screws, nails and keys.

'Bit late now!' said Tycho.

'No wait, I think there's something else.' Zafe reached again, and recovered a —

There was a gust of wind and their candles flickered out, it was time to leave. Tycho led the way back through the pitch-black tunnel, down the steps and stumbled at the doorway. He was held back from falling onto the rocks below by Zafe's firm hand, but his shriek had attracted the attention of a solitary cow-crab: smaller than the others but shoulder-height nonetheless — and clacky. Very clacky.

With no courgette muffins to distract it, Tycho whirled the inner tubes around his head, whipping at the creature, trying to frighten it away. It seemed to be enjoying his game and became even nippier, despite Zafe's attempts to deter it by yelping. And then he had an idea.

'Lasso it!'

Tycho lobbed first one (waited a couple of seconds) then another of the inner tubes. He timed it perfectly and the crab's enormous pincers were cuffed by the large rubber bands. The crab wandered away, perplexed and clack-less, and the boys hurried to the dinghy before it nibbled its way through its shackles.

The paddle back to the jetty was even more exhausting than their journey over and the pedal home was slow, but the boys' excitement at an evening well spent could not be dented, even when they arrived at the container balcony to see Nonna leaning over it, glaring.

Zafe dangled, frozen to the spot by the woman's expression and a whispered tirade ('*I don't even want to know where you've been! And there was I in bed after an episode of the Parjitters, assuming the two of you were asleep.* '), while Tycho slipped the remaining inner tubes over a piece of guttering (to be reclaimed in the morning).

Nonna finally fell silent, ushered them into the kitchen, made them a pot of chamomile tea and returned to bed.

It had been an interesting night.

36.

Shiny

Bleary-eyed at their desks the following morning the boys agreed they'd be doing nothing more than sleeping as soon as they got back from school (always assuming they survived the day).

They were just getting comfortable for a five minute kip when a ball of energy sat between them and whispered at them. Loudly.

'HAVE YOU HEARD THE NEWS?' Why Addie ever asked that, Zafe would never know. Tycho and Walf's shaking heads told the same story.

'Your grandfather has become President of the Space Alliance?'

'Your neighbour has become a full-time contributor to the energy station and doubled our output?'

'You've got a load of beetroot crackers and don't much fancy them yourself and were wondering if we'd like some?'

'No, no and no again. You give up?'

They nodded, their tired heads hovering over their desks.

'It's time for the show!'

Walf let out a whoop of delight, and Zafe said that that 'sounded nice', although when he saw the luke-warm reception Tycho gave it, he was less sure.

'ATTENTION PLEASE, CLASS!' boomed their teacher. 'Walf! I've already spoken to you once today and there are plenty of corners that need scraping. Okay … now that I've got everyone's eyes on me, I have a rather exciting announcement to make. The date has been set for the —'

'SPRING SOLSTICE SHOW' everyone duly replied. So, it seemed that Walf, Tycho and Zafe were the only ones who hadn't known about it (and Zafe was still none the wiser).

Mrs H told them that everyone was expected to perform, adding that their class would start practising in earnest that afternoon, as they were doing 'Ribbon Technical and Artistics'. Walf whooped again. (It was the beginning of a long morning spent scraping corners.)

Any questions Zafe might have had about this spring solstice show were answered (before being asked) by Addie, Knower of All Things.

'It's also called the Whirly Gig. It's a 'Celebration of the Sea' that we hold before the fishing season ends and we get to do exciting stuff.'

'Like what? Fishing?'

'Mostly whirling, a bit of singing … some sea shanties … eat a bit of fish if we're lucky.'

'And Ribbon Technical and Artistics? What's that?' Zafe asked, with some trepidation, recalling what he'd seen Walf's sister doing.

What followed was equal parts thrilling and terrifying. As his classmates twirled and swung from long ribbons suspended hundreds of feet above the sea, with a moth-eaten net to catch anyone who dropped, Zafe clipped himself onto a trapeze. And, with a lot of encouragement (and a few threats) he released the wall. He swung (with a lurch and a scream), away from the tower and out into nothingness. His stomach (and his rice-porridge breakfast) did a loop the loop. He then swung back at which point Mrs H (ignoring his cries for help) pushed him out again with surprising strength.

All the while, the school band played sea shanties on a variety of instruments that sounded like they'd been made out of bits of kitchen sinks and diving equipment ...

Two hours of swinging, perched on a narrow iron bar, holding onto thin ropes with a white-knuckled grip while listening to an oompah band play, was enough and Zafe's journey back was even slower than usual. His bottom was a rainbow of bruises. They returned home to celery and beetroot soup and bed.

Swinging in his hammock, Tycho spotted Zafe's beltbag. 'Hey, what was that thing you got from the hidey-hole in the cave last night?'

'It was another button,' said Zafe. 'A nice one though. Twinkly. I've added it to my beltbag.'

Sunday couldn't come quickly enough for the boys, who had decided to visit Aunt Nineveh and let her know what they'd learnt, but they had to swing down to the bay first and see if they could pick up a prawn to roast for Nonna. They zip-zigzagged down to the jetty and as they rearranged their belts, a waft of salty fishiness blew their way from a passing vessel.

Zafe stepped back in surprise, nostrils flaring, and Tycho just managed to grab him before he fell into the water.

'If you dislike the smell of fresh fish that much, I don't think we should bother going to see my second cousin, Thirstow.'

Zafe attempted to answer but he couldn't without opening his mouth and letting in more of the fishy miasma.

'Thirstow lives off South Utzeera Tower, which is where they dry the fish before they sell it overworld. Nonna says that hundreds of years ago they used to be canned. Now it's just dried. Even I find the smell a bit pongy.'

Zafe's eyes watered as he remembered the nose peg he'd worn when he'd first arrived, and the vague impression he'd had, groggy from his trip, of a tower covered in fluttering dark grey scales shining in the light. It had glistened like a great, armoured fish balancing on its tail fin, and he thanked his lucky stars he hadn't been sent to stay with a Vispan from South Utzeera.

Mouth firmly shut, he lifted his eyebrows in a questioning manner and Tycho told him Istanglia was where everyone came to get their fishing boats fixed. 'We've got the best mechanics.'

And, as if on cue, an untidy old boat rammed the quay.

'Let's see what they've brought in,' said Tycho.

The smell was overwhelming, but Zafe had never been this close to a boat before and he was struck by what he saw.

'The floor, it's … like a dream. A miniature rainbow,' he

mumbled, opening his mouth as little as possible.

'Huh? Oh that, that's not the floor, those are dvd's. There are loads of them around here. I've heard it was junk from a container that went down during the Great Remove. You wouldn't know it, but they're hundreds of years old and don't look like they've aged a day.'

'What do you do with them all?'

'Nothing much. You can snap them and use them as cutters … and some people use them for decoration. You should see Aunt Genevivia's place, on a sunny day it's blinding!'

'What will they do with them?'

'I don't know, but you can't make a tower out of them. Or a potato masher.' He went over to the fishing captain but returned empty-handed. There were no prawns to be had. 'Looks like it's going to be leak, carrot and paprika soup then.'

Tycho looked back at the catch, hypnotised by the way the sun reflected off the disks; a shoal of small, circular rainbows that mimicked the fishes' scales.

As they returned to the main jetty to go home, half a dozen seabirds swooped over to the boat and the fisherman in charge twitched the net, the sun caught on the disks again and the birds squawked in protest, flew off and perched on an overhanging zipwire.

'Why did they fly away from the fish, they're mad for it aren't they?' The two boys stopped and watched again as the birds railed around and then past the net again.

'They don't like the light, the way it glints off the disks.' Tycho bent down and picked a couple of them up, looping them over his thumb.

'It's frightening them away.' The boys looked at each other. 'Frightening them away like a scarecrow!'

And the disks were just the right size to hang off the nodules on Tower Adamant. What a sight that would be.

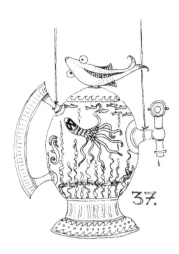

Return to Nineveh

Now that Triple-G had a taste for it, Zafe said he didn't think two chunks of C-H-O-C would be enough. Tensions were running high but Tycho was sure that two pieces would be enough, after all, chocolate was the stuff of legend and the woman had only had it once in 115 years, so she surely wasn't going to start being greedy about it now.

Unfortunately, Tycho had homework to do (planting he hadn't got round to), so it was Zafe, Addie and Gonzales who set off to visit Nineveh Puffbird in her rooftop haunt.

Aunt Battily was, as usual, fast asleep and only the word 'chocolate' (uttered in a ghost-like whisper by Aunt Nineveh) prompted even the slightest stir from the elderly, younger sister. Nineveh hid the two precious chunks away, relit her pipe and waited for a proper fug to envelop her before asking her visitors how they were and, once the samovar had come to the boil, getting down to business. 'What would you like to know?'

'About the Guardiax,' said Addie, 'Because we went to the Aquamarine Visitor Centre and —'

'Did you have one of their scones? My great-great nephew Geoffington grows the cauliflowers you know.'

In the interests of diplomacy, they assured her they'd had the scones and considered them the finest they'd ever eaten. Although Zafe thought Addie saying that 'Geoffington must be a genius' was taking it a bit far.

'— speaking of which, I've got some juice over there if you want some. Would you pour some please, Seafarb? Sarflip? … Addie, you pour it.' (The milky-green colour of the juice suggested that Geoffington may have been responsible for that too.)

'We noticed the nodules on Adamant and the dvd's and wondered if they were anything to do with the Guardiax?'

'They hung them all over!' She spoke as if it had been the most obvious thing in the worlds. 'You see they hoped it would frighten the creature away.'

'And did it?'

She shrugged in an 'I suppose so' kind of way.

'And when they made Tower Adamant, what did they do with the moving parts that were left over? You know, the engine?' Addie asked.

Triple-G blew out half a dozen smoke rings. 'That I don't know, although it would all have been valuable metal of course.'

'We thought perhaps it had been dumped in the sea, so we visited the little metal peak off Adamant's east wall.'

'The submarine they use for lobster fishing?' Again, Zafe couldn't help wishing they'd visited a week earlier.

'If only your grandmother had seen it in action,' said Addie.

'Yes, if only. Of course, she saw her grandfather in action, you see he was in charge of its arms.' The old lady blew a complicated series of smoke rings through her sister's floss of hair. 'He made the Guardiax arms swing back and forth while it wobbled and its eyes flashed and it made a terrible, burping sound.'

'What energy did they use?' Zafe asked.

'Cauliflower power for the most part! He was in charge of the limb garrison, much like a cox in a rowing boat. *Heave ho* and all that. Do you row?' They nodded obediently. 'Well, he told me that when he shouted *starboard* they ran to the right and when he shouted *port* they ran to the left. If they wanted the arms to move up and down, they pulled some levers and scrambled off the forearm. No good lifting the arm with the garrison on it, after all.'

'They actually moved?'

'I think they bobbed up and down a bit, something to do with putting all the manpower into the knees and careful balancing. She said she remembered seeing one of them fall over once, and they had to heave it upright again with two miles of rope strung around Istanglia.'

'So, no wind power or anything like that?'

'Well, I think it helped to jangle the disks about, but the Guardiax themselves were moved about by the crew like a big puppet.'

Perhaps the reason the present generation of Vispans knew nothing about the Guardiax was because they were too embarrassed to talk about them.

The machines had been nothing more than lolloping scarecrows — something Zafe must have said out loud, because Nineveh agreed, 'YES, yes, that's exactly what they were!

'Now, the treebucket project my great great grandmother was working on was much more exciting, only they ran out of metal. And time of course. She and Ragnar wanted the fourth Guardiax to be reshaped into a treebucket, but the mayor said no. The Wotwa had gone and there was nothing more to be done.'

'But now it's back.'

'Indeed, it is.'

'What was the 'treebucket' designed to do?'

'To finish the Wotwa off, once and for all. Not just scare it away.'

'But if the Guardiax were just scarecrows, how was the creature …?'

'Finished off? Perhaps they were hoping to scare it to death. Anyway, since it's back…' She reached for her headphones. 'Get collecting and you could have your own scarecrow up and running in no time at all, but you'd better get a move on. Who knows how long you've got!' She fixed them over her ears and shouted, 'YOU'RE GOING TO HAVE TO MAKE A WEAPON THAT WILL FINISH IT OFF ONCE AND FOR ALL!'

And with that pronouncement, the old lady jigged to a tune neither child could hear and then appeared to suddenly fall asleep. Addie released the pipe from Aunt Nineveh's thin fingers and carefully laid it on a plate, well out of the way of anything flammable.

It was Zafe who poured the remains of his cauliflower juice over it and they ran out as the room filled with toxic fumes, tripping over faithful Gonzales, who'd just managed to make it up to the roof.

They enjoyed the fresh air and Addie popped Gonzales on her shoulder. 'He's such a faithful snail when he feels like it.'

Zafe didn't say anything, but he felt a lot happier knowing exactly where Gonzales was.

That night there was a storm, the fiercest Tycho could recall and one of the rare occasions on which opening the shutters and letting the gales through wasn't enough. The entire tower made their way into the tower core, taking their few precious belongings with them. Grundi checked Auntie Nineveh was safe and sound and joined them as the wind began to roar, the tower shook and the containers' contents clanged, metal on metal.

Even seated in the hidden core of the tower, the sound of the gales froze their blood. While the residents wondered at the state of the weather, Tycho and Zafe wondered what was out there.

After three hours, the gong sounded the all-clear and tired groups returned to their homes. Their container didn't look too bad, although the storm had done nothing to make the tower any straighter, and it was just as well Zafe was used to traversing the beams as the netting had been whipped about mercilessly and was less of a safety feature than it had been.

Even by candlelight it was clear that the kitchen had suffered. Grundi suspected it was because one of Nonna's larger pans, firmly attached to the over-rod, had swung loose, battering the kitchen, denting all and sundry in the high wind. Grundi took it down and with the aid of a wooden spoon, got quite a good tune out of it, but Nonna was unimpressed.

In the morning, the full extent of the devastation became apparent. The water between the towers was awash with rubbish and the tattered remains of netting fluttered from every storey.

A multi-coloured fringe, dancing in the breeze.

Collection

School had become a never-ending series of PE lessons in preparation for the spring solstice show, and although Zafe was getting better at risking his life on a swing, he was no more graceful. Summoning up the energy to maintain an elegant pose whilst hanging dozens of storeys up in the air, was particularly difficult because Tycho and Zafe spent every night monitoring the skies.

Given the state of the towers (and their inhabitants) the class was spared PE the day after the storm, and recruited instead to join the cleaning effort, fixing what could be fixed and replacing torn netting.

At the end of a busy afternoon Suza, Addie, Tycho, Zafe and Walf met on the school roof to chat, as the rest of their class zipped, pedalled or abseiled away.

They had two plans. One was to make a scarecrow to frighten the thing away. The other was to make a medieval siege machine (that they'd never seen) out of metal (they didn't have) and finish the Wotwa off for good.

Zafe suspected they'd have to melt down the Visitor Centre café in order to make it and he wasn't sure how well that would go down with the Adamanters, but Tycho reminded him that if the Wotwa returned, there would be no cauliflower-scone-loving residents of Adamant.

Conversation swung back round to the scarecrow idea and they agreed that the most important thing was to collect dvd's.

Meeting over, they dispersed. Suza was off to Kodiak school to see if they had any useful books, and Addie and Walf were going to help sort out the nets (and get in some more trapeze-hanging practice at the same time). And Tycho and Zafe were going to hunt down the disk collection he'd moaned about ('But my aunt has given me *thousands*').

Expecting a deluge of shiny loveliness, Zafe stood back while Tycho carefully opened the high cabinet above the larder. What fell out was fishing paraphenalia, clips, harnesses and beekeeping bits and bobs.

After some rooting around with a fishing rod, he pulled a sack out from the cabinet's farthest reaches, and handed Zafe a silvery disk. He twirled it between his fingers, reflecting bright circles that shone around the room. 'How many have we got?'

'Huh?'

'How many have you got in there?' Zafe asked, pointing at the bag.

Tycho upended it and nothing fell out.

'None? But I thought you said that every time Auntie Mirrah goes diving near Tower Adamant waters she brings you a load of them back.'

'We've got … one.' He held up the solitary disk. 'Thinking about it, I'm fairly sure Aunt Mirrah was going to give us some more the other day, until I complained and we got the Walk and Talkies instead.'

'All together you should have thousands of them.'

'Yeah, only um, we tend to throw them about a bit. They look so nice when they slither through the water — you've seen them! We string them together and swim with them when it's sunny and then we let them …drop.'

'You chuck them back into the water? So every time your aunt gives you dvd's, she is in fact just returning them to you?'

'I don't think she minds.'

'Does she know? Is it good for the fish?'

Tycho shrugged.

'So apart from this one in the bag, have you got any others at all?'

'Nope.'

Zafe considered lobbing the one disk they did have into the waves below. Taking a couple of deep breaths, he quietly asked what they'd been used for before The Great Remove.

'Nonna says that they're old technology because before The Even Bigger Bang, the people of the Old World were far advanced. We don't think the disks were very valuable but they must have been useful once because Mirrah finds them by the hundred.'

'Only because you're chucking them back in. There might only be a dozen of the things.' muttered Zafe. 'What are they for anyway?'

'Information. Although I've tried writing on them but the squid-ink runs straight off.'

'What does it say on the one we've got?'

Zafe turned it over to look at the dull side and read 'Minutes of the Frampton Cotterell Parish Council, Part 2.'

'What does that mean?'

'Dunno. We might know more if we had Part 1.'

'Do you really think so?'

'Maybe not.'

There was a message from Grundi on the waxboard in the kitchen, instructing them to check the hive lines, they pedalled up to the roof and, satisfied that the lines were tight, so Tycho practised his balancing on the roof's rigging. As he teetered on the metal cables, they discussed the possibility of a sneaky trip to see the dvd-sparkling home of Aunt Genevivia.

Encouraged by the ease with which Tycho was balancing on the rigging, Zafe agreed to give it a go. He walked to the edge, tripped and disappeared over it. Gone.

Tycho ran over. His friend was sprawled on his back on the one scrap of netting that hadn't been wrenched away from the building during the storm. 'Are you all right?' he reached out a hand to help Zafe up.

'NO, I AM NOT! But – I have just had a thought. How will we illuminate the disks, if the Wotwa comes at night?'

'Do you usually have ideas when you fall off buildings?'

Back on the roof, the two of them sat in silence, until Tycho heard his friend's breathing return to normal. 'How did they make the dvd's shine before?'

'Perhaps you should fall over the edge again and work it out?'

The towers of Thames Sea were illuminated at night. Tiny points of light shone out around the base of each one to prevent shipping accidents. And that, along with the radio and the sewage system, was what used up their energy.

And where did they get that energy? On Vispa they mostly used hydro-energy generated by the waves — and coffee that was sailed to South Utzeera. There was talk of the fuel once having been drunk, but the few people who'd ever had a sniff of coffee agreed that it must have been something very different. It was either a spelling (or a smelling) mistake.

'We do have light, we just don't have much of it, and it's at the bottom of the tower, rather than the top.'

Zafe opened his beltbag and offered Tycho an asparagus shortbread. 'What was that call you got earlier?'

'It was Suza. She's going to show us the plans for the treebucket tomorrow.'

There were no cracks of light in the sky that night — which they found even more unsettling than the usual half a dozen or so. Why was tonight so quiet? Was the Wotwa hiding? Feeding on something? Gone?

Or was it saving its energy?

39.

Courgette Fancies

When the boys swung down into their classroom the following morning, they noticed a series of black flags whipping in the breeze. A fishing vessel had gone down. Mrs H hit the gong and asked the class to observe a minute's silence, the end of which was marked by the boom of a trawler out to sea.

'It doesn't make any sense,' said Tycho. 'The sea was like a millpond last night.'

It had been a small fishing vessel run by a family off South Utzeera who'd fished the waters for as long as anyone could remember. According to Mrs Hawtrey, not a single member of their family had ever worked off Vispa. All they'd ever known was boats and the briny.

The vessel had been lost with all hands on deck, including the parents of a girl many of them had played water polo with. Fishing levels had been hit in recent months and they'd gone out further than they usually did, desperate to meet their quota.

Zafe looked from one classmate to the next, their eyes were downcast. Both parents lost.

In a trembling voice, Mrs H announced they could, if they wished, abandon their wax-pads and have some extra time swinging, and she murmured something about shouting at the wind.

Some of the class swung violently, some swung thoughtfully, some did shout and some sang. Others simply sat quietly and got on with their work. Mrs H didn't mind what they did, but stood looking out to sea, tears coursing down her cheeks. Tycho was one of the loud, violent swingers and Zafe noticed Walf swinging nearby; unseen but there if Ty needed him.

Zafe felt angry about the hot heavy weight in his chest; he punched it, but it remained. A long way from home, he wished he could have spoken to his parents and told them how he was. Known whether they were safe. It wasn't an unfamiliar feeling, this 'not knowing', but when a girl his age lost her family so suddenly, he was reminded how fragile his relationship with his own family was.

After school they headed up to the hives for afternoon tea: Nonna had baked. None of them could recall why the small cakes were called 'fancies' and Tycho said he was sure there was another name for them. Zafe said he could think of a few more things to call them, but the others chose to ignore him and carried on chewing.

Under a glowing orange and purple sky, Suza carefully opened a roll of jellypaper, putting a cake on each corner to keep it flat. With Mrs H's permission, she'd visited Kodiak school and, with a month's worth of dried fruit, she had managed to persuade each of the teachers to show her their collection of books; amongst them a picture book full of kings, queens, soldiers — and castles, not unlike stony Amburg.

And there she had found a picture of something called a *trebuchet*.

It was a complex weapon, three containers high and five wide, and it was designed to throw a huge missile. Left to her own devices, Suza had traced the illustration she'd found on the precious piece of jellypaper she shared with them now. The squid-ink had run a bit and the drawing had obviously been done in a hurry, but it showed a machine made up of a series of beams arranged into a triangle.

And from the top of the triangle there balanced another longer beam, with a weight on one end and a slingshot on the other.

Slingshots were not unfamiliar to the group and they'd spent many an idle afternoon sending pebbles skittering over the waves to rustle up some fish for dinner. But if this thing was as large as it appeared, the counterweight needed at the other end would be enormous, although there was something familiar about the wedge shape. It was not unlike the café at the visitor centre ...

'Perhaps we could resurrect it?'

'What do you mean?' Zafe asked.

Tycho shrugged. 'You know, smarten it up, fix it — make it work again.'

'Make the café into a death-machine?' said Walf.

'I'm not sure we can make it into a weapon again.'

'But do you think they'd mind if we used the café to fight the Wotwa again?' asked Walf, flinging something green over his shoulder.

'It **is** a good café,' said Addie, 'They might not like it.'

Tycho suggested chucking cauliflower scones at the Wotwa might be the way to go, but his idea was poopooed. 'Besides, even if we found a swinging arm, we're still not sure how it worked.'

'But it's obvious, isn't it?' said Suza. 'This weight here is pulled back as hard as it will go by this great big wheel here, where those little stick figures are pulling and then they pull this switch to let it go, all that energy is let loose, the weight goes this way and the sling flings its missile that way. Simple.'

The fact remained that the 'A' frame was probably now part of the visitor centre, welded into the foundations of Tower Adamant. They would have to find something else.

'So how many dvd's have we managed to find so far, for the scarecrow?'

'I've got 47 in my gardening drawer,' said Addie. 'I've been asking around my neighbours.'

'I've got 29,' said Suza.

'That's um —'

'76,' said Zafe.

'And I've got 5,' said Walf, 'But I'm not sure my granddad will let me have all of them.'

'If your granddad does then that makes, um five plus 76?' Zafe and Suza waited for one of the others to work it out, but no answer was forthcoming.

'Well, it's a start. I mean, it's quite a lot. It might cover a couple of containers ... or a shin of Tower Adamant, but I'm not sure how we're going to attach them to the beams of our tower or yours, without any nodules!' said Addie, confident that their dvd collection was going to grow an awful lot bigger than it was.

'We could tie them on with gardening twine,' said Walf.

Zafe imagined hanging off the side of Istanglia for hours on end, swaying in the wind, disks clipped to his belt, fighting off angry goats while fiddling with twine. His stomach lurched until he heard Addie speak — and it lurched again. 'So how many disks have you two got?'

Tycho murmured something, and she asked him to repeat it. Zafe quickly stepped in and said they hadn't "had a chance to look at the numbers yet", which sounded sufficiently technical for Addie to fall silent, until Walf spoke up.

'Ty, have you actually got any?'

'YES!'

'No need to shout. You haven't got any, have you?'

'I have!'

'Oh yeah?'

'I've got one. THIS one.' And out of his beltbag he fished out his solitary disk.

'Well why didn't you say so?' said Walf, 'If we add that to what we've got, that means we've got a grand total of ... 94?'

(Surely the answer's 83! Or is it? Show your workings please.)

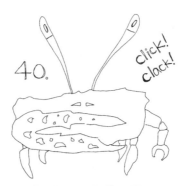

Crabs and Candles

Walf and Addie agreed to go to the jetty and collect dvd's from the fishing vessels, while Zafe, Tycho and Suza went from container to container explaining that they were collecting the shiny disks for a project. As the day went on it became clear that the disks had myriad uses: mirrors, decoration, wind-chimes, bird-scarers and coasters.

Only one person wanted to know what they were actually going to be used for; an elderly man on the 17th floor who interrogated them at length. Finally, Tycho cracked and told him that they were building a machine to beat a deadly sea creature that threatened to eat the planet, to which the man said, 'Well why didn't you say so?' He popped into his container and appeared two minutes later with a net full of them.

Suza said her aunt knew someone who'd used them to direct sunlight towards his carrots and said they'd grown at twice the normal rate, although she admitted that she'd been unable to confirm the story.

It was also Suza who pointed out that having the three of them carry 23 disks seemed like a waste of manpower. She had a project to get on with and as she was planning to visit Triple-G, she had to start thinking about what her offering might be.

(Like many in the tower, she was also related to Aunt Nineveh.)

Suza said there was something she couldn't put her finger on and she had a feeling that a trip to see Auntie Puffbird might help; and a jar of gooseberry jam was her ticket up there.

Zafe nudged Tycho, 'I'm not sure she'll be there long if she takes gooseberry jam. I've had some and it's not very sweet.'

'You've only tasted Nonna's,' Tycho replied. Perhaps Suza would be okay after all.

Two hours later they met up with Walf and Addie on the steps of Istanglia's inner core to count their haul. Addie had zipped over to Amburg to deliver some fish to her grandmother and was introduced to a family whose daughter was no longer a disk collector. Their collection had gone up three-fold.

'So how are we going to light them up at night?' Zafe asked. That was the million quintar question and one that they had been avoiding asking (or rather, answering) for days now. 'Candles?'

'Do you have any idea how long it takes a bee to produce enough wax to make a candle? We'd be living in the dark for seasons,' said Tycho.

'I still think we should talk to your grandparents about the tower-devouring monster that's threatening to wipe out Midlantic Towers … and how candles might save us from being eaten.'

'Mm, a scarecrow might not be enough, however many disks we manage to collect,' said Tycho, ignoring Zafe's concerns. 'I've been thinking that maybe we could make some sort of enormous slingshot that doesn't involve us remodelling the Adamant Tower Visitor Centre and Café'

'If we added up all our elastic bands, how many would we have and how far would they stretch?' Rubber was harvested from the Nicobar plantations and the elastic band in a slingshot was a big deal and not easily replaced.

Much like the disks conversation, everyone had some rubber bands, but they weren't going to add up to much, and even if they went round all the containers, they wouldn't raise very many. And there was no question of asking the tower-dwellers to donate their precious rubber bands, without telling them the reason why.

They were pedalifting back home, when there was a terrible scuttling sound and Zafe yelled 'CRABS!' He hadn't expected to see dog-crabs' eyes-on-stalks waving overhead and his shrieking was so loud it actually managed to drive them away, until he stopped mid-scream.

'They don't usually bother coming so high,' remarked Walf.

'Tycho, you could catch them,' whispered Zafe, 'Like you did before — with the black tubes we found. HEY! We don't need rubber bands, we've got those inner tubes we can use!'

Knots

End of their world or not, preparations for the performance went on regardless.

Walf was the best, closely followed by Habjema. While everyone else swung round on trapezes and climbed thick, knotted ropes, Walf and Hab climbed the thin hanging ribbons all by themselves, twisting the hanging fabric over one foot, using that *hold* to make it another an arm-length up, and another, and so on.

Once they were so high up that they could quite comfortably have had morning tea with Mrs Decker on the 21st floor, they began to spin, loop and twirl, snapping the ribbons with a loud 'crack' every now and again, on the off chance there was anyone not paying attention.

Tycho, Addie, Stirmatt and Jadri were in the middle ability group and hung from thicker ribbons onto which bulky knots had been tied, making it that much easier to hold on and pull the ribbon taut, so that they could 'stand' on the line.

Zafe's group was made up of him and Devik, and the two of them were firmly clamped onto their trapezes and instructed to swing from side to side, or forwards and backwards JOYFULLY. If they managed that they would go onto swinging whilst holding on by only one hand, and then the next lesson after that they'd let go.

Devik (who, as far as Zafe could tell, hadn't smiled since he'd arrived on the planet without any technology) suggested that if the two of them didn't smile while swinging they wouldn't have to do any of the trickier things their teacher was suggesting. He was overheard by Mrs Hawtrey, who insisted they do what they'd been asked while smiling AND singing sea shanties.

After an hour Zafe was beginning to feel quite comfortable, swinging back and forth, looking out beyond the corner of the tower at the rumbling reef and the sea, breathing in the air's saltiness and looking at the horizon's pink glow as the suns began to set for the day.

Swinging with the wind in his hair, back and forth, back and forth the next thing he knew he'd smacked heads with Devik and the two of them were tangled well beyond the safety of the tatty netting.

'POOPSLUGS! Zafe! You're way over from where you should be!' Devik was rubbing a blobfish-like lump on his forehead. Zafe's head hurt too but there was no way he was going to release a hand from the trapeze ropes to find a bump.

Mr Flintlo could find no easy way to sort out their tangled mess and decided that the most sensible course of action was to lower them onto a dinghy, which Zafe swiftly fell out of. And so, he returned home from school, soaking wet again. (Nonna remarked that his 'space suit' was beginning to look quite Vispish.)

Zafe was relieved to hear that they were spared a morning of rehearsals the next day, as Mrs H and Mr Flintlo were taking them on a trip to Kodiak, to see the pineapples. Tycho was the only one not excited by an excursion that spared them a morning of rehearsals and radish identification.

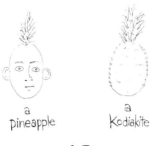

a
pineapple

a
Kodiakite

42.

Kodiak

While the rest of the class boarded the boat to Kodiak, it was suggested that Tycho stand at the prow like a figurehead, albeit a vomiting one. The captain had given him strict instructions to keep the boat clean, so in the end Mr Flintlo borrowed an ear trumpet (from one of the older jetty masters) for use as a funnel; to direct the flow of sick over the side – if or when Tycho was sick.

Kodiak began in much the same way as Istanglia, Amburg and Bakossi. It sat on a huge limestone pinnacle, rising from the waves majestically like a gnarly, geological finger pointing at the sky, but this was a finger surrounded by a bamboo forest, regularly trimmed and logged by the bamboo-jacks who had melted their potato mashers long ago and forged axe-heads.

While the grandparents hacked and chopped bamboo, it was the Kodiak schoolchildren who were given responsibility for the tower's principal crops; its pineapples, rambootan and chives.

The tower itself was, unsurprisingly, entirely built out of bamboo, and while the other towers had a fixed design — metallic tendrils, container remains, jammed together lumps of stone and glass, Kodiak was something different.

The tower had an inner core from which the homes sprouted, dangled or grew, but it looked to Zafe as if every row of homes had been built without any thought for its neighbours. In fact, the stranger, the better.

While some homes were spherical (like the globes of Adamant) others were cylindrical or cone-shaped. Some of the homes were smooth to the touch, some were wavy, some were plaited or woven; and others were rough and unkempt, using fresh green, aged grey or golden blades of the giant grass.

There wasn't an ounce of metal in the whole thing, and Zafe marvelled at the broad bamboo beams, soaring walkways and wide bridges that led down to an impressive series of jetties.

They arrived, the boat was tied to a bamboo post and the children jumped across to the jetty, while Mrs H helped Tycho onto dry land. He'd survived the trip but was pale, almost as pale as Zafe who was having difficulty dealing with the fishy smell drifting across from nearby South Utzeera.

They walked up a long walkway to a bridge leading to the pineapple groves, the fruit processing plant, the drying racks and the tasting centre where, according to Tycho, they would be eating the sharp fruit sprinkled with salt. *(It made it taste sweeter.)*

It would be a long day, and there were no prizes for guessing what they'd be having for lunch.

Planted within towering bamboo fences, the spiky pineapple tops stuck out at right angles from fencing dotted in amongst homes, and the green-mohicaned Kodiak children swung from one small plantation to the next, clambering up and down the pineapples.

The class had spent an hour admiring pineapples under the tutelage of a couple of girls no older than themselves, when Suza injured herself and Mrs H was forced to leave the class to their own devices while she accompanied her back to the ferry. Suza had slipped on a piece of pineapple, but told the others it had been part of an elaborate plan she had for skipping the fruit tour and visiting Triple-G instead. None of them questioned her motives, but they agreed that the chances of Suza tripping were high.

With their teacher away, half the class was swinging from bamboo, practising moves for the show, while the other half had sneaked off to the jetty to see if they could make their dinners a bit more interesting. And it was Zafe and Tycho's chance to talk to the only person who might be able to tell them whether the magna-eels had made any difference to the way Kodiak experienced storms. Nineveh Puffbird's brother.

There were only a handful of men sat on the bamboo slats, one of them noticeably older than the others. He had bright blue eyes that twinkled like waves on a sunny afternoon and laughter was etched into his face in a way that made you want to smile just looking at him.

His fishing rod was much-repaired and his twine was frayed but he had a bucket full of sprats, and Tycho wondered what his bait was.

But the main reason they guessed he must be Triple-G's brother, was the bilious cloud of cheroot smoke that surrounded him.

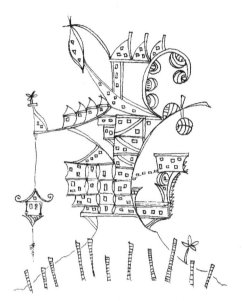

43. NO CHEROOTING

'Excuse me, sir.'

'LOOKING FOR SOME FISH?' he yelled.

'No, no, we -'

'SPEAK UP!'

'NO, WE'VE COME OVER FROM ISTANGLIA!'

He yelled back for them to wait a moment, and fished out of his bucket a beautifully decorated bamboo cone, engraved with small pictures of sea creatures. Holding it up to his ear, he asked the boy to speak again.

'Do they all hear here with ear trumpets?' asked Zafe, thinking back to the funnel Tycho had used on the boat.

'Ssssh,' whispered Tycho, 'He can hear us now!'

'Indeed, I can,' answered the man, cheerily. 'Now, how may I help you?'

'We've come from Istanglia and we were just wondering if you were, um, if you might possibly be, um …' He'd completely forgotten the name of Nineveh's brother! Goglabite? Gigglymit? Bilgygonk? He had to say something, the man was waiting for a name. 'Gilgibart?' The gentleman's face lit up and he began coughing and cackling amid a cloud of rancid smoke.

'I haven't been called that for years! Just goes to show, I'm not spending enough time with new people. Everyone round here seems to have got the hang of my name and it does make things somewhat uneventful.'

'You're Nineveh's brother?'

'I am indeed. And who might you two be?' The boys introduced themselves. 'So you're friends of Ninny are you?' After a few vigorous sucks of a cough-sweet, he spoke again. 'Yes, she enjoys a chat. Battily is a bit quieter. You're a long way from home, what are you doing in Kodiak?'

'We're on a school trip but we've lost our teacher and were just waiting here for her.'

They weren't sure that telling him that they'd deliberately wandered off would be a sensible move, although if the large NO CHEROOTING sign the man was sitting next to whilst puffing on his pipe was anything to go by, he wasn't a great one for following rules himself.

'What's the weather been like here, recently?' began Tycho. Something about the old man's expression told Zafe he was a bit taken aback by the question.

'You've come here to talk about the weather? If it's weather you want to hear about, we've had a fair few storms over the last couple of months.' The boys stood looking at each other in silence and the old man interrupted their awkwardness. 'Is it actually fishing you want to discuss?' He sized them up with a beady eye, closing the lid of his bait box.

'It's nothing about your fishing, sir, I promise,' said Tycho.

'Glad to hear it.'

'It's just, we've noticed the storms too. In the middle of the night. And we know you were an engineer, and interested in Adamant and we visited the visitor centre and almost drowned, and, and — ' As Tycho floundered to finish the end of his sentence, Zafe noticed, among the many animals etched onto the gentleman's bamboo cone, a figure, much bigger than the others, that appeared to be standing on legs.

'Your cone, I mean, your ear-trumpet, I was wondering about its decoration.'

'It belonged to my grandfather. He burnt the decoration into the wood himself, pictures of the old stories he used to tell me.'

'That figure in the sea, the giant one on legs.'

'Sshhh!' hissed Tycho.

But the old man's eyes twinkled and, encouraged, Zafe whispered, 'We've come to speak to you because we think the Wotwa is back!' He'd forgotten that he was still holding the gentleman's ear trumpet in his hands, but the look on the man's face suggested he could lip-read.

As Zafe handed the trumpet back, his shoulder was jerked down by Tycho who thought he'd seen Mrs Hawtrey's tutti-frutti headdress. They bobbed up again and whoever it was, had gone.

'Someone you didn't want to see?' asked the gentleman. They vigorously shook their heads. 'So, the beast wasn't beaten. How do you know it's back?'

While Tycho told the man about the weather, the giant clams and what they thought they'd seen, Zafe studied the image on the ear trumpet again.

The looming figure was one of four, the other three were depicted in the background, and underlining them all was a long snake-like creature with a spiny back and a double row of sharp teeth. The other sea creatures burnt into the wood were swimming upside down. He shivered in the sunlight.

'… if that's the case, then time is of the essence.'

'Well, we, we're collecting dvd's….'

'For what purpose?'

'We're going to make a scarecrow.'

'I hope it's a jolly big one!'

'We had a look at Tower Adamant and how it's covered in nodules, and after talking with Great Great Great Aunt Nineveh we decided that the Guardiax must have been scarecrows.'

'Before they were taken apart and made into the visitor centre?'

'Yes. So, we were thinking about turning them back into scarecrows by covering them with the disks. Only the problem we're having is that the Wotwa comes at night and the sun won't reflect off the disks at night.'

Nineveh's brother blew a noxious smoke ring. 'Mm, I'm not sure that's your only problem …'

'Anyway,' Tycho piped up, 'It wasn't all we wanted to talk about.'

'Go on,' said the gentleman (whose name was still something of a mystery).

'We wanted to know if you could tell us anything about what happened to Kodiak while the Wotwa was around?'

'That's a very good question, and the answer is nothing.'

'Nothing? So the Wotwa … what?'

'As far as I can tell the Wotwa had Kodiak in its sights, but didn't attack it.'

'Why not? It attacked Istanglia and Bakossi and destroyed Helsingor! What made Kodiak different?' Zafe asked, 'Was it the bamboo groves?'

'Well it could have been that, or the slightly warmer waters hereabouts,' said the man.

'Or the pineapples or chives?'

'Don't forget the rambootans!' said Zafe.

'I suppose it could have been any one of those things. Or a combination of them.'

There was a gust of wind — a breeze from South Utzeera and Zafe's nostrils expanded wildly. 'HOW CAN PEOPLE LIVE IN THIS FISHY SMELL? I FEEL LIKE MY NOSE IS GOING TO EXPLODE!'

A tutu rustled and Mrs H stood glowering over them. The interview was over.

Magna-eel

44.

Help?

They were marched back to join the rest of their class on the boat back to school, and while Tycho stood on deck, Zafe sat with Addie and Walf and told them what they'd found out.

'You say he didn't sound impressed by the scarecrow idea?'

'I think he thought we were going to have to do a very good job of it,' said Zafe.

'Will he tell on us?' asked Walf.

'I doubt it.'

'Otherwise we'll tell on him and his cheroot!'

'That pipe he was smoking was horrible, but it was a picnic in the park compared to the smell of South Utzeera!' protested Zafe.

'And what did he say about the magna-eels?' asked Addie.

'OH BLOBFISH! We didn't have a chance to ask him before Mrs H got to us.'

When the gong finally signalled the end of the school day, the four of them retreated to the gloom of the inner core and shared a packet of beetroot and 'baykon' crackers, care of Walf's grandmother.

'What were you going to ask Triple-G's brother about the magna-eels?' asked Addie.

'We wanted to know if they still hang about near Kodiak,' said Tycho. 'If they do, they might be the key to all this and the reason Kodiak wasn't attacked.'

'Aren't they outside the reef, with the rest of the sea-creatures?' asked Zafe.

'They've been known to get through. There might have been some about when Triple-G's grandmother was a girl.'

'Yeah, but that was hundreds of years ago,' said Walf.

'I'm not sure she's *that* old,' said Addie.

They munched their crackers, all of them considering their homes and how nice they were when they weren't being threatened by an enormous sea-creature. And they wondered what they'd devoted their time to *before* they'd devoted all of it to trying not to be devoured.

'What are magna-eels like?' asked Zafe.

'They're the length of a container,' said Suza.

'A small one or a big one?'

'BIG,' said Addie, 'Not that it matters. I wouldn't much want to meet one the length of a small container.'

'And they emit an electrical discharge if they're threatened or bored,' said Suza.

'Bored?'

'Apparently. The electrical charge is generated in their body with the aid of sodium. Something to do with the polarity.'

'What do they eat?' asked Tycho.

'There used to be one at the aquarium and my grandpa, Grandpa Norris, said it was crazy for fruit.'

'Any particular fruit?'

'If it's pineapple you want to know about, then I'm not sure.'

'Wait a minute,' said Suza, 'They need sodium to generate the electrical charge? Maybe the kind of sodium they put on pineapple?'

'Sodium?' said Addie.

'Yes, sodium chloride! Salt! They sprinkle salt on pineapple to take the sharpness away. They told us that while we were going round, and they let us try some.'

Things were beginning to look up. 'So how do we control the magna eels?' said Zafe.

'Well, we shouldn't have to. We just fill the Thames Sea with salty pineapple chunks and let them protect us,' said Addie.

'Protect us till the end of time? Fill the already salty sea with salty fruit and incredibly dangerous sea creatures until what?

The Wotwa gets bored, its fangs decay and drop out or it dies of old age or wrinkliness?' asked Tycho.

He had a point.

'Anybody got any other ideas?' asked Zafe. No one said anything, so he suggested it might be time to talk to the grown-ups about the Wotwa. Zafe's concerns and his suggestion were disregarded by the others with an impatient wave. How about asking the other children at school? The rest of the class? This was waved away with a slightly less impatient hand, but waved away nonetheless.

'Anyway, we've still got the scarecrow idea and that's going to take a lot of putting together,' Addie reminded them. When Zafe asked how many dvd's they were up to, Walf said he thought they had almost four hundred. Enough to cover a Guardiax shin and knee.

They agreed another trip to the Istanglia jetty was needed to boost dvd numbers. They had to cover two kneecaps at least.

'And if that doesn't work then —'

'— we finish off the Wotwa with a missile thrown by the treebucket!' said Walf.

'Which we have yet to build,' said Tycho.

'Or design,' added Zafe.

Return to Puffbird

Nineveh's metal home was solid, dark and perched on the corner of the uppermost floor, at such an angle that access from the central shaft opened up to the container's balcony. Suza knocked on Great Great Great Aunt Nineveh's door and heard the pulleys straining to open it.

Everyone else's door was a fairly standard size (not quite tall enough for a grown-up to walk through and rounded at the edges), but Aunt Nineveh's door was heavily decorated and was the full height of the half container she and her sister inhabited.

The panels around the door were scratched with the story of the sky-sedan's assembly and a series of SuperBlobBoy stories (that Suza wasn't sure her aunties would have appreciated). There was also a half-finished Morpheo which she'd have to remember to tell Walf about.

Suza knocked again and the door opened into the shadows, the pulley strings pulled taut, reaching from one corner to another, stretching across the ceiling and walls. Suza watched as the machinery worked, and she stepped over the threshold agog. How had she never noticed it before? Great Great Great Auntie Nineveh lived in a siege engine!

It was, admittedly, a machine (with small, curtained windows) adapted to the serving of tea, the rocking of chairs and the smooth running of a small home for two elderly women, but still a container that held fearsome potential. Fearsome potential energy.

She presented the jam and a tin of asparagus fancies to her elderly relative, settled down cross-legged on the floor and watched her turn one of a number of handles connected to the samovar.

Cables tightened and loosened, pulleys turned and squeaked and the copper kettle lowered just level with Auntie Nineveh's elbow, where another handle was turned and it tipped into the teapot that had risen from the floor. Suza asked Auntie Nineveh about her home.

'Well, of course I was born here, as were Battily and our four brothers Gilgabont, Jettering, Bliddalo and Lamchop. Our father was born here too. Mother came from Kodiak Tower; her family were bamboo-loggers. I'm fairly sure my paternal grandmother grew up in this container too, in fact, now I come to think of it, she must have done.' She began coughing and absent-mindedly turned a lever, and a set of bellows sucked away the smoke until the room was clear enough that they could see each other once more.

'Zafe told me about your grandparents' project.'

'My grandmother's grandparents,' corrected Triple-G.

'Ah yes. How they worked with Ragnar on the catapult and the treebucket.'

'Indeed, they did. Anything you needed fixing, they were the people for the job. Forever tinkering with things. I was told you daren't perch on anything for fear they'd changed it into something else. I remember once, one of my brothers perched on his usual seat, it dropped down a pinch and he went flying over the table! My mother was working on an ejector seat for the sky-sedan. It didn't catch on, but oh, how we laughed. Not that Lamchop did … anyway, yes. Engineers.'

'Is he an engineer?'

'No. Lamchop was a wrangler, and he disappeared during a surge in mantis shark numbers due to the Overharvest of '73, when the fruit fell into the bay and the sea-creatures went beserk. And Bliddalo and Jettering went off to space and then emigrated to Aurinko, and Gilgabont lives in Kodiak.'

Before Suza could tell her aunt that the boys had met him, Great Aunt Nineveh reached for her headphones and popped them on. Suza took a moment to study the designs on the container's walls and realised that something about the time of this visit must have been different, because the room's lighting had changed. The suns illuminated the walls in a way they'd never done before.

Engravings of little figures, animals and towers danced before her eyes as light rippled around the room, moving with the clouds outside. Images of dugongs and whales swam across the floor, giant cow-crabs cantered across the walls and seabirds flew across the ceiling.

She wondered whether the engineers who'd constructed the tower were the ones who'd scratched the story pictures into the walls or whether they'd been done later. Perhaps Battily and Nineveh had had a hand in them? She looked from one chapter in the planet's story to the next, and her eye was caught again by a larger figure, much bigger than the others.

Was it a man or an animal? It was hard to tell but it appeared to have arms. Long arms. But then again, maybe not. Or maybe it was —? With a passing cloud the image was gone and by the time it had moved on, the light had faded and the animated wall was still again.

Suza was beginning to wish she'd held the tin of asparagus fancies back. She had to find out more about the treebucket in order to beat the creature she may have seen lurking on her aunt's walls.

The only way to tempt Triple G away from music hour now was to present her with the offering she'd brought and kept in reserve. A honey chew her grandfather had given her, that she'd been saving for a special occasion (although if trying to save Vispa wasn't a special occasion she didn't know what was). She wished she could have cut it in half.

Delighted with the gift, Triple G suggested they have another cup of tea to go with their nibbles, and Suza's spirits lifted until Nineveh produced a plate of luminous green kale crackers. Of the chew, there was no sign.

'So, how is your little gang doing? Have you found a way to save the towers?' Suza was unable to reply because her mouth was full of dry, green 'goodness', so Auntie Puffbird carried on. 'I've heard them pottering about on the rigging at night. I don't sleep as well as I might and that boy Stayforth isn't light on his feet. Please do tell Tycho that if they want the storm records for the nights they sleep through, they're very welcome to mine.'

She patted a small notebook that had slipped down the side of her seat. It was made up of tiny scraps of paper (real paper?) and was very old and very rubbed out by the look of it.

'Nyum nyum-' said Suza, trying to speak through the dryness of kale crumbs. 'The construction of your container is very interesting; all the pulleys and things.'

'My grandmother's grandparents, Hetti and Norwich Puffbird, who designed and built it, loved learning about the time before the Great Remove and The Even Bigger Bang, when there were *compyotars* and, dare I say, *roobotics*.' She and Suza both took a loud sip of their tea. 'Anyway, they pretty much added a pulley to everything. Battily and I barely move a muscle in here now!' she said.

She flung out her spindly little arm and accidentally flicked a switch which prompted yet another curly teacup holder to hover at her elbow, along with a heap of knitting, and a tinkling sound as a small chain hung with teaspoons emerged from under the rocking chair and began to curl up, up and away, possibly never to return.

'The thing is, Auntie Nineveh, I found a diagram of a treebucket.'

'Oh yes?' The lady's eyebrows rose.

'Well, Triple G, I was wondering whether this bungalow, your home … was the treebucket?'

'There we are! You've got it! I thought Tycho and his friend Stayput might get it, but well done Suza. I should have known it would be you. Yes, Hetti and Ragnar's plans weren't allowed, so they began modifying their container. They'd half-built the thing by the time the mayor found out and had the project closed down. Fortunately, the committee didn't have the heart to request it be dismantled and said they could keep the container as long as they pacified it.'

'Pacified the Wotwa?'

'No, the container, to make it a little less... threatening.'

'As far as the Vispans were concerned there was nothing to battle any more and they were afraid that if the technology got into the wrong hands ... Anyway, you can see how, if you rerigged the samovar pulley here and attached it there, changed the sink attachment to that point there and then joined the slingshot to the hive rigging outside and attached a weight to it up there, you'd have something pretty big to play with.'

Suza wondered why the woman had waited for them to find it out themselves, given that she was keeping records of the lightning strikes and knew how close the Wotwa was to breaking through the reef! The expression on her face must have betrayed her again as the next thing Nineveh said was, 'I'd have told you if I thought things were getting serious. The Wotwa is at least a week away, if my great great grandmother's diary is anything to go by.'

46.

Dear Diary

Suza's news was greeted with joy, confusion, questions, alarm and more questions.

'Triple-G lives in a weaponised bungalow?'

'How is she allowed to live in a weapon and I'm not?'

'So, every time she puts the samovar on, Great Great Great Aunt Nineveh is rigging up a missile?'

'How dangerous is a cup of tea at her house?'

'Do you think she'd let us blow up her container to destroy the Wotwa?'

And 'What did you learn about her great-great grandmother's diary?'

Finally, from Tycho, a question she could answer.

'Great Aunt Nineveh said it was kept in the library.' They all groaned. 'Of course, it turned out she was talking about a cabinet in her container.'

'Why did she call it the library?'

'There must have been at least a dozen books in it. She turned a couple of levers, the pulleys kicked in and the doors opened.'

'So even her library is a weapon?'

Addie ignored Walf and asked, 'What sort of books?'

'Mostly cookery, and she had a couple she called "thrillers".'

'Frillies?' said Walf.

'— and then there were three books that were unmarked and they were her great great grandmother's diaries.'

'Did you look at them?'

'Better than that. I borrowed them!' Suza opened a rucksack she had hanging under her desk and brought out a waxed cloth wrapped parcel and revealed three slim booklets numbered 14, 15 and 17. She cleared her throat and began (in her best 'reading a diary' voice) to read number 14.

'*Dear Diary,*
I had broccoli scampi today, followed by banabbage trifle. The weather was warm and I have swimming tomorrow.

Dear Diary,
I had swimming today at the ghats and was included in the life-saving crew. Bakossi are rubbish at swimming. Left-over broccoli scampi for supper, followed by left-over banabbage trifle.

Dear Diary,
I wish I'd had swimming today. Goat herding was more exciting than unusual because Uncle Binjom had forgotten to fasten their magnetic shoes, so he drove them out and they all fell off the edge and dangled in and out of people's containers for twenty minutes before there were enough of us to haul them up again. A couple of them got into Old Mrs Bartlebot's container and ate her hammocks and she was MAD about it. But apart from that it was quite funny. Goat curry for tea.'

'Seems a bit harsh,' remarked Zafe.

Walf couldn't get over the age of Mrs Bartlebot, but the others agreed it must have been one of her ancestors and that it was unlikely to have been the Mrs Bartlebot they took care to avoid. Unless she was 150 years old. (Perhaps that was why she was so crotchety?)

Suza flicked through the rest of the booklet and they realised that (apart from the banabbage) their lives were remarkably similar to Triple G's great-great-grandmother's, when the diary mentioned lessons in herbology, carrot study, flower boxes, honey filtering and 'WAIT!'

'Dear Diary,
The silent storms are becoming more regular but Mama's guardians are nearly finished. Daddy and the limb team are so funny to watch and they make such a lot of noise but he thinks that will make all the difference.

Mama says that they're betting on the fact this dreaded creature makes so little noise itself, that it won't like the din we make.'

Walf shouted out, 'See! If you know one thing you know the opposite!' Which they agreed (again) made no sense at all. Suza read a couple more pages.

'Ragnar Best came over tonight and ate a great deal of roast shrimp. Papa was most annoyed as he likes roast left-overs for lunch. They were talking about his treebucket and they got into a bit of a flap about it.

Mr Best says it's almost ready, Papa doesn't think they'll need it and Mama says what they ought to be doing is finishing the Guardian of Helsingor, just off the reef. Papa said he couldn't understand why that wasn't the first one they'd finished because of its position and they got into a bit of a barney again. We had gooseberry tapioca for afters. A whole spoonful each!'

Zafe asked what they'd learnt.

'That they had tapioca?' said Walf.

'That a spoonful each was enough?'

'That Ragnar was greedy and should have eaten less?'

Tycho glared at them. 'THAT ALL THIS STUFF REALLY HAPPENED!'

They ruminated on that for a moment. It wasn't a cartoon on an ear trumpet. It wasn't an old family story bent out of shape over the years. It wasn't a space station fairy tale or a bit of bad weather. And it wasn't something distant, half-seen. And it wasn't Zafe shouting about it (for a change).

A battered diary had brought the fight to life in a way nothing else had so far.

These were real people just like themselves, eating broccoli scampi and gooseberries (just like they did), building huge machines to fight off a threat to their civilisation (just like they weren't).

Without diaries number sixteen to hand, Suza started on the last diary. Number 17.

'Dear Diary,

It's so nice to be home, despite the sea of Wotwa flesh our boat had to wade through and the terrible smell — like that time Uncle Lubjoy forgot about the blobfish in his fishing bag and it lay there all term, until he found it three months later.

But I think the Wotwa smell is worse than that, because there's nowhere to get away from it, apart from moving back downland and living with the wasabi pickers again. NO THANK YOU!

I didn't notice Helsingor had gone until Mama pointed it out. Felt bad about that. The wranglers are out looking for the missing people.

There's a space where it was and a small rock above the waves. They're dredging the bay to use its bits to add to Amburg tower which isn't tall enough. And they might build a new one. Shame about the seaweed skating rink though.

Wotwa risotto for dinner, followed by beetroot surprise. I hope the surprise isn't that it's being served with Wotwa. Or that there's no beetroot.'

A collective shiver went round the group at the thought of the meals she'd endured. The next couple of day's entries were about more Wotwa-related breakfast, lunch and dinner horrors, until a more significant entry caught Suza's eye.

'Dear Diary,

Ragnar is leaving. He came round for tea and brought a thick spool of jellyfish ribbon which he's given to my grandmother. He told me he's going away to sculpt and when I asked him why he wasn't helping with Amburg Tower, he said that the beast's destruction was not the key to our survival and that the Wotwa was nothing more than a distraction. He also said he needed a breath of fresh air. The Wotwa smell is bad, but it'll go away soon, won't it?'

'And?' said Tycho.

'That's it,' said Suza.

'How are we supposed to survive if we don't beat the Wotwa?' Walf asked. 'Would have been handy if she'd written a paragraph on the likes and dislikes of the huge great "distraction" that's going to eat us.'

Zafe leapt to his feet. 'But don't you see? WE HAVE TO FIND THE JELLYFISH RIBBON! It must have been the plans for the treebucket. It's the answer to everything! How to rebuild the treebucket and shoot the Wotwa away! Triple G will have it and it'll tell us everything. We WON'T be eaten!'

There was an awkward silence and a lot of nudging. Finally, Tycho spoke. 'They only last a couple of years, Zafe.'

'What do you mean?'

'Jellyfish ribbon doesn't last all that long. It gets thinner and thinner and finally just goes mouldy. Whatever information was on that ribbon is long gone.'

'Yeah, we could still be eaten,' said Walf, unhelpfully.

Neighbour

The storm that night was like nothing Zafe had ever experienced, but he and Tycho stayed where they were, huddled under a tarpaulin. The breeze was cold and the wind stung their ears making them sore, but the storm was silent. There was no thundering from the Mega Clams and the lightning show was stunning and terrifying in equal measure.

Thin fingers of bright light scraped the sky leaving red and pink scratches, although it was difficult to tell whether that was merely the effect it was having on the boys' eyes, and not something the sky was doing at all. The fingers became bigger, like the broad branches of a monstrous tree.

There was a low, rhythmic, rumbling sound and the sky tore in two again and Zafe saw it.

A long, menacing shape looming out of the darkness. It was enormous.

It didn't have the arms he'd imagined. What it did have, looked more like tentacles; at least half a dozen of them attached to a broad serpentine body rising from the waves. It was closer than he'd imagined, much closer. Just beyond the reef, just beyond their defences. The marks of lightning dissolved from the sky and the thing was gone.

'Did you see it?'

No sooner were the words out of Tycho's mouth than he realised what a silly question it was to have asked. Zafe was sitting with his mouth open, like a fish gasping for water, his finger pointing at a now untroubled sea. At first his words were unformed, a rasping sound, but he coughed violently and they gained traction.

'It's going to eat our tower and us in it. We have to tell somebody. We could bring them up here now and show them.' But the air was still, the electricity in the atmosphere gone and the sky mended. The storm was over and there was nothing to see, but still Zafe's eyes nervously scanned the horizon. 'Tycho, we can't stop this thing without more help. It's HUGE!'

'It's a lot closer than the first time I saw it. Is it like you imagined? Although didn't you say it had laser eyes and gnashing fangs?'

'It's worse because it's **real**, even worse than reading the diary. It's out there and we just weren't close enough to see the fangs. I'm sure it's got them. We HAVE to tell the grown —' His hand shot out as he pointed towards Amburg: no, beyond it. 'There's someone there. LOOK! There's someone with a lamp on the roof.'

Tycho whipped round and saw a retreating light, but couldn't make anyone out. 'Someone else was watching too?' Zafe saw the look of disappointment on his friend's face but couldn't help feeling relieved. Whoever it was MUST have seen it. It wasn't their secret any more.

'We'll talk to Grundi about it tomorrow.'

Walking down the stairs of a lopsided tower, exhausted, the two of them almost slid down a whole floor when they heard the click of a door nearby, and noticed a nubbin of wax on a step. Had someone else also seen the storm but decided to sit it out in the central corridor?

The next morning Tycho and Zafe got out of their hammocks extra early, so they could perch with Nonna for a while before school. Waiting for their tea to cool, they glanced at each other to see who'd speak first. After much nudging, it was Tycho.

'I don't suppose you saw the storm last night?'

'Storm? I didn't hear anything!' said Nonna, stirring some gooseberry porridge.

'That's because it was a silent storm.'

There was more stirring of porridge. 'Haven't had one of those for a while.'

'Well, there have been a few of them recently — wait! You know about them?'

'Of course! We used to have them when I was a child.' She added some more *green* to the steaming, gloopy mass. 'It's an amazing light show, but if you're tired at school and I get a telepipe call from Mr Antibus there'll be trouble! Besides, if the siren doesn't sound, it's safe and you ought to be sleeping.'

'No, no, we're fine. It's just that we saw something out there, something big. A creature.' They left the word hanging in the air.

'Have you packed your beltbags? It would be a shame to be late for school given how early you got up this morning.'

'Yes, yes, we did Nonna, but about the creature —'

'Do you have any quintar left over from last week? The tuckshop's open today isn't it?'

'NONNA! WE SAW A MONSTER!' Tycho yelled, his voice pinging off the beams and travelling across the waves.

'There's no need to yell, Tycho,' said Grundi, in an entirely reasonable tone of voice, as he entered the room.

'A monster, Grundi!'

The shocking thing was that his grandfather didn't look shocked at all; in fact, he looked interested. Tycho peered deep into his grandfather's eyes. 'You know, don't you?'

Zafe stood frozen like Tycho, his heart racing, but the old man had said nothing. He took a deep breath and spoke. 'Whatever brought down Helsingor is back. We saw something last night and it's getting closer. Closer to the reef. We've got to do something or it will ...' He didn't know what to say, so he ended the sentence with a shrug, which he hoped conveyed the despair he felt.

Grundi took a thoughtful bite of his beanbread toast and a sip of his Earl Grey. 'Nonna, would you mind making a telepipe call to Mrs Hawtrey to let her know the boys will be late?'

The man walked over to the balcony, looked up and shouted something about 'a cuppa'. He took the largest teapot off its hook, tested the hotpipe's temperature, put some Vispish Breakfast tea leaves into the pot and waited for the hot pipe to come to the boil. Grundi smiled at something beyond them and they looked around to see an elderly man on the balcony.

Tycho regarded Walf as one of the quietest 'landers' he knew; he could abseil down and take off as gently as a sea-spider on its web, but this man was in a class of his own.

He'd wafted in with a light breeze, wearing a tie-dyed kilt (which served only to highlight the chickeny nature of his assam-coloured legs) and a voluminous shirt of many colours. He was a dandy and, they guessed, the man whose door they'd heard click the night before. The man who'd waited out the storm in the central core last night.

Tycho had thought he knew all of his grandfather's friends, but Grundi explained that he and his friend Dinesh had performed at a hivekeepers' aerobical display (on opposing teams), long before Tycho was born, and that they usually met once a week at Dinesh's container to sample the week's honey.

Nonna announced she was going to join her goat-herding group and after the introductions were made, she swung off the balcony and insodoing made Dinesh's silent entrance all the more impressive. (Tiny as she was, the woman moved like a herd of walruses.) Grundi poured the tea while his guest perched with the boys.

'So, I gather you two saw something last night?'

'We've seen the Wot-,' Zafe wouldn't have said anything but the man's bright green eyes had landed on him and for a moment it was as if he'd had no choice.

'And you know its name!' he exclaimed, rubbing his paper-dry hands together, 'Tell me more about the beast.'

Zafe fell off his perch, but Tycho managed to hang on, a look of thunder on his face. Not only was their secret out, it had never been a secret at all.

The Plan

They returned to school just before lunch and met up with Walf at the tuckshop. Chatting over a bag of sea-spider flavoured Turnip Bites, Zafe told him about the storm, and the morning they'd spent with Grundi and Dinesh.

'He's been studying the storms, and knows about the Wotwa, and last night he almost sounded the alarm because he thought it was so close.'

'Grundi and his friend know about it?' asked Walf, glancing around at Tycho as he paced behind them, saying nothing.

'Yep.'

'But Zafe … how long have they known?'

'They said they realised it had returned a while ago but wanted to keep it quiet.'

Tycho stopped his stomping just long enough to unfold his arms and let out a loud and angry 'WHAT?'

'Didn't they think they could trust us?' asked Walf. Zafe suggested that perhaps they'd made a promise to Aunt Mirrah too.

'So why aren't they building a war machine? Don't they think the Wotwa is dangerous?'

'They thought that they could get rid of it without worrying anyone, just like we did. They've told us their plan but we're under strict instructions to tell no-one. So, it is still a secret.' He glanced over at Tycho. 'They don't want people to panic.'

Walf, Suza and Addie promised, hand on heart that they wouldn't repeat what they'd been told, especially as the two boys had promised Dinesh and Grundi they wouldn't repeat what they'd been told. And, as far as they could tell, they'd all promised Auntie Mirrah they'd do nothing about any of it. (And Addie wondered what promises Mirrah must have made.)

'Dinesh said they're waiting for a container of wasabi to be delivered.'

'Yum!'

'They think it'll keep the creature away.'

'Is that their plan? But what if it likes wasabi?'

'Apparently the Wotwa has never been seen in the south-west quarter, where wasabi is grown.'

'Has it definitely been seen in the other quarters, I mean, aside from Tower Quarter?'

'He didn't say.'

'Is Mirrah bringing the wasabi in?' asked Addie. When no-one answered, she asked what else they grew down there, that the beast might be avoiding.

'Well, there's coffee.'

'No that's further up.'

'Tea?'

'Nope, that's in the south-east.'

'BANANAS?'

'Walf!'

Could it be the wasabi that was keeping it away from the south-west?

'Well, it is *a* plan,' admitted Tycho, idly kicking a plant pot. He accepted a radish chew from Suza and did a bit less plant-pot-kicking.

'What did they think of our plan, Ty?' said Walf.

'They think we should keep going. We have to approach Triple-G about transforming her container into a weapon and we've got to finish the scarecrow.'

'AND we haven't found a light source!' added Zafe.

'Mm, I've been thinking about that.' Suza took a roll of jelly paper out of her beltbag, which showed a tower (labelled Bakossi) with a large candle inside it, and light shining from the crystal which had been repositioned.

'So Bakossi is home to the biggest crystal. That's the one we use to direct our light to Istanglia and Amburg, and from those two towers on to Adamant, where it will reflect off the dvd's,' said Suza.

'How are we going to make a candle that big?' asked Walf. 'It must be the size of a container!'

'We're not. I just drew one big one to symbolise a lot of them because I was running out of squid-ink. We're going to need a lot of candles, as many as we can get.'

'Why use Bakossi for this?' asked Zafe, 'Why not Adamant if it's got all the crystals in it to start with?'

'Bakossi's filter system and core is bigger than any of the other towers,' said Suza. 'The huge lightwell in the middle of the tower would be the perfect place to put the candles and then *redirect* the illumination up to the top crystal, the big one, and reflect it over to the other towers and the disks, where it would be reflected one hundred times over … or 403 times, depending on exactly how many disks we've got. Besides, we can't illuminate the outside of Adamant from the inside, however good Adamant's crystals are. If anyone's got a better plan, I'm happy to go along with it.'

It was kind of Suza to ask, but no one else had anything to contribute that was anything like as well thought out as this. The more they looked at the scarecrow diagram, the better the wasabi plan began to sound, but Dinesh and Grundi had been encouraging and had said they were all going to have to pull together if the beast was to be stopped.

When they got home, Grundi said that he and Dinesh were going to meet up with the Towers' Committee the following day, tell them about the threat and suggest that the towers work together to beat the Wotwa. The more plans, the merrier.

After dinner, a couple of games of chess and an episode of 'A Book at Bedtime', Tycho and Zafe retired to their hammocks. They had a lot to talk about and it should have been difficult to sleep, but Nonna's potato fajitas were very filling and both boys nodded off long before the shipping forecast finished. Tycho's dreams were of sky-blue skies, trouble-free waves, raisin cakes and perfectly trained goats — until they went on the rampage wearing magnetic shoes. Were they eating Mrs B's kitchen again?

In Zafe's dream he was with his parents in a spacepod being driven by a monkey in goggles (who was concentrating so hard his little, blue-black tongue was sticking out). Zafe wrestled the controls from the animal and steered them away from the two suns.

While he was being congratulated by his parents (but not by the monkey), Zafe tapped his glowing data-arm and ordered them a feast of multi-coloured foodcubes. They'd just finished the first course when they heard Zafe's father begin drilling into the metal wall. He was fitting a wall-bed. A nice, secure, stationary wall-bed.

The drill was loud, but it wasn't a wall-bed being fitted – and he wasn't in a spacepod. Could it be Gonzales? Zafe sat up in his hammock and yelled, 'HE'S SOMEWHERE NEAR. I CAN HEAR HIM NIBBLING CUTTLEFISH!'

His eyes met Tycho's and they both realised it was something much, much bigger and an awful lot worse than a goat, a drill or a rampaging snail. The grinding sound was real and it was coming from the reef.

Just beyond the circle of breaking waves, lurked a black, glistening shape, a mess of angry limbs and coral-grinding teeth, hell-bent on destroying their protective wall.

The sky was angry with lightning, impatient flashes ripping it apart, illuminating a giant black serpent. A nightmare made real, swimming in the water surrounding their home.

The Wotwa had arrived.

49.

More Panto

The boys looked up, down and across at their neighbours, all of whom had been awoken by this horror, a horror for which they might have been ready in a week's time, but not yet, not now. The younger Vispans were ushered into the towers' cores and an emergency council meeting was held in the Great Hall.

It was agreed that the Venerable Poet should broadcast an impromptu pantomime to let the tower-dwellers know about the Wotwa, the status of the reef, the plans they'd forged to protect Thames Sea and, above all, to calm everyone down.

Grundi told Nonna, Tycho and Zafe he was going up to the roof to tend to the bees but that he'd listen to the radio programme whilst up there, and they nodded as if they didn't know exactly who the VP was (and hadn't just had breakfast with him).

Without the light show, the many chanted responses and Mrs H causing a riot, they knew the Venerable Poet's programme could have fallen a bit flat, were it not for its monstrous message. They sat tight, nibbling celery-bean porridge-sticks, waiting for the radio to crackle into life.

'THE TIME TO LEAVE HAS NOT COME!

'The people of Ancient Earth may have known a time of catastrophe was near, but we do not. We still don't have any Naked Mole Rats, but we have plenty besides, which we'd rather not see mashed to a pulp by the diabolical creature that lurks beyond our reef defences.

'Do we wish to see our towers toppled and our homes

destroyed?

'I'LL TAKE THAT AS A NO!

'Each of our mighty towers has a surfeit of beetroot and a strength all its own, whether it be dried fish or fruit.

And so, each of our towers has its own unique form of defence. Indeed, a fluky five of our youth have chosen to construct a giant scarecrow out of Tower Adamant to frighten this Demonic Hell-haddock of the Seas away, and with that in mind I would like everyone to take apart their spangly bird charmers, let go their coasters and donate their dvd mirrors to the cause. Collection points will be arranged.'

(At this point a determined few, Mrs Hawtrey among them, yelled out the usual 'GOATS, GOATS, GOATS!' as was traditional.)

'As far as the goats are concerned *[pause]* we'd like them rounded up, along with any herds of crabs, and kept under strict supervision. We've got a lot to do and they *will* be more of a hindrance than a help. Geoff-Bert, the Venerable Poet is talking to you.

'Even as I speak, a container of wasabi is being transported to our imperiled shores. The beast will be vanquished, but not without a great deal of help, and it is with this in mind that I'd like everyone to have a cup of tea (if they have not done so already) and consider what they might do to help the cause. We welcome your ideas and your enthusiasm.

'We must find the spirit that moved us to undertake the Great Remove, and indeed, the same spirit that prompts our lesser Removes.

'This monster is no meteor, but no less of a threat if it crushes our kettles or eats us in our hammocks. We do not want to go BOOM or be extinguished Just. Like. That. Lucky we are to have this life. Let us not squander it with indecision and inactivity, and fall into the jaws of fear.

'I fear myself, that I am waffling on when there is a great deal to be done, and so good tower-dwellers, that is all.

'WE MUST GET CRACKING BEFORE THE WOTWA DOES!'

The radio fell silent, and although the Wotwa's loud munching could no longer be heard, there followed a series of screams and the sound of breaking china and ripping nets. Far from calming the residents, it may have served to make things worse, and Zafe looked downright confused. 'Fluky five? He called us "The Fluky Five"! What does that mean?'

'Didn't he say "poopy",' asked Addie.

'No, he definitely said, "fluky",' said Tycho.

'Which must be better than "poopy",' said Walf. 'But what does it mean? Is it a worm?'

'It means "lucky",' said Suza. 'Although I don't know what's so lucky about finding a sea monster? Perhaps the Venerable Poet doesn't know what "fluky" means... he could have called us "The Fortuitous Five".'

'Or "fearless",' said Tycho. 'That's a good word, a MUCH better word!'

'Were we fearless?' asked Zafe.

'He could have just called us "The Five",' said Walf.

Grundi returned ten minutes later, his sleeves covered in honey. He went for a wash while Nonna made a pot of chamomile tea and they told her what 'the Fluky-Fearless-Poopy Five' had been up to.

'The scarecrow plan I like, but I'm just not sure Old Auntie Nin will take very kindly to you dismantling her home. What exactly did you have in mind?'

'Well, we worked out —'

'Suza worked out,' corrected Zafe.

'— that her container may have been designed, originally as a weapon. A huge catapult. The only problem we've got is the lack of a catapulty bit. A lack of twang.'

'A rubber band, you mean? Like the ones you were wearing round your necks when you got back from your midnight trip to Puffin Beach?' Nonna smiled at their reaction. 'Come on boys, you know you can't go anywhere without a member of my Repainting Society or Band of Knitters seeing what you're up to.

'And besides, if you'd asked me for a large rubber band, I'd have told you about that cave. I was playing in there sixty years ago. What do you think Mrs Krankwurst's netting is made out of?'

Tycho thought back to a friend of Nonna's whose container he'd visited when he was little, and how he'd bounced his way off the twentieth floor. Fortunately, there had been a dragon boat passing underneath that had picked him up. They'd never been invited for tea at her house again.

'So, Nonna, what happened to the Uiskers?'

'What do you mean *what happened to them*? Puffbird is a Uisker name.'

'Nineveh is a Uisker?' (It was the only time Zafe ever saw his friend come close to falling off a perch. Needless to say, he himself was tangled in netting on the floor.) 'POOPSLUGS! But I thought they were famed for their height?'

'Tycho, there is no need for that language. And the Uiskers *were* famed for their height. Their lack of it.'

'So, does that mean she's ...'

'No, it does not.' She turned to Grundi. 'The Venerable Poet told us to put our backs into it and get a move on, so perhaps we ought to get going.'

'I'm fairly sure we were asked to "do what we might to help the cause",' remarked a slightly miffed Grundi.

'With that in mind, it might be an idea to get a hold of those big rubber bands you were talking about and put them to use,' remarked Nonna. 'I've got an idea.'

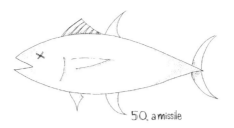

50. a missile

Wotwa War

Grundi met with the other Istanglia Council members as part of a delegation to visit the home of the oldest living tower-dweller (Countess Nineveh Adriatica Jonquilla Puffbird) to see whether rumours of her living inside a weapon of some sort were true.

While CNAJP was more than happy to have her home blown up or twanged across the Four Seas, several council members were outraged. Some of them had never been inside the home of Triple-G (she was notoriously picky about her visitors) and although they were interested in the pulleys, the hovering samovar, the door and the seating machinery, it was the decoration and ornate metal work that caught their eye.

Istanglia lacked the architectural grandeur of Amburg, the sweeping lines of Bakossi and the individuality of Kodiak. *This* was its architectural gem. After a quick vote, they agreed that a home of this calibre could not be disassembled. It was just too nice to take apart, even if the future of Vispa was at stake...

By lunchtime each of the towers had settled on a plan. Tycho had passed the second wakl-and-talkie to Grundi, along with Suza's jellypaper plans, which he copied for the council's consideration, and by the afternoon's end the towers had formulated strategies to ready themselves for the Wotwa's onslaught. They were all agreed that a 'Jack of All Trades' approach was best; a bit of this plan and a bit of the next, as no one plan looked like it might succeed.

South Utzeera had all-hands-on-deck, drying and storing fish at a furious rate. Once they were fully dried, they became very hard and someone pointed out that the bigger specimens would make fearsome clubs. This person was gently taken aside and told that the dried fish was being produced as a continued source of *food* (given that they'd now acknowledged that fishing levels had dropped, due to the Wotwa). The other council members nodded in agreement but, once the meeting was over, admitted that the idea of dried tunny fish being a weapon shouldn't be discounted if the Wotwa got within bashing distance.

Kodiak was crazily planting bamboo (the fastest growing kind) and Nonna had suggested that if they continued at their present rate, they'd soon be able to walk over to the tower. Tycho was quietly excited about that, but didn't think it much of a plan.

Pineapple-harvesting efforts were also redoubled as Kodiakites began covering their homes in crushed pineapple, under the belief that the monster would find it too sour and retreat (ignoring the councillor who'd suggested the acid of the pineapple flesh would, in fact, dissolve their housing).

The Fluky Five wondered what Nineveh's brother was up to and agreed he'd have been more likely to lob pineapples at a beast than feed it.

Amburg Tower stopped carving, which was unheard of. Someone had suggested that the constant tapping might be misconstrued as a friendship call and actually attract the Wotwa. Efforts to find more dvd's were stepped up and, on hearing about the Istanglia cave, a climbing team swung around their foundations, only to find a doorway leading to a staircase, leading up to a room in which they found a stash of stained glass. The architects were delighted and the decorative panes of glass were taken up to the Great Hall and immediately put on display.

It was only after most of the inhabitants had been to see the new finds that they admitted it wasn't going to help beat the Wotwa and they began frantically harvesting beetroot and other colourful vegetables instead.

At midday, the children of Hundredwater were assembled for twirling practice. So, in addition to saving the world they had to practise for the show, otherwise they'd be in detention when their tower was eaten.

Bakossi redoubled its broadcasts, asking the narrators and newscasters to speak at twice their normal speed. They'd also redoubled their dried fruit efforts, with slightly better results. Were they hoping to trade sultanas for weapons, or did they think that if the Wotwa ate too much of the stuff it would leave with a sore tummy or a bad bottom? Either way, they were busy.

The residents of Istanglia started a small army although it wasn't clear what marching up and down the central core would achieve. Someone had taken against the Venerable Poet's words about the goats, deciding they were as good a task force as any, and was attempting to train them to butt, nibble and nip on request (rather than doing it all the time as they usually did).

Nonna, Zafe and Tycho abseiled down to the jetty, only to see the boxes of rubber inner tubes from the cave being floated up to the roof under helium balloons, so they pedalifted back up. By the time they'd reached the roof the boxes had been sorted, reboxed and were about to be lowered back down, when Nonna got her hands on them.

'As I'm sure you've gathered, Auntie Puffbird's home isn't to be turned into a weapon, much as she'd like it to, but I think there's still a way we can use these to devastating effect.'

Under Nonna's directions, the boys looped as many giant rubber bands as they could over their shoulders, taking the zipwire over to Amburg and then on to Bakossi. Given the extra weight they were carrying, their swing over was faster than usual and the trip was thrilling for Tycho (less so for Zafe, who zipped with his arms around Nonna and his eyes tight shut).

They were met by Mr Flintlo, who said, 'I've been swinging off my balcony ever since your grandmother gave me the call, and I've identified eight homes that are rigged just right.' He looked down at some squid-ink scribbles on the back of his hand, and they took the pedalift and the heavy bands, up the tower.

'What were these things actually for?' asked Zafe.

'We believe these rubber bands or *inner tubes* are related to bicycling. We know they used tyres on the metal wheel rims, but had no idea what part these played until recently. They may have been part of an ejection system for giving pedallists on bicycles a bit of extra oomph when they set out. As far as we can tell, they were hung around lampposts, which is where bicycles were kept, and were used to catapult the pedallist at the beginning of their journey.'

'Sounds a bit dodgy,' remarked Tycho, a boy who swung hundreds of feet up in the air for pleasure.

'No more dangerous than cycling which is, after all, balancing on two thin wheels,' replied Mr F, 'It doesn't bear thinking about.'

Bakossi Tower's homeowners were more than happy to be part of the war against the Wotwa, especially as their entire plan had been mostly just broadcasting and the gathering of dried fruit. The first home they arrived at had a magnificent balcony, around which Mr Flintlo looped a black rubber band, pulling it tight.

Leaning back with one eye closed, Nonna aimed at the reef, adjusting the band where necessary. They carried on in this way until they'd set up all the bands and had a siesta while they waited for a shipment of ammunition from Kodiak. It was going to be a long day. And night.

Alarmed by the diameter of Zafe's nostrils (which had flared to an unfathomable size), Walf was the first to notice that the missiles had arrived two towers away, on Bakossi. Enormous nets of tunny fish; huge, sharp, dried tunny fish as hard as wood, to be used as spears in the war against the Wotwa. And it was Triple G's brother, Gilgabont, who led the group distributing the smelly arsenal. (Much to the boys' relief, Mr Flintlo had greeted the gentleman by name.)

Addie was anxious to help and had wanted to join Tycho and Walf, who were attaching dvd's to Adamant's legs after a late surge in donations, but she'd realised that once the stockpile of fish was distributed to the rubber band balconies on Bakossi *someone* would have to fire them ...

An hour later the reeking, rock-hard fish had been delivered and Addie had an inner tube in her grasp and the reef in her sights.

A couple of tower-dwellers twanged off the tower's side during the practise session (something they were keen not to have happen once the Wotwa reappeared) but after an hour's practise they were firing fish (rather than people) in roughly the right direction.

Crystal Tilting

Suza and Zafe had done the calculations for the crystals' angles while the others had created the sticky putty that would hold the 'lenses' in place, in a bamboo frame. It was a mixture of dried fruit, pineapple and jellyfish ink. A couple of hours later the crystals of Istanglia and Amburg were upright, held tight and pointing the right way to illuminate the dvd's. It was time to tackle the last, and most significant crystal.

Unlike the others, Bakossi Tower's pride and joy, known as 'The Mother of All Crystals', was a single gem of monstrous proportions, and moving it was going to be a delicate and difficult job.

Waves of light danced off the facets, filtering out into greens, yellows and blues as Tycho, Zafe, Addie and Suza tilted their heads, enjoying the lilting light it produced.

'OH POOPSLUGS!' Walf had lit all the remaining candles but one, which was rolling away and heading towards the edge. It disappeared, there was a gust of wind and almost all the candles went out. There was another OH POOPSLUGS! to mark the occasion.

Taking a deep breath, they stood in a circle around the lens, slid their fingers under the crystal and undid the catches that held it securely. They were now the only things keeping the mega-crystal in place and they struggled to hold it as Zafe muttered something about not being sure that the bamboo frame would be strong enough.

Their hands were tacky from the fruity, fishy goo and Suza said she was stuck to the thing and couldn't unstick her grip. She pulled and wriggled, getting one hand off and then the other as the first stuck again. Zafe tried to help her but he was stuck fast too.

Walf was the only one who managed to wrench both his hands free of the goo — and in letting go of his bit of the crystal, he made it that much heavier for Addie to his left, who unstuck her right hand, leaving the others to bear the huge weight which was now threatening to pull them all down into the central core.

Their backs breaking, they finally yanked their hands free amid screams and shouts; and watched in horror as the crystal dropped, twirling hypnotically. Ever-decreasing circles of light twinkling all the way down: The Mother of All Crystals hit the stone below and shattered into a million, beautiful pieces.

They'd barely been able to hold it before; they could have carried it around in their beltbags now.

Silence.

Walf sniffed. 'Well, the way I see it, it was us or the crystal. But Bakossi's water treatment is going to be bad for a while.' He was right but they had even more to worry about at that moment than the poo-chute. Their source of light was gone. The scarecrow was no more.

They remained frozen, staring down at the beautiful mess that had been The Mother of All Crystals. Silent apart from a rhythmic 'Oh no oh no oh no oh no' rumbling from Suza. The Talk-and-Walkie crackled into life.

'How are the Fluky Five doing?'

They looked from one to the other, hardly able to believe Grundi hadn't heard the crystal smashing into a million mini-mother pieces — there'd been nothing fluky about that.

Tycho opened his mouth to speak, there was some static on the line, it cleared and they heard Grundi again. 'The wasabi has done the trick! The Wotwa's arrived but it's passed Istanglia by.'

'And where is it now?' squeaked Tycho, his mouth dry with shock.

'... the current and the wasabi slick is headed towards Kodiak.'

'Grundi! We can't —'

Interrupted by crackling, they heard the words "Adamant's safe but not Bakossi", there was more interference on the line and then Grundi's voice again. 'Best of luck with the Bakossi Mother. It's heavy and it'll need careful handling.'

Tycho began to speak but the device had gone silent. He shook it, but it was as dead as a Dromban sand frog, and Walf helped him to unstick it from his gummy hands.

'What do we do now?' said Addie.

With nothing better to do, Walf had set about blowing out the few candles that remained lit; tiptoeing over the others. No point wasting the wax if the number one crystal was now numbers one to 3,017. But there was another gust of wind and his job was done for him.

The sky had darkened. It was strewn with patches of inky-blue and back-of-the-pantry black, cut in two by spears of lightning. Combined with the invigorating wind roaring around their ears, there was a strange buzz of excitement about them. Eat or be eaten? This was it.

Walf was jumping up and down like a vartig beetle on a hot brick (with the odd armpit squelch thrown in) and Zafe was surprised to see Tycho and Suza join in. Then he realised he was jigging too. Madly jigging. It was Addie, arms firmly crossed, who brought them to their senses.

'Grundi Gillhew said Adamant's safe but BAKOSSI ISN'T. STOP making that noise Walf! And Zafe, now is NOT the time for jazz-hands.' She furiously recrossed her arms, knotting them into submission. 'There's nothing we can do about the crystal so we're going to have to do something else. Tycho, I don't want this to be the most exciting day of my life. I want it to be the most exciting story I tell next week, when I'm still alive! We have to do something and you have to calm down!'

They paused mid-jig, Tycho cleared his throat and smoothed his shorts. There was a crunching sound and they turned to the balcony edge. There, in the waters between Amburg and Bakossi, thrashed the beast. Its dark, silvery scales glinted at every lightning strike and it writhed and shimmied, much like the children had just moments before. It looked like it was enjoying the chaos and fear (much like the children had, just moments before).

Screams from the towers were lost in the billowing wind before returning tenfold. The Adamant 'scarecrow' wasn't sparkling as they'd hoped it would.

Tycho crossed his arms. 'Addie's right. This CAN'T be the end of our plan! There must be something here we can reflect the light with.' He turned to each of them with a raised eyebrow. 'Hasn't anyone got a spare dvd?'

Tempted as Zafe was to say that was *a bit rich*, given the way he'd chucked so many of them into the bay, he and the others dutifully patted their pockets. All the disks they'd collected were attached to Adamant. Waiting to be illuminated.

Then Zafe patted his beltbag and felt, among the nobbles, his collection of buttons. He emptied the contents of his little bag onto the floor and there, in amongst the pieces of chalk, bamboo splinters, coils and crumbs were his buttons. Two were tiny and mother of pearl, but the third was quite different and much bigger. Even as the storm whirled around them in the gloom, the crystal button appeared to glow.

Addie gasped. 'Where did you get *that*?'

'It was in the cave where we found the inner tubes. It was on a little shelf, hidden.'

'No wonder,' she said. 'Someone must be missing it. It's like … the Daughter of All Crystals!'

'Yeah,' said Walf. 'Although we probably wouldn't have dropped this one.'

'Mm, I'm not sure it's big enough to help, but it is beautiful,' said Suza. 'Funny, it looks almost as if …'

They watched as a proud, little flame of pink light appeared within the crystal's heart, changing to green, then blue and fading before it grew again. The tantalising gleam held their attention until, riding on a gust of wind, a high-pitched whistle pierced their ears; and Suza spotted a figure standing on Amburg's roof.

Horst Altvassa.

For a moment, his gaze was fixed on them much as theirs had been on Zafe's jewel — until he looked down at the thrashing waves again, still playing the painfully high-pitched notes. The flute he played was extremely long and so fine an instrument, that, until its metal gleamed in the lightning's radiance, it looked like Altvassa's fingers were dancing on the wind.

And then they all saw it.

The Wotwa had broken through the reef and was writhing in the waves below them. They watched the creature arching violently back and forth, until a booming sound stilled the beast's movements for a moment. The flute's shrill notes had been dampened by the mangled tones of an inexpertly-played brass instrument. The Fourth Form had absconded with Mr Flintlo's tuba again.

They looked over to where Horst had been standing, but he'd gone. Zafe put his crystal button away.

Three Floors Down

Year Four were a bunch of misfits and several teachers had left to seek employment in back-breaking coffee fields and gum plantations rather than return to that particular class. There was a wildness about them that made Walf look like a member of the Headmaster's Association, and they always seemed to have weapons in their hands. Or a brass instrument.

They were making a huge amount of noise.

'Quick!' said Zafe, 'We have to help them!'

He obviously hadn't got to grips with the horror that was Form Four, but they agreed that Horst's flute-playing wasn't helping to quell the beast, and there was a distinct chance it was making things worse.

There was also a small chance that Year Four's tuba-mangling was dulling the flute's shrillness — and calming the beast. Besides, if Tycho's class found Year Four frightening, then perhaps the Wotwa did too.

So many ziplines had snapped in the wind or been sheered in two they had to hold Addie's legs as she leaned over the tower's edge, trying to work out which floor the closest wire projected from.

'There's a line six floors down, we can cross from there.' Hauling her back up they ran down the six flights, racing with the raindrops cascading down the core and when they reached

225

the container's door they shouted and banged, and shouted some more.

They tried one floor up and one floor lower down, but there was no-one at home.

'We'll have to find another zipwire.' Zafe sat down on the steps.

Tycho pulled at his top and began dragging him back upstairs, back to the top of the tower. 'You'll be fine. It's only a few floors down.'

'YOU'LL be fine Tycho, I won't! There's no way I'm climbing six floors down the outside of the building.'

'We're not going without you. When the new pantomime is written you'll be in it, just like the rest of us. Ragnar Best will be forgotten and it'll be Zafe the, the …'

'The One who Stayed Behind?'

'Come on!'

'The One who Fell Off?'

'Mm… hopefully not.'

Walf was the first one over the edge. He climbed like a mountain goat, without a moment's hesitation.

Sitting on the edge, Addie and Suza waited their turn close to hysterics, although it wasn't clear whether their laughter was due to extreme joy or fear. Zafe joined in, his wild cackles caught by the wind.

'Zafe, that's not helping.' Tycho thumped the boy's shoulder and Zafe thumped back and a small ruckus ensued, which was stopped by a roaring sound that scraped at their hearts.

The creature was so close now, that the name 'Wotwa' seemed altogether too silly. A made-up thing, the stuff of little children's nightmares. Not a colossal sea-beast intent on destroying their homes and killing them all.

'Come ON Zafe! We've got to go!' Tycho added, unhelpfully, 'Better to fall off than be eaten.'

They got to the edge, their toes curling over the precipice, and the urge to jump was so great that Zafe began to sway and it was only Tycho's firm hand on his chest that stopped him joining the creature in the salty water of Thames Sea.

'Do as I do,' Tycho commanded. He sat down on the deck and shuffled towards the edge, until his knees were bent and his feet were dangling. He waited for Zafe to join him.

'Right. Feel with your feet for any ledges. This tower's just a giant climbing frame.'

'I can't feel anything!'

Tycho glanced down at Zafe's feet. 'You're going to have to ditch your shoes.'

'My shoes?'

Tycho nodded. 'Don't worry, I'm sure Walf will find them.'

Squeezing them off his feet, Zafe heard someone yelp as they dropped the length of the tower.

'Can you feel any bits of metal?'

'Yes, yes I can.'

'Hold onto the nearest metal frond with both hands and slowly swing round and down until you're looking at the tower and hold on fast with your toes!'

Zafe's heart was in his mouth, or his tongue was in his chest. Either way, he didn't feel good, but he had to join the others. He glanced over at Tycho's face; he couldn't let them down, it was just that there was nothing to clip onto.

'Forget your clips!' shouted Tycho, reading his friend's mind. 'If you can twirl on a trapeze, you can do this.'

'The only time I've actually twirled I was out of control and it was by accident, AND I've always had a safety net!'

'You've got one now —' Tycho cast an eye at the netting that hung between the two towers, torn and flapping in the breeze.

'I've always been clipped on!'

'No, you haven't. I didn't clip you on once last week.'

'You didn't?'

Tycho gave him a shove and Zafe swung round and down, yelling all the way, and slammed into the tower's side, his hands burning against the metal, his t-shirt up around his neck, where Tycho had a hold of it. 'See, you're fine!' And with that, Tycho let go of the fabric, clung to the deck's edge, swung round and began to climb.

Zafe was alive but if he didn't begin moving soon, he'd be stuck there for good, when the rest of the towers had been devoured and he was the only morsel left. He moved a hand, and then a leg, and then a hand …

Hold on tight, keep on going, don't look down. GO!

Suza grabbed Zafe before he overshot the sixth floor down. She pulled him close and guided him to a small shelf, urging him to open his eyes.

Zafe asked where Walf had got to and followed Suza's pointing finger across the stormy, rain-soaked chasm that divided the two towers and there, clinging to a curvy and badly chipped caryatid that adorned an Amburg balcony, was Walf. It wasn't clear whether Walf had knocked the caryatid's nose off, or whether she'd been like that for a while, but she wasn't grinning like Walf was. *(And, if you're wondering, a caryatid is a female figure carved from stone, supporting a roof — or a zipwire balcony.)*

Suza, Addie, Tycho and Zafe perched on the balcony next to the zipwire. It was a fruit and veg wire designed for only the lightest deliveries, and so it was the lightest of them who went next, Suza followed by Addie.

Although he was lighter than Zafe and should have been the next one across, Tycho stepped back for his friend to take his turn. It was only when he looked at his friend's face that he realised that Zafe had never zipwired alone before.

Neither of them said a word as he clipped Zafe on, told his friend to hold on tight and pushed him into the driving rain. His screams were muffled by the storm and Tycho watched anxiously as Zafe … landed safely on the other side. Tycho waved to them all to go up to the school, which they did. Everyone but Zafe.

The zipwire on the Bakossi side was making a tinny, twanging sound. Several of the small wires that made up the bigger cable had come undone.

Tycho looked for other zipwires but there were none. Zafe was waiting on the other side, clinging on with one hand and waving with the other. Tycho took a last look up at the sky, at the beautiful, cracking sky lit by explosions of light, clouds illuminated in plum-pink, bruised purple and warring navy.

He hadn't told the others that he'd snapped his clip on Bakossi, and that it was useless. He ripped off a pocket and one of his sleeves, and twisted the scraps of fabric into a loop. Held firm with his right hand, he passed it over the cable, and tried to twist it around his left, but it was a fraction short. His hands were knuckle to knuckle, pressing against the metal.

He always tugged on his clip before setting off, a habit he couldn't shake, which he thought perhaps brought him luck, but Tycho had a feeling that if he were to do it this time, it wouldn't be lucky at all.

DANG

53.

The creature bellowed in the water below and Tycho closed his eyes for a couple of seconds, took a deep breath and eased himself off the edge. Just for a moment he felt a terrible fear crush his heart and he wondered how Zafe had managed to do what he'd just done. He swung through the wind, and there was a TWANG halfway across and Tycho was dropping, falling.

The metal ripped the fabric around his knuckles, the heat of it unbearable, and he snatched at the cable as he fell, twirling around and around, swinging towards the stone of Amburg. Tycho closed his eyes, waiting for his body to crunch into the tower, and with a *thwack* he was shoved to one side. He shrieked as he hit — what?

Not rock! Netting? And he carried on sailing through until he landed with a smack on a floor. Tycho opened his eyes and could see nothing. He tried to move his arms and legs but was powerless. He yelled and screamed and felt his arms begin to move a little. He carried on thrashing until his body was unbound and he was let loose from an acre of black fabric. He found himself looking into the faces of a group of animals. Puppet animals — and Zafe.

Surrounded by the remains of the Great Hall curtains, his friend was out of breath and holding a long bamboo rod that Tycho's bruised ribs recognised.

'I didn't mean to hit you hard, but you were coming so fast.'

Zafe and Tycho's hug was short-lived. Tycho was in a great deal of pain, but he knew everything would have hurt a lot more if he hadn't been jabbed towards the Great Hall (and away from the stone wall). His palms were badly burnt but there was nothing to be done about them now, so he shoved his throbbing hands into what remained of his pockets and they climbed back up to school.

The tuba had been abandoned and Mrs H led the noisemakers with a big drum, while everyone else was chipping away at the school. Tycho and Zafe were handed a couple of potato mashers by Walf and encouraged to join in.

'HEY WALF! What are we supposed to be doing?' asked Zafe.

'ATTACKING SCHOOL.' Walf knelt back down and got on with his work.

'BUT WHY?' Walf reluctantly got up and led Zafe and Tycho into the hallway to explain – it was quieter there.

'Form Four have decided the best way to get rid of the Wotwa is to drop the school on its head. They're chipping it away, trying to break the balcony off.' They poked their heads back in; everyone was covered in rock dust. The school did stick out, although how they would time it correctly and get the Wotwa underneath the ledge when it fell wasn't clear.

Zafe and Tycho leaned over the school balcony. The sea was an angry, foaming vortex and all that could be seen was the odd flash of a wrangler's oar or the flick of a giant black tail or tentacle.

'IT DEFINITELY DOESN'T LIKE WASABI!' It was one of the smaller Fourth Formers, a girl called Jebnit whose hair was decorated with shards of stone. Her fingers were clotted with dust and dried blood, but her eyes shone with excitement and she held an axe in her hands.

'Reminds me of the Fourth Form's end of term celebrations,' remarked Tycho. 'Makes you wonder what they'd get up to if they didn't have school to go to.'

Suza and Addie stood out due to the relative cleanliness of their clothes, but they were also busily attacking the floor, while Mrs Hawtrey danced and drummed, singing a battle-cry of encouragement as her trusty band of destroyers toiled. Twirling with her hands on her hips — hands up in the air — on her hips — up in the air, Mrs H was getting increasingly overexcited and she accidentally hit the lunch gong with the potato masher she held in her hand.

The huge copper disk was loud at the best of times (it was usually struck with a waxboard scraper) but this time the din was out of this world and Zafe thought his ears would shimmy off his head.

DANGGGGGGGGG-GGG-GGG-GGG!

Walf was hacking away at the far end of the classroom, near the balcony, and was almost propelled into space by the gong's vibrations. Zafe yelled in his ear, 'Walf, I don't see how this is going to work if the Wotwa isn't right below the balcony when it breaks off.'

'Yeah, it might just destroy the school and I know that doesn't bother the Fourth Form, but it would be a shame to destroy it without also getting rid of the beast,' said Tycho.

Walf shrugged. 'How can we make sure it's underneath when the school is set free?'

'Set free?'

'Liberated from the building?'

'You mean, chipped away from Amburg Tower and sent hurtling into the water below, perch desks, soil samples, waxboards and all?' asked Tycho. 'I've got no idea.'

DAAANNNNGGGGGG-GG-GGG-GGGG!

'We have to keep the creature down there, exactly under us, but I don't see how.' They looked down and saw a couple of dragon boats reversing at speed. There were large dents in their brightly painted dragon figurehead where the Wotwa had lashed out with its huge tentacles.

'It'll work if it stays exactly where it is now.'

Which was true. The creature was thrashing around the bottom of the tower, repeatedly whipping at the lower floors, doing its utmost to destroy Amburg's foundations and send it into the Thames Sea. Just like Helsingor.

'We have to stop it trying to chop the tower in half —'

'— while we're trying to chop our school in half.' Zafe's

hair was now white with dust and he ran his fingers through his fringe, only for it to remain where it was, stiffened by the chalk. Pointing at the ceiling.

The three of them watched the creature below, listening to the chopping, hacking, banging, drumming and wailing going on behind them. There were a couple of resounding DANGGG-GG-GGGGs as Mrs Hawtrey danced into the gong again. And for a split-second the writhing stopped and they got a better look at the beast; its vast bulk and scaly, black skin.

'WAIT! I've got an idea!' It was Zafe. 'Do that again, Mrs H.' She joyfully struck the gong and a rousing cheer went up from a small group of *chippers*. 'Did you see what the Wotwa did when the gong went off? It stopped lashing out and just, kind of … swayed for a moment.'

Zafe unhooked the gong as Walf and Tycho carefully lowered it to about an inch off the floor – and then dropped it. Another great DAAAANNGGG sounded as the gong hit the floor and the creature slowed its thrashing again as the note rang out. Once the din had tapered off, they turned their thoughts to how they were going to move it down the tower, and closer to the Wotwa.

'We could carry the gong between the three of us,' said Tycho.

'Or we could lower it down the outside of the tower using these hooks?' Zafe suggested, but they looked over at the zipwires swaying in the violent storm outside and they weren't convinced. What to do, what to do?

'Seriously?' It was Suza. 'You are such blobfish-brains sometimes!' Suza wasn't taken to outbursts like this and the three of them stood (blobfish-like) hoping she wasn't going to call them any more names. 'ROLL IT LIKE A WHEEL!'

'Oooh!' 'Yes.' 'Right, we could do that.'

They sheepishly pushed the gong towards the door and could be heard all the way down as it DONGed, DINGed and DANGed, trundling over every step, and past the smaller children of Amburg and their grandparents, who were sheltering in the tower's core.

By the time they got down to the first storey, their ears were ringing and they were using sign language to communicate. Walf pointed at the door, Tycho nodded and Zafe was about to knock when Tycho indicated he should wait until their ears had stopped vibrating.

Finally, Zafe knocked and the door opened but he couldn't understand why Tycho and Walf had frozen, standing stock still, staring at the householder before them.

'Mrs Bartlebot! You've moved!'

Ah.

The Perfect Home

Arms crossed over her chest and a none too encouraging expression on her face, the inhabitant of this container was the woman Walf and Tycho had spent the best part of a year avoiding.

Being eaten by the Wotwa was better than this.

'Tycho Gillhew. Walf Pomfret. After a certain incident in my *own* container,' (she paused here for dramatic effect) 'I decided to move to Amburg, an altogether more pleasant tower, and yet here you are.' The boys had nothing to say. 'Well? What are you doing and why are you making so much noise?'

'Well, we, we, I'm sure you're busy, we'll go back up.'

The thought of trundling up the stairs with the gong and losing more precious time trying to regain their hearing when they should be battling the Wotwa was too much for Zafe, who was also the only one of them with a chance of winning this woman over. He cleared his throat and, doing his best to adopt the tone and timbre familiar to fans of the Venerable Poet, he addressed Mrs Bartlebot.

'Allow me to introduce myself, my name is Seyfert Garret,' he held out his hand and shook hers (admittedly not a hand she'd offered for shaking, but the politeness was the thing). 'I imagine you've heard the ruckus going on outside and are curious to know what is going on?'

'I am, indeed I am,' said a flustered Mrs Bartlebot.

'We're having a bit of trouble with a sea creature you may have noticed, and we wondered if we might use your balcony to save the tower-dwellers' lives. Would you be willing to take on the role of "Saviour of Amburg"?'

This request did nothing to lower the woman's level of flusterment or bewilderation. To be fair, Tycho and Walf were as surprised as Mrs B by the 'nice young man' by the name of 'Garret' (?) who'd taken charge of the conversation. They'd never heard Zafe speak like this before, but it seemed to be working.

Tycho took a step back, urging Walf to do the same, hoping she'd forget he'd knocked on the door, or that either of them had ever been there at all.

Zafe's silky words did the trick and, doing their best to hide behind the gong they were rolling, Walf and Tycho manoeuvred it onto Mrs Bartlebot's balcony while Zafe advised her to take shelter with the other Amburgers.

Zafe gently shut the door behind her and joined the boys on the balcony. They were enthralled by the scene in front of them. So close they could almost reach out and touch it, tentacle after tentacle waved and smashed before them; the wreckage of a dragon boat flung up with every thump.

It was so awful it didn't seem real. Like a story over the radio, a puppet show or a pantomime legend. Leaning over the edge, Walf caught sight of a small group of wranglers clinging to the tower's foundations. 'They won't last long if the beast sees them,' he shouted. But it was Zafe who suggested the creature couldn't see at all.

What appeared to be eyes, were elaborate markings on the side of its head, and they may have been ear-holes, but the creature seemed to be moving in the wranglers' direction all the same.

Zafe shouted over the waves' roar and sound of breaking timber, 'WHAT ABOUT THE DOOR?'

'HUH?' They moved away from the balcony.

'The door to the cave!'

'Zafe, that was on Istanglia! We're on Amburg now!'

Walf remarked that if there was a 'ground floor' to the base of Istanglia, there might be one for Amburg. There must be a tunnel, they just had to find it! Running back into the container, they looked behind every wall-hanging, shelf and tea cannister Mrs Bartlebot had.

Finally, a netting-tapestry in the main bedroom pulled aside to reveal the door to the foundations, the door to Amburg's own cave. Now all they had to do was get it open. They had left their potato mashers upstairs for the feral Fourth Formers and their demented chipping, so what did Mrs Bartlebot have that they might use to unlock it?

'What did you use before?' asked Walf.

'A bamboo stick.'

'Has she got any kebab sticks in her kitchen?' They searched high and low but Mrs Bartlebot was evidently no fan of fish-on-a-stick, so they tried out a couple of forks, leaving them bent. They had more luck with a chopstick but not enough luck to actually open the door. Time was running out for the wranglers stranded outside.

'We need to THINK!'

'We need to to EAT!' wailed Walf, 'I can't think without food.' They were all starving and they reasoned they weren't going to save anyone if they fainted from hunger.

'I haven't got any crackers in my bag,' said Zafe. 'Have you got anything Tycho?'

Nestled in Tycho's beltbag, amongst bits of broken, dusty beetroot biscuit, a ribbon of jellypaper and a couple of pebbles and shells, was the rusty key he'd been given by his auntie (the one that hadn't worked on the Istanglia door).

His damaged hands shaking, he managed to make the key fit in the lock and his face broke into a wide smile. 'It works!' It was Walf who pointed out that it only truly worked if you could turn it and it opened something. Tycho's hands were too weak, so Zafe wrenched the key round, fortune smiled on them and the door unlocked.

They were through. Through the first door, running past jars of honey and boxes of imported interspace toothpaste, down more stairs, (round and round) and through the second door — carefully avoiding the shards of coloured glass that dotted the floor — through a third door and — Tycho's arm shot out just in time to stop Walf from walking straight into the Thames Sea.

They huddled in the doorway, poking their heads out and shouting at the wranglers every time the creature appeared to be distracted, but they were getting nowhere. The wranglers hadn't heard them (but the creature had) and they were pinned to the face of Istanglia's rock as the Wotwa's tentacles pummeled the water. It created waves that threatened to drag them from their narrow shelf, and scraping fragments of stone into the depths of the Thames Sea.

Inching his way round the corner, Tycho gripped ledges and handholds, clutching at seaweed and nests to keep from falling into the water; until he felt Walf's hand in his and looked across to see Walf anchored by Zafe. They edged their way as unobtrusively as they could, holding each other's wrists firm, afraid to make any sudden sounds that might attract the attention of the glistening black monster.

Their human chain got just close enough for the three wranglers to spot them, when the creature, with its unseeing eyes, mere markings on its head, turned in their direction. They froze: and a familiar stench assailed Zafe's nostrils. The creature slipped back into the water, and turned towards the volley of dried fish, and into the Bakossian line of fire.

Together, they retreated to the safety of the doorway. The exhausted wranglers were led inside, to Mrs Bartlebot's container, where the boys settled them in the sitting room.

Tycho rooted around Mrs B's container looking for blankets while Zafe put the kettle on. It was Walf's job to find food and Zafe watched, impressed, as he looked for something edible in the furthest recesses of Mrs Bartlebot's larder while teetering on a perch-stick.

Walf announced he'd seen a bag of biscuits at the back and was just balancing on one leg to reach it, when he was struck by something black and shiny. It moved at a speed Zafe found difficult to fathom, and he found himself enthralled by the fetid limb as it writhed around the room, slamming from wall to wall.

It shoved Zafe to the floor and, blindly searching for something to hold, its tentacles curled around Walf's ankles and the beast dragged the boy towards the balcony.

Not Quite So Perfect Now

Zafe wrenched the perch-stick out of its socket and plunged it into the fat, thick, gelatinous limb, again and again, as the creature attempted to pull Walf over the railing and into the foaming sea. Green goo squirted from its wounds and with each stab of the stick there was an unearthly squelching sound. Walf was dropped and the lacerated tentacle slammed around the kitchen as it retreated. Zafe wiped his sticky hands on his trousers and Walf staggered to his feet and did a bit of jogging on the spot and a few stretches. Neither looked at each other.

Tycho popped his head round the doorway and cheerily asked what they'd found in the way of treats.

After a hot, sweet cup of tea and a celery cracker, the boys' thoughts turned to the banging of the gong. They needed something to hit it with. It had to be loud to overcome the roar of the sea, the bashing of Form Four, the beast's shrieks and an ear-splitting note that fought for its attention – the sound of Horst's flute.

One of the Bakossi wranglers asked what they were looking for, and when Walf told him, the man abruptly wrangled a music-stand off Mrs Bartlebot's wall. Oh. Mrs Bartlebot was not going to like that. The boys cast a critical eye over the container and realised things weren't looking half as smart as they had when they'd arrived.

What with the seawater and the state of the upturned kitchen, the best thing that could happen now would be for the Wotwa to smash the entire container to pieces (them included).

The beast's fearful reign of destruction continued. Despite the tentacle incident, Mrs Bartlebot's container was one of the few Amburg homes with a remaining balcony. The sea was dotted with chunks of masonry and a film of rock-dust. Nonetheless, the boys had a gong-beater and it was time to see if their theory worked.

DDDAANNGGGG — GGG — GGG

DDDAAANNGG — GGG — GGGG

DDAAANNNNG — GGG — GGGG

DDDDAANNNG — GGG — GGGGG

The gong rang out, swallowed by the sea and howling wind, but still they continued, taking it in turns, their shoulders burning with each strike as it reverberated up their arms. Was there any sign of the beast slowing down? Should they try a different rhythm? Zafe suggested they try matching their gong-hitting to the beast's heartbeat.

'Which would be what exactly?' asked Walf.

'Well, assuming it's got one, it's going to be slower than a small animal, so slower than us. A lot slower than us,' said Zafe.

'I'm not sure but I reckon we've been making it speed up. Look at it! If we carry on going as we are, the entire tower will be destroyed within the next ten minutes.'

Zafe might have had a point. The beast seemed even more excited than before. Beginning afresh, they took it slow, allowing each blow to be absorbed by the sea, soaked up by the creature they were trying to placate.

DDDAANNGGGG — GGG — GGG

DDDAAANNGG — GGG — GGGG

DDAAANNNNG — GGG — GGGG

DDDDAANNNG — GGG — GGGGG

'HEY TY, IT'S SLOWING DOWN!' said Walf, 'It really is slowing down!' It was as if the creature was dancing now, swaying through the water, moving to the rhythm of the beat. And the shrieking had died down too, all the better to hear the gong. Unfortunately, the boys had slowed down too, their arms shattered with the continual banging and the shockwave that travelled up the metal music-stand each time they struck the gong. 'If it gets too slow the Wotwa might get bored and decide to eat something,' said Tycho. 'We have to keep going!'

After every ear-shattering note, they passed the stand round, their arms as weak as blobfish. And just when they thought they could carry on no longer, one of the wranglers appeared at the doorway, a cup of Earl Grey held between her no longer shivering hands, asking if she could help. If her muscles and those of her colleagues were anything to go by, they'd be able to keep the rhythm up for hours.

Fortified by Mrs Bartlebot's tea and cauliflower scones, the wranglers sent the exhausted boys upstairs, with heartfelt assurances that they would keep the beat going.

Walf, Tycho and Zafe did the best they could not to reveal the devastation wrought on the container as they edged out of the door. Mrs Bartlebot wouldn't be winning 'Container of the Year' any time soon, but then, neither would anyone else. It was time to return upstairs and see how the Fourth Form and Mrs

Hawtrey were getting on.

The walk back upstairs did to their legs what the gong-smashing had done to their arms and by the time they'd made their way from Mrs Bartlebot's container of destruction up to the smashing of potato-masher on stone, the three of them were as wobbly as a foodcube.

They were greeted by a thick cloud of stone dust and a slightly over-excited Fourth Former. 'We've nearly done it, it's going to drop. Hundredwater is going to be SMASHED!' yelled the little boy, and Tycho wondered whether the Fourth Form knew *why* they were chipping away at school.

Mrs H was the first familiar figure they saw, her wig weighed down with dust and her toga held over her mouth as she continued to sing shanties and encourage the children's reign of destruction. A couple of chalk-white potato-masher smashers approached the boys, wiping the powder from their eyes, their hair stuck up in dusty horns on their heads. But it was only when they spoke that they were revealed as Addie and Suza.

'We've been working solidly since you left. My arms are killing me, but every time I stop, a small child threatens to take my masher off me,' complained Addie.

'If you're that tired, why don't you give it to them?' asked Walf, which seemed fair enough, although Addie didn't seem to think so.

'A load of them have crumpled to nothing, or the metal bit has flown off the handle and been lost over the side. There aren't many functioning mashers left. This is like gold dust!' she said, holding up a handle — with nothing attached to it. 'Oh, poop slugs! What am I going to use now?'

'So, what have you been up to?' asked Suza.

'Oh, you know, saving a team of wranglers, attacking a tentacle, lulling a diabolical monster to sleep and trying to avoid showing Mrs Bartlebot the remains of her wrecked home,' Zafe replied with a shrug that sent shooting pains down his lifeless arms.

Something about Suza's response implied she'd taken that as a joke but the boys didn't have the energy to correct her, so they followed her to the balcony to see what the beast was up to. Holding onto the remains of a thin rail, they took it in turns to lean over and look, through the swirling cloud of dust, at the Thames Sea's increasingly calm waters and the recumbent body of a huge, tentacled sea-serpent.

The DANG-DANG-DANG of the slow gong wafted up, regular and soothing to the cold reptilian soul.

Suza shouted the news at Mrs H, and the tall, powdery figure brushed the dust off her limbs, shook the gravel out of her hair and clapped her hands violently. The banging, shouting, knocking, jeering, chipping, hollering and hacking died down and Mrs H told them the news.

'Children! It's below us! Are you all listening? Right, well the Wotwa has been subdued by the school gong. We need one last GARGANTUAN effort for our beloved Hundredwater to land on the beast's head and finish it off.'

One of the younger members began to cry, saying it was the closest he'd ever got to having a pet and that if he'd known they were going to kill it he wouldn't have hacked as hard as he had.

Another pointed out that if he'd wanted a pet so much, why hadn't he kept the hermit crabs they'd decorated the other day, rather than giving them to his Nana to fry (which made a couple more children start to cry). Another quite rightly pointed out that it's no good having a pet you want to eat (or one that wants to eat you).

Mrs Hawtrey calmed everyone down (everyone apart from Jebnit who was still doggedly chopping away at the floor with her axe) when yet another small, fearsome member of the chalky tribe complained that his masher had been smashed, and he held up a handle very similar to Addie's.

They all raised their tools (or what was left of them) and a scuffle broke out over the one remaining masher that was intact, as well as accusations that the person holding it hadn't been working hard enough. Unfortunately, it was Suza. Walf dragged her out of the pile of angry bodies and Mrs H clapped again.

Mashing Mashers

'The mashers have done their duty and are no longer useful. What else have we got?'

The children looked around, up and down through the fog of stone dust, unable to see anything that might help. Standing in silence, they heard the distant gong shaking its note through the dust, slow and sure just as it had been when Tycho and Zafe had left.

Distracted by the beat Mrs H began to tap her toe in time to it, adding a flourish here and there and a swing of her hips.

'We can have a dance off!' suggested Walf.

'A LOVELY idea, Walf, for another day but can we focus please!' said Mrs H, swaying.

'No, I mean, you know, jump up and down on the balcony until it breaks off!'

There was a great cheer from the Fourth Form.

'If we time it right, and keep an eye on the crack, it might just work,' said Suza, 'We'll need two children clipped to the sides of the balcony, looking underneath to assess how things are going. We don't want the balcony to fall with us on it. They'll need to listen for a splintering sound because when it begins to go it'll be quick. We're going to have to move fast if we don't want to fall down too.'

Tycho nodded. 'And we're going to have to get a move on. We don't know when the beast will get tired of dancing.'

'Or decide it's hungry,' said Zafe.

There were a couple of points along the line on the floor that, on further examination, had been hacked all the way through. The balcony was hanging by a finger's width of stone and it would require careful timing if they weren't all going to join the Wotwa in the waves below. Two of the more responsible Fourth Formers were clipped onto zipwires and edged down just below the balcony's underside, while everyone else stood in a group in the classroom.

'Right,' said Mrs H, 'If we can all stamp one step in front of the wonderful groove we've already carved out, and hold hands? Now, this is going to be a bit like The Hokey-Cokey.'

'What's that?'

'Don't worry Zafe, it's easy. It's a dance the ancients used to do to encourage the worms and increase crops.' (Suza's expression suggested Tycho hadn't got it quite right.)

Mrs H clapped her hands to get everyone's attention. 'Now, I'd like each of you to put your right foot in. **STAMP**. And then return your foot to the normal standing position. We don't want to join the beast down there, do we? PUT THE AXE DOWN JEBNIT!'

The little girl harrumphed loudly, sinking cross-legged to the floor at Mrs H's feet.

'Are we all paying attention? Good. Now, you put your right foot IN.'

They stamped in unison and quickly jumped back, waiting for the balcony to shatter onto the creature below. Nope, nothing.

'You put your left foot IN.'

When everyone was safely behind the line again Tycho shouted to the Fourth Formers dangling over the edge, who reported that a small amount of dust had dropped from the bottom, but nothing significant.

'All right, everyone, EVERYONE! We're going to have to do it with a bit more gusto. Right, on the count of three, IN OUT IN OUT!'

There was no count of three and the group was a jumble of jumping, stamping and general hilarity until some more of Mrs H's violent clapping brought them to their senses.

'Anything, girls?'

A small, distant voice replied, 'It's working! School is going down!'

'Thank you, Rosanthea. On the count of three, again? Although I think we'll miss out the chorus. I'm not sure "'shaking it all about" is going to make any difference to the balcony. So —'

This time they were ready and they stamped like maniacs, first with their right and then with their left – and there was a splintering sound.

Zafe held up his hand and Mrs H indicated he could speak. 'Perhaps if we all hold hands and every other one of us jumps while the other one stands still? That way, if anything happens while we're stamping there's a chance the jumping half of us can be pulled back in time... you know, to stop us from falling over the edge.'

'Good thinking, Seyfert! Right, can we arrange that?'

And so, hands held firmly, half of them jumped, half of them stood firm, and they heard the balcony crack again.

Mrs H inspected the groove. There was nothing to see but they'd all heard the terrible, exciting, awful, wondrous sound. 'I think we might try that again. Everyone at the ready?'

A black, scaly limb swept across the balcony — and Jebnit raised her axe and hacked at the floor. The tentacle retreated abruptly as Mrs Hawtrey roared in pain, jumped up and landed beyond the line. There was a resounding CRACK.

The balcony disappeared, along with Mrs. H.

And the tip of her toe.

The Aftermath

Twenty grubby hands held Mrs H's toga fast, as she dangled over the edge of what remained of their classroom. Her wig was long gone and because she was holding onto her entire, unfurled costume, Mrs Hawtrey was quite, quite nude. Eyes averted, the Fourth Form quietly pulled her back up, and they all stayed that way until one of the younger children asked 'Can we open our eyes now?'

Mrs H told them all to stay away from the edge, while she retied the long sheet around herself, and tore a strip off the end of the cloth and bandaged her foot. She then began a slightly limping celebratory dance in time with the wranglers' joyous gong-banging. They were banging much faster than the lullaby-din they'd done to calm the beast, and the Fourth Form raucously sang in time with the manic DANG-DANGETTY-DANG from below.

> *No prizes for guessing what we're -*
> *HAVING FOR TEA!*
> *Dinner! Dinner! Dinner! Dinner!*
> *WHAT'S FOR TEA!*
> *It's Wotwa for Dinner and it's yum-yummy!*

By the time they'd sung it a third time the tempo had slowed and it had taken on a melancholy air, as if the reality of relentless Wotwa dinners had struck home. Or perhaps because it wasn't a very good song.

The sound of the balcony hitting the Wotwa in the waves below was something none of them would ever forget. A deep BOOM followed by a shriek that shattered windows and still echoed around their skulls. The monster must be dead; it had to be. The adventure was over.

Suza stood frozen to the spot, hands still covering her ears, eyes lowered, hair coated with dust, body shaking. Addie put a trembling arm around her cousin's shoulders, too tired to join in with the younger children's hooting calls of celebration. Walf was swinging off a zipwire, in and out of what was left of the school's entrance way, mournfully squelching his armpit. He had a faraway look on his face as he gazed up at the sky and clouds, determined not to look down.

And Zafe and Tycho? Tears of sadness, pain and relief streamed down their filthy cheeks leaving dirty streaks.

'I don't think my eyes will ever be right again.' Tycho rubbed them with what remained of his sleeve.

'It's a sight that will live with me forever. And you know, I'm not sure she minded being nude in the least.'

'I was talking about the dust from the chipping.'

'Oh.'

They took their time walking up ten flights of stairs to a container from which a new zipwire was being set up. When it was ready Zafe happily clipped on and sailed across the enormous gap between the two towers, back to Istanglia. The water below had turned an ominous, oily green and the giant chunks of rock which had crushed the creature had long since dropped to the bottom of the sea, through greasy waves.

As for the creature itself? They could see no sign of it. Perhaps the wranglers had dragged the body away? Maybe Wotwa wasn't on the menu after all.

In their hammocks that night, Tycho and Zafe looked out at the calm, untroubled sky. No streaks of purple, turquoise or red, just a vast darkness pricked with twinkling stars.

'What do you think Horst was up to with that flute playing?' asked Zafe.

'I don't know but he's definitely not on our side. Thank goodness for Mr Flintlo's tuba.'

They listened to the waves crashing against the battered, slightly nibbled reef.

'I've been thinking about it, and I reckon the Fourth Formers actually destroyed more than the Wotwa did. And Mrs H encouraged them,' said Zafe, with a note of awe.

'What do you mean?'

'The Wotwa was very frightening, got a lot of homes and houseplants wet, dissolved a bit of Amburg's lower half and smashed up a dragon boat, but it didn't *actually* destroy the school.' Zafe almost attempted a swing in his hammock before thinking better of it. It would be a shame to survive the Wotwa (and a gang of small children) only to fall through the netting now.

'Are you suggesting that Form Four are more dangerous than the Wotwa? Do you think they regarded the Wotwa as competition?'

'You've seen what they're like. The only thing the Year Fours weren't doing was nibbling at the reef.'

'Mm.'

'They may even be the reason the tower is at this angle.'

'Night night, Zafe. Sleep tight, don't let the Fourth Form bite.'

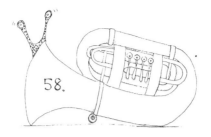

58.

The Winners

The next two weeks were unpleasant.

The weather was warm but swimming was discouraged due to the wasabi-Wotwa slick lapping the towers. There was much relief when it rained, and yet more relief when vats of crushed pineapple were plopped into the sea. It did nothing to clean the water but it certainly made it smell better.

Needless to say, there was no school for the children on Amburg or Istanglia. They were invited to join classes on Kodiak, but there wasn't a single child prepared to adopt their dress code (a green mohican). Instead, Addie was writing up the planet's recent history for the Hundredwater Herald, an epic entitled *'From the Depths of Vispa'*, which Walf was scratching into the towers, at the sedan stops.

The others spent their time repairing netting, replanting plants, cleaning the Thames Sea of bits of their old school (for recycling) and practising for the Spring Solstice Show.

Neither Zafe nor Devik could quite believe that Mrs H still intended to hold the twirling display, and they glumly swung on tattered cables. The festival was usually held on the jetties of all five towers; the show-goers moving across from one to the next to see the bits they were interested in, but because of the pineapple and rotting fish smell, the show was moved to Kodiak's jetty and its long zipwires across to Bakossi.

The Fluky Five watched the children from Kodiak performing their puddle tap dancing routines – and the way their green plumage swayed as they jigged about.

'The name of their school has never made any sense to me,' remarked Tycho.

'TenWater?' asked Walf.

'Yeah. It makes it sound like our school has been destroyed ten times more than theirs. What do they do all day?' And Addie suggested that perhaps they went straight from form three to form five.

While the Whirlygig Festival-goers enjoyed fish kebabs, baked beetroot, celery toffees and pineapple and onion smoothies, the Hundredwater children took their positions.

Walf, his sister and Habjema were to perform from the highest zipwires while Tycho and most of the others were scattered around the middle, and they climbed up the tower's bamboo to find their places. Devik and Zafe had been put at the bottom, along with Suza who'd slipped on a half-eaten kebab and had asked to be given lighter twirling duties as a result.

'What's the gong about?' Zafe's hands were firmly clamped on the trapeze ropes as he craned his neck to look at the huge metal disk that had been hoisted up and hung from a long bamboo beam on which Mrs H was sitting. (Was she holding Mrs Bartlebot's music-stand in her hand?)

'Didn't you hear?' Suza sat alongside him. [DAAAAAAAAAAAAAAAAAAAAAANNNNNNG]. 'They've ditched the yodelling because the gong playing went down so well.'

Devik said a loud 'thank goodness' and then almost fell off his swing when Mr Flintlo let out a large "PAARP" from his tuba.

The twirl began quite well. Zafe managed to sneak a look up to the lofty reaches of Kodiak and saw Walf and Habjema doing amazing things upside down, requiring feats of strength and coordination the others could only dream of. Tycho's group weren't doing much better than Zafe's (in his opinion) but they had the advantage of being higher up and being coordinated.

The only advantage Zafe, Devik and Suza had was the leftover dvd's from Adamant strapped to their legs. The suns reflected from them as they twirled, and they hoped the sparkling effect would make up for their performance, which consisted of swinging and smiling at the huge crowds who'd come to watch.

They were three verses into the routine when Suza asked Zafe whether he thought the tempo was getting quicker. With every chorus the children were having to work harder to keep up with the song.

Walf's group were doing things that were complicated enough without the additional speed, and there were so many in the middle group that things began to get a bit hectic.

Sweat dripping from his forehead, Zafe was relieved to hear the gong slow and clatter to a stop as Mrs H dropped her beater. It also sounded a lot like Gonzales had slithered into the end of Mr Flintlo's badly dented tuba (his favourite hideyhole, according to Walf).

But when those sounds died away, it was apparent the other sounds had too.

The clapping had stopped. The audience were watching in silence, their mouths open in a way that suggested things had become a lot more 'interesting'.

Zafe glanced out to sea, scanning the waves for the Wotwa, certain that the audience's reaction must indicate the return of the creature that had threatened their lives, but the sea was calm, there was no threat. Until he looked up.

Above the three twirling novices, was a huge, struggling scrum of ropes, limbs, ribbons and hair; the focus of the audience's rapt attention.

'You're standing on my EAR!' (That was Tycho.)

'Well your ear's in the way of my FOOT!' (That was Addie.)

Devik remarked afterwards that if it had been a competition, they'd have won because everyone else was very definitely eliminated.

Prompted by Mrs Hawtrey, Zafe, Devik and Suza carefully stood on their trapeze bars and bowed. The crowd went wild and only died down when The Venerable Poet began his closing Pantomime speech, addressing them from a bamboo orb bobbing alongside Mrs H's gong. He cleared his throat in a most distressing manner, was handed a honey lozenge, and finally spoke with the help of a large, engraved ear-trumpet he used as a megaphone.

'Thank you to the wonderful twirling children of what was Hundredwater School. They may have lost their school, but they've lost none of their … fortitude.' [The audience regarded the bunch of bickering children being lowered onto a net for disentanglement.]

'And so, we bring the Spring Solstice Show to an end as the fish begin their migration to wherever it is they go. The harvest has been good this year, possibly the best beetroot any of us has ever eaten and, more to the point, we weren't a part of anything else's harvest.

'Thanks to the valiant efforts of the tower-dwellers and, in particular, a certain Fearless Five, we did not go BOOM or indeed, CRUNCH!' [There was a 'whoop!' from the mess of children.]

'We found our spirit, we were not extinguished and our goats wander free once more. Geoff-bert, I'm talking to you.'

[GOATS! GOATS! GOATS!]

'The diabolical creature who sought to destroy our way of life and bring down our magnificent towers is no more, but of course we did not come away unscathed. As I mentioned before, Amburg has given up its didactic, craggy beak and another location will have to be found for the HundredAndTenwaterSchool.' [There was a loud groan from the tangle of children on the net below.]

'But all of Thames Sea played a part in our victory; from the beekeepers who supplied the candles that [ahem] kept the Wotwa from Adamant, to the pineapple growers of Kodiak whose fruity soup saved their waters from its fearsome jaws.

'The wranglers from Bakossi and South Utzeera wrangled, and gave their dried fish for use as missiles which the archers of Bakossi so expertly fired in our defence. And then of course, there was … Form Four, without whom …' [The Venerable Poet cleared his throat again and there was a brief interlude while he had a coughing fit.]

'Enjoy the candied sprouts and let us hope next season is a thoroughly boring one.'

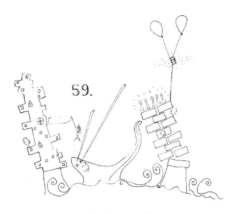

Time to Go

It was the end of term, and Aurinko beckoned.

Just when Zafe felt he'd got to grips with Vispa (or what was left of it, at least). It was time to go and he had another big change to face – although things had changed on Vispa too. None of his school friends had time to hang out together anymore. They were all too busy harvesting, planting, painting or herding and, given that Zafe was no good at any of those things, he spent his time practising his zipwiring.

The fear and adrenaline he experienced as he sped from tower to tower blocked out his sadness and anyway, it was something to do.

Nonna had asked whether he would miss Vispa, but aside from that nothing had been said about his departure at the end of term, and that was what hurt the most. Neither Walf nor Tycho had mentioned him leaving at all. He would go and their lives would continue as if they'd never even known him.

His last evening on the planet, Zafe was packing the remains of his clothes and reviewing the contents of his beltbag, when Tycho swung in the window.

'I was thinking you might like to go and say goodbye to Auntie Puffbird?'

'Yes, yes, I'd like to do that. Say my goodbyes.' Tycho began whistling a cheery tune and picking at the tattered and stained, vaguely blue scraps of fabric Zafe had carefully folded. 'Because it will be really sad to say goodbye and not see her again. Leave Vispa behind, and the school and, you know, all the people who I probably won't see again. They might think it would be sad to have me leave.'

'Well of course they'll be sad.' Zafe's heart leapt, until Tycho cheerfully resumed his jaunty whistling and said 'Still, it could be worse, I mean you're not leaving many friends behind.'

'I'm not?'

'Well, why would you be? It'll be sad not to see Aunt Nineveh of course, and then there are the Drinkwaters, if you count them as friends. And Dinesh I suppose. Anyone else you'll miss?'

Zafe realised that what he would miss, was having a family. This family. A group of people he could rely on to tell him what to do, make him tidy up, eat his greens, chew with his teeth, wash his hands … help him up when he was hanging over an ocean ready to fall. A friend to listen to his beast-beating ideas, encourage him when he was the worst twirler the Hundredwater School had ever seen and just generally… be there.

And they wouldn't 'be there' any more, because he was going away. But that wasn't the worst thing. Tycho, the best mate he'd ever had, didn't seem to care.

Zafe gripped his hammock and a great wave of sadness threatened to overwhelm him, and tears flooded his eyes.

Leaving his parents behind had been hard, and not knowing what they were doing was harder still, but he'd come to Vispa and been a part of something. The Fluky Five!

They'd worked together to save the planet and the boy he'd shared a room with for a whole term was now telling him that the only friends he was leaving behind were Dinesh (Grundi's mysterious friend), the Mayor and her kitchen-crushing husband, and Nineveh Puffbird who'd eaten all his chocolate. Well, almost all of it.

Tycho said he had to help Grundi with the hives so he'd probably see Zafe up on the roof, and he jumped out of the window to clip onto the pedalift. Everyone seemed too busy to spend any time with him at all and Zafe was tempted to curl into his hammock. Wiping his eyes, he began the long walk up to the roof.

He could have taken the pedalift, but he preferred the quiet and darkness of the central core's stairs. Besides, he needed the time for his tears to dry.

He knocked on Triple-G's container door and there was a cough, a splutter and a brusque 'who is it?' He gave his name and was asked to enter. The old lady was beaming from ear to ear, and Zafe's heart began to firm up again.

Nineveh's cabbagey hug and smile reminded him that he did have friends and her warm welcome was no less warm for her enquiry as to whether he had any chocolate.

She lit the gas under the samovar and, glancing across at her snoozing sister, she asked him to lift the blinds that covered the window at the far end. The suns were setting and although he'd been enchanted by Suza's description of the pictures engraved into the container, he wasn't prepared for what he saw.

Star systems, creatures of all kinds, heroes, heroines, harvests and feats of engineering danced across the walls, and then Nineveh told him to look at the space to the left of the shutter.

A teetering tower had been scratched into the painted surface. At the bottom of it, thrashed a leviathan, its huge scaly, tentacled body beating the waves, its fangs dripping with foam. Lasers shot from its (non-existent) eyes. A small armada surrounded the creature: the hulls of the boats were dented, their sails torn and there were people struggling in the waves. He heard a familiar crunching sound — the reef!

No. There was something moist nuzzling his ankle. It was faithful Gonzales and his midmorning cuttlefish snack. Carefully extracting his soggy foot, he turned back to the cartoon.

Halfway up the tower a beak projected out, a balcony barely hanging on due to a large crack and dozens of small figures crowded onto it. From the end of the teetering stone a thin line dangled down and hanging on the end of it, a mysterious figure who *may* have been clothed...

And on the tower's roof? Five figures standing next to the container in which Zafe now stood. Rays of light radiated from them and their small faces showed smiles. His heart swelled.

Before Zafe left the container, he gave his hostess the last of his chocolate as a parting gift.

Auntie Puffbird's eyes shone and she told him to be sure to get a place on the right-hand side when he took off the next day, because he'd get a better view of things. He nodded, but before he could ask 'what things?', he hit his head on the samovar, spilt boiling water on his shoulder, caught his elbow on a pulley, heard a crank begin to move and saw Auntie Puffbird move faster than she'd ever moved before.

She pulled on a lever to the side of her rocking chair and glanced over Zafe's shoulder at something pointy pointing at his head. She giggled nervously and he wondered just how harmless her container was?

Zafe thought about his flight over to Vispa. It had been late at night and after a much-delayed departure (something about some replacement berries) he had slept through the whole thing, but he did recall there had only been room on board for him and the pilot (who'd sat on the right).

Not wanting to spoil her fun, Zafe smiled, gave Aunt Puffbird a hug goodbye, carefully left the container and ambled downstairs.

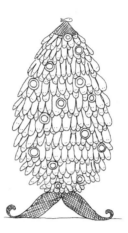

60. Farewell Vispa

In the morning, Nonna suggested Zafe consider whether he *really* needed to take his 'enormous, great-big, heavy-as-a-Ghat-stone' bag with him to Aurinko, and after much umming and aahing, he left behind one of his tops and a pair of trousers. He'd lost his spare pair of shoes to the Wotwa, so with just his beltbag (crammed full of beetroot crackers for the journey), he had very little to carry and was ready to go. Tycho looked after Zafe's bag as they abseiled together with Grundi and Nonna, and took the sky-sedans across to South Utzeera Arrivals & Departures.

They landed on a jetty crowded with people whose eyes were watering and Zafe was grateful for his nose peg. He could only imagine the smell of the dried fish that adorned the tower, flapping in the breeze. Hung on hooks like the dvd's on Adamant, the fish sparkled in the morning light.

'There are a lot of people here, is there something coming in?'

'I shouldn't think so,' said Tycho.

'So, where's the pod?'

'You mean the rocket?' There was an unruly cheer and they noticed the Fourth Form milling about around the base of the tower, flicking fishy flakes at each other. Just for a moment Zafe felt a small tinge of relief that he was moving on, and then realised they'd joined a long queue weaving its way into the tower itself.

Tycho, Grundi and Nonna were busy talking to neighbours as Zafe was pushed along with the crowd. Maybe the pod set off from the tower top? He looked for Walf, Addie and Suza but could see no sign of them, nor of Mrs H. Tears welled up and Zafe rubbed them away, taking a deep breath.

The other towers were made up of homes around a central core, but South Utzeera was an empty metal husk. No balconies or poo-chute pipes. While the tower outside was covered with drying fish, its inside was covered with people.

Tower-dwellers entered and began climbing up, until they located spare hooks and clipped themselves on, finding a rest for their feet. With a nudge, Zafe climbed, following Grundi, who'd found a spare row of four on the right-hand side and asked Zafe whether he wanted a seat next to the 'window' (a gap in the fishy outer covering). He made himself comfortable and Nonna checked he was clipped in tight before making room for Tycho to sit next to his friend.

'You're clipping yourselves in too?' Zafe asked.

'Well, we aren't leaving on separate flights!' Tycho tightened his clips. 'Vispa doesn't produce enough energy for two big trips. Besides, it's more fun if we go together, isn't it?'

'You mean you're coming to Aurinko too? With me?'

Zafe's cheeks had turned a deep scarlet and he looked almost as puzzled as Tycho — until his friend began to laugh. Nonna promptly leaned over to embrace Zafe, crushing her loudly-protesting grandson in the process. 'Oh Seyfert, OF COURSE WE ARE! You surely didn't think you were going on your own? We're nomads! Of course, we're coming.'

'But what about Auntie Nineveh? Battily? The Drinkwaters?'

Tycho had begun giggling again, so it was Nonna who explained how a cohort of people stayed behind, those who didn't like the travelling or whose expertise was required to keep the planet ticking over during the seasons when there was no fishing to be done. There would be a second, smaller journey undertaken in a few weeks, and they'd see Auntie Mirrah on

Aurinko then.

Anxious to change the subject (if only to stop Tycho laughing) Zafe asked, 'So, what are the people of Aurinko like?'

Grundi, Nonna and Tycho looked perplexed, until Grundi raised an eyebrow. 'Ah. I see. Yes, you'll know as soon as we arrive, because you'll be one of them.'

'I'll be an Aurinkovite … Aurinkunian … Aurinkovian?'

'We'll all be Aurinkans as soon as we land, just in time for the first harvest.'

'Are Suza, Addie and the others coming too?'

Tycho pointed three tiers of passengers above them, to where Walf was sharing a bag of *baykon* bits with Devik, and Addie and her cousin were sitting another row behind. 'The fish will migrate any day now and it'll be the monsoon season, so there's no point in staying unless you really want to.' He shrugged, 'It's time for us to move on.'

Time for a change.

Happy as Zafe was to be with his friends, he felt a small knot of worry in the pit of his stomach. 'I suppose that means there'll be a new school?' No sooner had Zafe said the words than he heard their teacher quite distinctly in the upper reaches of the rocket, starting a sing-song. 'And I suppose that means the Fourth Form are coming too?' Zafe shuddered at the memory of Jebnit and her axe, and he was suddenly reminded of somebody else.

He scanned the tiers of people, some familiar, some less so. The hairs stood up on the back of Zafe's neck; a sudden rush of fear that had nothing to do with him sitting in a space rocket with no obvious landing gear. Although he couldn't find Horst's face among the multitude, Zafe had the distinct feeling that the mysterious librarian knew *exactly* where he and the rest of the Fearless Five were.

Zafe shifted his feet to make himself more comfortable, shoving his bag firmly behind his knees. 'When did you put your luggage on board then?'

Nonna, Grundi and Tycho fished about in their beltbags and

showed him their toothbrushes.

A couple of minutes of sing-song later, the din died down and was replaced by a countdown. A huge balloon of air was inflated by a whirring fan below them that Zafe hadn't previously noticed and, with twenty seconds to go, the balloon filled the tower's cavernous insides, blocking their view of the Vispans clipped opposite them. There was a brief but loud PARPPP when the fuel ignited and a sound of disgust as the passengers without nose pegs were subjected to the acrid smell of burning coffee and singed fish.

Smoke swirled outside and Zafe felt his heart beat in a way it hadn't for days. He was amongst friends and, despite the fact he was about to hurtle through space in a fishy tin can being propelled by beans (*and no idea how the contraption was going to land*) he felt light, happy and excited.

There was another great PAAARP and another puff of smoke and he was reminded of Auntie Nineveh and her instructions. Zafe gazed over to the distant towers of Kodiak and Bakossi and, looking down, he saw the sea boil and turn an ominous brown. The giant tuna torpedo they were all sitting in shook, and as it began to rise, something else caught his eye.

Two elderly ladies twirling from long silk ribbons; their lips brown with chocolate, they trailed purple smoke, waving wildly at South Utzeera as it took off.

Up.

Up.

Up.

Juddering in their seats and gritting their teeth they rose — until, after what seemed an age, the shaking and acceleration stopped. They were in freefall, and it was the closest Zafe had felt to home since he'd arrived on Vispa — which he realised with a pang of his heart, he had just left.

Everyone else was moaning and groaning and Zafe was surprised Tycho's stomach hadn't reacted to the sudden change. He'd definitely gone a funny colour, though. (So, *this* was what the little bags clipped to the seats were for.) But Zafe was comfortable in zero gravity.

He gazed at the stars outside, looking for signs of life; space pods and delivery shuttles, but he saw nothing, until he awoke to a loud yell, 'HANG ON!' It was Mrs H, and her command was followed by a jolt as the tower began to fall.

Down.

Down.

Down.

To Sweaty Aurinko.

And immediately in front of them there loomed a planet that was a mass of hot, swirling orange.

A planet that appeared to be on fire.

Zafe's new home.

Acknowledgments.

Thank you to my gorgeous boys, whose stunning illustrations pepper the chapter headings, and who were always on hand to comment on the relative sizes of fictional crustaceans.

Thank you to my husband, Stuart, for all his patience, love and support.

Thank you so much to my parents and family for their unending enthusiasm.

A huge thank you to Kirsten McKenzie, whose writing is an inspiration and who so kindly beta-read this book. (You're thrilling!)

And thank you to Ruth Weinekoetter for her camaraderie and patience in making it happen. (And for making it look **so** good).

Thank you for reading my book, I hope you enjoyed it, and I'd be very grateful if you'd leave a review on Amazon. A review is like a long-forgotten piece of chocolate. Prized beyond measure.

Thank you, thank you, thank you!

P.T.O.

Author's Note.

If you enjoyed reading about Zafe's adventures on Vispa, you'll LOVE

"Across the Sands of Aurinko"

"Into the Forest of Strom"

and

"Beyond the Ice of Fyel"

Please visit **goats_in_space_saga** on instagram, if you'd like to know whether the first book in the Goats in Space Saga really was written by a snail living in a tuba *

*With your parent or guardian's permission

Made in the USA
Las Vegas, NV
15 September 2021